The Regan McHenry Real Estate Mysteries

The Death Contingency
Backyard Bones
Buying Murder
The Widow's Walk League
The Murder House
A Neighborly Killing
The Two-Faced Triplex

PIP Inc. Mysteries

The Glass House
The Funeral Murder
The Corpse's Secret Life
Dearly Beloved Departed
Donor 73101

Other books by Nancy Lynn Jarvis
Mags and the AARP Gang

Edited Anthologies
Cozy Food: 128 Cozy Mystery Writers Share Their
Favorite Recipes
Santa Cruz Weird
Santa Cruz Ghost Stories

Buying Murder

A Regan McHenry Real Estate Mystery

Nancy Lynn Jarvis

Good Read Mysteries
An imprint of Good Read Publishers

This is a work of fiction. Names, characters, places, and incidents are either products of the author's imagination or are used fictitiously.
Any resemblance to actual events, locales, or persons, living or dead, is entirely coincidental.

**Good Read
Mysteries**

Good Read Mysteries © is a registered trademark of Good Read Publishers
301 Azalea Lane, Santa Cruz, California, 95060

Copyright © 2010 by Nancy Kille

Library of Congress Control Number: 2010931813

ISBN: 978-0-9821135-6-1

Printed in the United States of America

www.GoodReadMysteries.com

Books are available at special quantity discounts through the website.

To home inspector Barry Turner, for suggesting the perfect hiding place for Jimmy Hoffa. Of course there had to be a book about it.

And to Meg Powell: we miss you.

Acknowledgments

Acknowledgments always start with Craig without whom I couldn't do this. He deals with computers in a way normal mortals cannot. He's also the go to guy for initial editing, book cover implementation, and encouragement, and most importantly, it's his eyes I see when I'm writing about Tom's blue eyes.

Thanks to Paul at Land Rover Experts in Santa Cruz for explaining about brush guards and their installation; to Don French, the manager of the Watsonville Airport, for his information on airport operations; to Morgan Rankin for her copy-editing skills and advice; and to Pat Pfremmer who always knew the answer to: "Where would Regan look if she wanted to find out …"

Thanks to Danish author P.V. Glob, whose 1965 book *The Bog People,* with its details about Tollund Man and other mummified bodies, obviously made an impression on me.

Buying Murder

Nancy Lynn Jarvis

As always, the disclaimer is true: this story is fiction. But there are some things you should know before you read it.

California was deep in its second year of drought when it caught fire in the summer of 2008. At the height of the conflagration, over 1700 separate fires raged throughout the Golden State.

California is a huge place. Santa Cruz County is not. It's the second smallest county in the state, tiny as counties go, only 445 square miles if you don't count the parts that are under water.

We had three fires in three weeks within our county borders during the summer of 2008: The Summit Fire, the Trabing Fire, and the Martin Fire.

During the Summit Fire, Tom and I invited a young couple with a week-old baby to stay with us. They were friends of our son, Ben, and had been forced out of their home. Thirty-five houses were claimed in that blaze. Luckily the young couple's home was not one of them.

We did the same for some clients when their house was filled with smoke during the Trabing Fire. That blaze took ten houses and ten barns.

We learned all about mandatory evacuations and smoke from wildland fires thanks to the Martin Fire in Bonny Doon. Our house wasn't damaged, but the blaze came within a wind shift of overrunning our home and neighborhood.

The Martin Fire started on June 11th, a Wednesday that seemed too early in the year for fires. Wednesdays are days off for real estate agents like us.

1

We planned to take our truck to Sacramento that day and pick up an antique wardrobe I found on Craig's List and visit friends who recently moved there.

We left Cinco in charge even though it was Harry's turn for the honor — that was Tom's idea. Cinco and Harry are our cats. Cinco's a resourceful little country cat. She's good at catching mice and too good at catching birds; she doggishly drinks water out of toilet bowls.

And Harry — well we don't know what Harry's good at yet — except that sometimes it seems like he can understand what we're talking about. He's a recent adoptee, a city cat with a history ... but that's another story.

Like I said, it was Tom's idea to leave Cinco in charge. Tom's not known for his prescience, that would be my department, but he just had this weird feeling and thought it would be ironic if a fire started while we were away in the truck ... the truck we got to evacuate our favorite possessions in case of a wildland fire.

Tom likes to attend to details. He knows you're supposed to close doors and windows when you leave ahead of a fire and decided it couldn't hurt to do that — or to leave Cinco in charge with instructions to watch out for Harry if there was a fire, since he's new here.

Tom and I left in the truck in a light-hearted mood, secure that all the hatches — or in this case doors and windows — had been battened down. It was a good move as it turned out because by the time we got back, a mandatory evacuation order was in effect for our neighborhood.

Cinco did an outstanding job attending to her responsibilities. She and Harry weren't terribly hungry when we were finally allowed to go home; we found some feathers on the dining room rug. The cats didn't seem to be particularly thirsty, either. We figured Cinco taught Harry how to lap water out of a toilet bowl.

2009 brought the Lockheed Fire to Bonny Doon. It was ten times bigger and took much longer to control than the Martin Fire, but the weather aided the remarkable firefighters again, as it had in 2008. Our home escaped the inferno for a second time. Luck of the Irish.

I acted cool while the fires raged — I'm good at hiding what's going on inside my head when I need to — but I was unnerved by them. People died in the 2008 and 2009 wildfires. Fortunately, none of the deaths occurred in Santa Cruz County.

But one body was discovered here as a result of the fires — and it was closer to home than any of the flames were.

Regan McHenry

Regan presented her final argument for buying the cottage to her husband. "The house is the last one on the street, as far back as you can go from where 11th Avenue joins East Cliff Drive at Twin Lakes Beach, so even though it's only steps to the sand, it's quiet and private. Schwan Lake is behind the house; that makes it both a beach house and a lake house. It's got location, location, location," she cited the realtor's mantra.

She had endeavored to be as logical as Tom was, but now she entreated. "Besides, I really want to do this."

"Is what you're suggesting even ethical?" Tom asked. "The owner called you to list the house, not buy it. You said she lives back east and hasn't been out here for years. She could say that since she had no knowledge of our market, she relied on you completely and that you manipulated her into selling to us for less than she should have."

"But she isn't just relying on me for market value. She talked to other agents, too. The owner said we all came up with similar market pricing for the house.

"She also said getting a quick sale is more important than

getting top dollar. Her oldest brother is in financial trouble. He needs cash fast, and she and her other brother want to help him out. They want to be realistic. She asked for a price that would produce a sure sale within a couple of weeks."

Tom shook his head, "There is no such thing as a sure sale in a couple of weeks in this market. Even a bargain price doesn't guarantee an immediate sale."

"That's exactly what I told her. She said they would have to think it over and decide which of us to hire, but they would definitely be using one of the lower prices we agents proposed. If we offered them the highest of the low numbers, how could that be unethical?"

Tom's chuckle was more an expelling of air than a real laugh. "OK, so we can come in and buy ethically and save the owner who needs cash. I don't want to be so charitable that we overpay, though."

"That's where the true brilliance of my plan comes into play," she offered a triumphant smile. "We take six percent off the high offer we're going to make. The seller's bottom line is the same because they won't be paying commissions, and we get a six percent savings to insure we aren't paying too much. Win-win."

"You've got an answer for everything, haven't you?"

Her giggle was mischievous and her eyes danced, "Of course I have. I want this house. I want a little escape pod, you know, somewhere we can go if there's another fire in Bonny Doon. Besides, I'm sure we can make the house really special. It's already quite charming — it just needs a little work — a wall knocked down here and there to open it up inside, maybe a new roof, and some new finishes in the kitchen and bathroom. I've even got an idea where a half bath could go."

"Sweetheart, what are you getting us into?" Tom's question indicated he already knew he wasn't going to dissuade his wife.

"The backyard is mostly Schwan Lake. We can keep a canoe there if you like. And the house isn't very far from the Yacht Harbor launch ramp. Maybe we could keep a little boat there, too. You've always wanted a boat, haven't you?" Regan enticed.

Tom made a sound that fell somewhere between a groan, a sob, and a laugh. "I assume you've already figured out how we're going to pay for this *little escape pod* that we'll need if there's ever another fire in our neighborhood that coincides with all the hotels and motels in Santa Cruz being full?"

"Trust me," she cooed, "it's all worked out."

"Trust me. Those are famous last words if ever I heard any."

Regan had a cardinal rule for buyers: always have a house inspected before buying it. But she and Tom had owned their little get-away cottage for three days, and she was just meeting Barry Bradford, the home inspector, for a belated look.

Her reaction to seeing Barry was the same as it always was. When she first spotted him, the opening cords of *Hail to the Chief* ran through her mind. His voice wasn't anything like his look-alike's, and the startle of recognition never lasted past his outstretched hand and his upbeat greeting, but so incredible was his resemblance to the former president, that from the moment she saw him until he spoke, she was in the presence of George W. Bush. She'd had clients elbow her as soon as he turned his back, or frown and quietly ask, "Doesn't he ...?" before she stopped them with a nod of her head to acknowledge, yes, he did.

What amazed her was that Barry didn't see his resemblance to the former president. He was a member in good standing of ASHI, the American Society of Home Inspectors, a designation that required the development of excellent observational skills, yet his face seemed to remain a personal blind spot as he looked in the shaving mirror and dismissed the stares of strangers.

As usual, Barry's greeting of, "How are you on this fine day, Regan?" banished her urge to address him as Mr. President. She smiled back a peer's greeting.

"I'm doing well, Barry." She couldn't resist interjecting some reality as she pushed a wind driven strand of hair behind her ear. "How are you on this blustery November day?"

"I'm ready to work, but I'll put off a look-see at the roof until the end of the inspection and hope the wind dies down in the meantime. I don't want a good gust to blow me off the house."

She laughed, "Has that happened to you?"

Barry grinned and the uncanny resemblance grew. "Only once, but I never want a repeat. I landed in some bushes that broke my fall, but it scared the blazes out of me."

"Tom and I just bought this house; since your inspection is

for us, you can skip the cosmetics. Tell me about the plumbing, foundation, electrical, and if we can get along for a while without a new roof. The interior is pretty chopped up; we want to knock down some walls and open it up, so we need to know which walls are bearing and which can come down easily."

"Sure, no problem. I'll take a good look at the structural members from the attic."

Regan unlocked the front door and stepped inside. Barry followed, carrying his neat tri-fold ladder and a satchel filled with his inspection tools.

"Could I ask you a question before you get started?" She led the laden Barry across the living room. "I'm curious why the house is built like this; maybe you'll be able to explain it to me. The fireplace isn't centered on its wall; it's close to being set in the corner, but it isn't quite. There's just this short wall between the fireplace and the side wall; it can't be more than three or four feet long, but see how it angles from the edge of the fireplace? There are conventional straight walls on the kitchen behind here and on the hall to the left. There aren't any openings for a closet or storage of any kind on any of the sides. I've checked. It's seems like there's just a blank triangle of space here. Why doesn't this wall parallel the back wall and make a square corner?"

Barry put his gear on the floor and tapped on the angled wall. "It sounds hollow. It's plaster like the surrounding walls, not sheetrock like it might be if it was added later. It looks original, like it was built that way. Now you've got me curious. If you don't mind me maybe getting a little insulation or dust in the house when I come back down, I'll start in the attic, take a look at this area and let you know which walls are load bearing before I look at anything else."

"I don't mind a little dirt — I'm anxious to understand the house's construction."

She walked Barry to the back bedroom and pointed out the attic access hatch in the closet. Barry set up his ladder and climbed up high enough to push off the hatch door. Then he put his hands on opposite sides of the opening and pulled himself up and through it like a gymnast.

A moment later his head dropped back down through the opening. "You don't have any insulation up here, Regan. This house is going to bake in the summer and be expensive to heat in the winter."

"I'll add insulation to my list."

His head disappeared again. She briefly saw his upper body highlighted by a beam from his flashlight, and then she could hear faint scraping sounds as Barry disappeared from sight and moved along the ceiling joists toward the triangle space.

"Can you hear me?" he yelled.

"Yes, I can, easily." She followed his movements, walking under him through the house.

"You're going to have lots of options for opening things up. So far it looks like the only bearing walls are the perimeters and left of center, front to back. Wiring is Romex, not knob and tube. Looks good. Looks nice and clean up here; one or two desiccated mice, but that's normal. No signs of a rodent infestation.

"OK, I'm to the triangle space. It's open to the attic. I don't see any reason for the construction being the way it is.

9

I'm trying to shine my flashlight into the space for a look, but I can't see anything much … it's got stuff in it … I don't know what exactly … it almost looks like … like cat litter. And … there's garbage … a black plastic garbage bag, at least. Hey, Regan, I know what it is. Somebody hid Jimmy Hoffa in here," he laughed. "You want me to pull the bag out and see what's in it?"

"Sure. Maybe you'll find pirate treasure — we are near the beach. I like the idea of finding treasure better than your suggestion."

"This bag is harder to get out than I thought."

She could hear muffled grunts — Barry trying to pull the bag up to the attic, she assumed.

"It tore," he said. "There's a piece of material in it … it's dirty … it looks rusty." A heartbeat later a guttural cry of, "Uhh … Ahk!" exploded through the ceiling above her.

"Barry, are you OK?"

She heard him scrambling along the ceiling joists back in the direction of the attic hatch, moving recklessly and without concern for the plaster ceiling he would damage if he slipped off the beams. She ran through the house to the closet, arriving just in time to see him lower his head through the opening. He was clearly in distress, coughing and gagging, and pale, even though the blood rushing to his lowered head should have been flushing his cheeks.

He fought retching. "No joke!" He poured out his words rapidly, like he didn't want what they described to linger in his mouth. "Somebody's in there. Maybe not Jimmy Hoffa — but somebody. He was looking up at me with empty eyes."

10

Regan knew she should call Dave. Her friend's official job title was Santa Cruz Police Department Ombudsman. He'd accepted that designation and the career adjustment that came with it after the loss of an eye in a shoot-out ended his more conventional policing career. Dave would know what to do. But she needed the comfort of Tom's presence and the reassurance she would find in his deep blue eyes. Need trumped judgment; it was her husband's number she hit on her cell phone speed dial.

"Tom, Barry found ..." her voice choked.

"Uh-oh. Does the foundation need to be replaced?"

"Barry found ..." she hesitated. Then her words tumbled out swiftly. "There's a dead body in the house."

"What? You mean like a dead raccoon in the crawl space? Oh, not a dog under the house?"

"No. A dead body. A person."

Tom said nothing during the moment it took him to absorb not only what Regan told him, but the way she said it. "It shouldn't take me more than twenty minutes to get there, sweetheart. I'll call Dave — then I'm on my way."

"I'll sit with Barry in his truck until you get here. He's pretty shaken up." She didn't say any more.

"That sounds like a good idea. Keep one another company," he worked on sounding reassuring. "Twenty minutes," he said again and hung up.

Within a few minutes, a patrol car pulled across the driveway blocking both Barry's truck and Regan's car. An officer got out, gave his holster a quick adjustment as he walked toward the truck, tapped on Barry's window, and made little counter-clockwise circles with his hand in a signal Regan recognized as "roll down your window."

"Officer Jamison, sir. Are you the one who found the deceased?" Barry attempted to speak, swallowed instead and nodded in the affirmative. Officer Jamison took a small notepad and a pen out of his shirt pocket and started asking the still-queasy home inspector how he spelled his name.

Officer Jamison's arrival was quickly followed by the appearance of another police cruiser, this one carrying a compact female officer who got out, adjusted not only her holster but also her no-nonsense bun hairdo, and after the slightest heads-up acknowledgement to Officer Jamison, went into the house.

Next on the scene was the County Coroner. He and his crime scene crew, bedecked with cameras and loaded down with tool boxes, snapped on latex gloves, and acting like the very epitome of efficiency and professional procedure, also went into the house. Moments later two of the crew returned for a stretcher and took it inside. Regan focused on the arrivals intently in an attempt to not listen as Barry told Officer Jamison the details of his discovery.

Tom pulled his car into the one remaining parking space before his promised twenty minutes were up and strode at a double-time clip to the passenger side of Barry's truck. Regan's composure abandoned her the moment she saw him. She jumped out of the truck and huddled in his arms until she felt well comforted.

When Dave arrived, Regan was standing with her head downcast, running through the morning's trauma with Tom. She had been so successful in avoiding the grimmest details of Barry's narration that her tale required her own imagined gore. Making it up required her full attention; she didn't notice Dave go into the house or his quiet approach minutes later.

His greeting of, "God, Regan, not again," abruptly brought her head up and her eyes level with his. "How many times can you get your name in the news because you were on-site when a body turns up before it starts hurting your business?" He was bemused and grinning, obviously not sharing her agitation. "What are we going to do with her, Tom? This is three bodies for her, isn't it?"

"Four, if you count the Native-American burial," Tom replied.

"Nah, I say only three," Dave corrected. "I only count murders."

"Are you sure this is murder?" She realized the moment the words were out of her mouth how absurd the question was. She had just handed Dave, who never missed an opportunity to tease, ammunition he was about to gleefully aim at her.

"Whadda-ya think, Regan? The guy climbed up there,

slipped on a plastic bag, fell into it, and starved to death? Of course it's murder." His mouth turned up further on one side, exaggerating his amused enjoyment of her question.

Dave may have intended his mockery as part of their ongoing needling sport, but Regan found it reassuring. They were verbal jousters, constantly teasing one another, but Dave was too much of a professional to indulge in the game during a crisis. His taunting signaled he wasn't particularly alarmed by the morning's events.

Tom's comforting arm around her shoulders and Dave's joking went a long way to restore Regan's mettle. Her distress at finding a body in their cottage was replaced by curiosity to know how it came to be secreted there.

Dave worked his mouth into a serious pose. "You've got to stop meddling like this, though. I thought after your last little adventure you decided not to play detective anymore."

"Umm, I don't think so. As I recall, we left it that I was going to keep you in the loop whenever I was preparing to solve a murder."

"Ha!" Dave's hoot of laughter was explosive.

"It seems we own this house, Dave. You might say we bought this murder," Tom explained. "That makes me as involved as Regan is, and technically, she wasn't looking for this one. You could say this murder found her."

"So I'm not meddling ... am I? And isn't it going to be part of your public relations job to keep us informed about this investigation, since we're home-owning principals?"

Dave's mouth reformed once more, this time into a serious turned-down-at-the-corners pout. "Well, maybe. I might keep you up to date with our investigation if you, and I am talking to you, Regan, promise not to get," he ran his tongue along the inside of his lower lip, "involved."

🏠🏠🏠🏠🏠🏠🏠🏠🏠🏠🏠

Barry's questioning was completed for the time being and he had calmed down sufficiently that Officer Jamison no longer considered him a hazard to himself or to other drivers. The officer moved his patrol car enough that Barry could leave.

Officer Lizzie Perez, the female cop on the scene, finished a brief interview with Regan, collected contact information, and told her she was free to leave whenever she wanted.

The coroner's crew wheeled out the stretcher. There was something on it, something covered with a black drape. It seemed too compressed and trivial for a body, yet everyone knew that's exactly what it was. The crime scene team made several trips between the house and their van to carry out their equipment and plastic containers and bags. Officer Perez began taking down the yellow crime scene tape from around the house. Once those tasks were completed, the only passersby, a couple taking their dog for a walk, who had paused to watch the activity, left as well.

Dave had disappeared during Regan's questioning and returned with coffee from Black's Beach Café for the three of them. It seemed all of the activities inside their new house had taken only moments, but when Regan checked her watch, she realized it had been a little more than three-and-a-half hours since she had called her husband.

"What happens now?" Tom asked as he sipped his coffee.

15

"Well, first I make sure the colors in my Hawaiian shirt are flattering for when the cameras start rolling. Then I do my job as police spokesman and explain to the KSBW and KION reporters how Regan here's found another body." He laughed and dodged the slap she aimed at his arm. "And then we get down to the serious stuff: we figure out who your houseguest was, when he died, and how he died. After that, we try to figure out who put him in your new house." In his usual manner of speaking, Dave made himself central to the police investigation.

"I want to go inside," Regan said. "Is that OK?"

"Tape's down, I don't see why not. It's your place. Let me go in with you just to double-check nobody left anything behind that you and Tom shouldn't disturb." Dave led the way toward the open front door.

The plaster and studs of the angled wall in the living room had been removed. A few tiny remnants of plaster still clung to the ceiling where the angled wall had attached, and the top and bottom plates where the studs had been nailed remained. Other than that, the triangle wall was gone.

"That wall definitely wasn't load bearing," Regan breathed the words too softly to be heard. Not load-bearing: what a strange first thought to have. Yet, they certainly had borne a weight ... for how many years?

She expected there to be more disruption to the house — a filmy coating of plaster dust clinging to the fireplace mantel, bits of chipped-away wall lying on the floor, maybe even discarded bits of a black plastic bag and whatever material had surrounded the body — but the coroner's crew had meticulously taken away every last trace of the triangle and

16

what it held. It had all become evidence to be carefully inspected and analyzed.

But, though only the outline of the triangle space remained, Regan's always vivid imagination created an invisible vestige. She imagined she could smell a slight, lingering odor where the triangle had been, the unmistakable odor of death.

Dave was right, of course — she shouldn't get involved. The body hidden in the triangle had nothing to do with them. She should let the police do their work and determine the who, when, and why of the remains. There was no need for her to poke around or ask questions. Leave everything to the authorities. That was what she should do; that was exactly what she planned to do. That, and work hard to squelch the annoying little voice in her head that kept connecting two thoughts in such an irksome way: *Your house, Regan. Your murder.*

Dave called Regan at work late the following Thursday afternoon. "Autopsy prelims are done. You interested?"

Prelims. In her world, prelims were preliminary title reports. Not so in this other realm where bodies were found in the walls of a newly purchased home.

"Yes, I'm interested."

"OK. Vic was a white male, early twenties, slender build, five-foot eight to five-foot nine. We got a reasonable idea what he looked like, too. Even though most of the remains were skeletal, his head and upper torso were partially mummified."

The room swirled around her. Now Regan understood Barry's reaction to the body in the triangle. It would be bad enough finding a skeleton, but the word "mummified" conjured up special horrors — and grisly fascination. Tutankhamen. The 500-hundred-year-old freeze-dried mummy of an Incan girl discovered in the Andes. The Caucasian mummies of Urumqi in China.

"That can happen sometimes under the right conditions," Dave continued. "Turns out where he was, in a hot dry area with decent ventilation, kind of dehydrated the top of him before he rotted. Oh yeah, the cat litter didn't hurt, either."

Dave had such a knack for saying things in a way that got a shocked reaction out of her, that she was sure he must rehearse what he was going to say before he talked to her. It was part of their verbal sparring — and she didn't want to let him know how much his description disturbed her.

"Barry was right?" she asked with all the nonchalance she could muster. "That really was cat litter?"

"Oh yeah. Helps us with dates a little bit, too. It was the clumping kind, which my sources say wasn't invented 'til 1984. The silica gel kind of litter was invented in 2000. It works a whole lot better at controlling moisture and odor than the clay clumpy stuff, so if I was going to go to the trouble of pouring tons of cat litter around a body, I'd use the latest wizbang kind I could get. Wouldn't you?" Dave didn't wait for a reply. "That says the Vic went in after 1984 but before 2000."

"You actually have a cat litter expert, a source?" Regan asked incredulously.

"OK. You caught me. I Googled cat litter," he confessed. "Turns out the history of kitty litter is very absorbing," he laughed loudly at his witticism.

"Looks like the guy got whacked over the head. A nice chunk of two-by-four with some of the Vic's blood and tissue remains on it was found at the bottom of the wall space."

"So he was killed by a blow to the head?"

"Nope. Looks like he had a lot harder end than that. His arms were duct-taped to his body and his feet were taped together, too. The coroner can't tell if that was done before or after the two-by-four, but it looks like either way the

19

murderer didn't count on the head-bash to do the job. Vic had a cord with a big silver medallion on it tied around his neck. We think the Vic was wearing the murder weapon as a neck-lace. The cord was cinched up real tight — the medallion was used to twist and tighten it. To make it simple so you can understand, it looks like he was garroted with his own jewelry."

Regan took in a sudden gulp of air.

"Anyway, the Coroner is calling it death by ligature strangulation. He thinks the guy might still have been able to suck in a little air, but the coroner says blood flow through the carotid arteries would have been cut off by the cord — that'll get you in a few seconds, at least cause unconscious-ness, even if death takes a few minutes — and that the Vic couldn't fight back, either because of the head-whack, or because of the duct tape.

"You're kind of quiet, Regan. You heard enough, or you want me to tell you more?"

She still had the book, *The Bog People*, a required and intriguing read for a college anthropology class. It was a small book by an author whose name she didn't recall, but the cover photo and the book's opening line had stayed with her: "The man lay on his right side in a natural attitude of sleep." The book described preserved bodies discovered imbedded in peat that was being harvested for fuel. The cover was a photograph of Tollund Man, a remarkably well-preserved leathery-looking Iron-Age man found in a Danish peat bog. He seemed to be asleep, his puckered mouth and forehead suggesting he might be having an unpleasant dream, but a closer look revealed a tight noose around his neck.

"Regan?"

"Yes. Yes, I'm still here … and up for some more gory details."

"Great, 'cause I've got more. The Vic was rolled in a sheet and stuffed into a plastic bag. Then the killer filled the bag with cat litter. The coroner thinks it was done within three or four hours after death or at least a couple of days later because the Vic was bent up into a fetal position so he'd fit in the bag. That means pre or post rigor mortis. The killer was cat litter happy. He poured a bunch of it into the wall space before he put the Vic in, then finished filling in around him. A lot of kitties were inconvenienced just so the guy stayed high and dry.

"We got some fingerprints off the plastic bag. Most of them were new — your inspector guy's — but there was one they managed to pull that may be from the killer. They used some process to pull it that I'm not even gonna try to explain to you."

"Which means you don't understand it yourself. Am I right?" she needled.

"No, you're not right. Well, it's not like I'm a CSI guy. Anyways, I don't have to understand all the details. You derailed my train of thought here."

She was delighted. He'd been messing with her throughout the call. It was satisfying to know she had just scored a point.

"Oh yeah … the way they got the fingerprint … the record for that method picking up anything useful is fifteen, sixteen years after the touch. That knocks some years off our timeframe.

"Our reasoning is that somebody had to know the house pretty well to know about the wall space. We're starting by looking for people with that kind of knowledge. You and Tom aren't suspects, by the way," Dave laughed. "I put in a good word for you."

"How can we ever thank you?" She tried for a tone that blended sincerity with sarcasm.

"We got ownership records of your house. It's been in the same family since it was built. A Lucille and James Schmitt built it in 1978. He died in '91; she went the next May. Cancer got both of them; pretty tragic, huh?" Dave spoke of the Schmitt's deaths with genuine sadness and real heartfelt sympathy. *He was a softy after all, wasn't he*, Regan mused.

"That pretty much rules them out for being the ones to leave the fingerprint." Wham. Dave slammed the door to his sensitive side with amazing abruptness. "Their kids inherited. They had a son Robert and a daughter Margaret who both live back east and a late-in-life kid named James Junior. Junior was still in high school when his mother died, but he was already eighteen and about to graduate, so big bro and sis felt OK leaving him alone in the house. He stayed on after he graduated and started the junior college route at Cabrillo, but he only lasted a couple of months. He quit Cabrillo and joined the Army. He's career military now."

"I dealt with Margaret Harper about the house," Regan said. "Harper is Margaret's married name?"

"Right. We tracked down fingerprints for the soldier; military has a set. He's not a match. Big brother and sister said they'd go to their local police station to give us theirs. Sis was a good girl, no match there either, but we're still waiting for big brother." Dave affected a high-pitched fussy voice. "'He's so very busy, he'll get to it just as soon as he can,'" Dave mocked, "so he hasn't been ruled out yet.

"We haven't been able to talk to the youngest son; he's doing a tour in Germany right now. Big Bro and Sis say they haven't been out to the house in years. They say they left it empty for three, four years after their parents died and baby brother moved out. The idea was they could all use it as a vacation house. None of them ever did, though, and they finally rented it in March of '96. They've only had one tenant, a little old lady who gave up living on her own earlier in the year and moved to a retirement place near her children in Florida."

"Yes, that all sounds like what Margaret told me."

"Well now, that narrows things down some more. It's hard to think somebody could stuff the guy in the wall while the L.O.L. was taking a nap and she wouldn't even notice. So we're thinking the guy got dumped after January of '93 when Junior left for boot camp, but before March of '96 when the tenant moved in.

"We pulled DNA and got a picture of the Vic; sketch artist is trying to fix it up for what he might have looked like with a little juice in 'im. The medallion used to choke him had initials on it, C.J.R. They could be his. We'll check missing person reports from '93 to mid '96 for starters. With a little luck, we'll get a name.

"We got another little mystery here, too, Regan. Vic had a key to your place in his pants pocket. Now just how do you suppose he got that key?"

The message Dave left for Regan the following Friday was short and direct: "We know who your long-term tenant was. Sandy says come on over to our place for dinner tomorrow; I'll tell you all the details." He sounded pleased to let them know the police were making serious progress on what he now referred to as *their murder*.

They arrived with a gift, a bottle of pinot noir from the McHenry Winery in Bonny Doon. "This year took gold as Best of Region in the Bay Area Appellation at the State Fair," Tom explained. "Unfortunately, you can't buy it any more. I tried to persuade the owners to share any they had in their private reserve — no luck. Then I shamelessly played the relative card and told them I thought they were related to Regan to try and get them to part with a couple more bottles, but they swore they were truly out of it."

"Tom, I never knew you were such a schemer," Sandy, Dave's wife, winked at Regan.

"You have no idea how good this is and how badly I wanted more," Tom smiled and wet his lips. "Wait 'til you taste the wine, you'll understand. This is our last bottle.

We've been saving it for good friends and a singular event."

"You mean like finding out who your houseguest was?" Dave chuckled.

"It certainly qualifies as an unrivaled event … at least I hope nothing like this ever happens again." Tom aimed a raised eyebrow at Regan.

Dave laughed louder. "Good luck with that, Tom."

"I have a request, honey," Sandy said. "Please stick to basic facts tonight. We don't want to hear any messy details over dinner."

"Thank you," Regan concurred emphatically.

"Just the facts, ma'am." Dave held up his hands as he quoted Joe Friday's famous line from *Dragnet*. "So here goes. First: the guy's name was Julien Rochette. We got a positive I.D. from the Vic's mom."

Regan was instantly horrified. "The police made her identify her son's body? After Barry Bradford's reaction …"

"We identified him from dental records, Regan." Dave smirked. "We got 'em when he was reported missing. We didn't even have to go to the expense of using DNA. The mom identified his medallion, the one that was used to …"

Sandy shot him a look.

"Well, you all know what it was used for. Seems a girlfriend gave it to him as a gift for his twenty-first birthday. It was his initials, C.J.R. — his real first name was Christian like his dad, but everyone called him Julien from the time he was a baby. He put it on a black silk cord and wore it every day. Ironic, huh?

"We narrowed the time frame for the murder way down, too. The guy had his own place, but he always went home to

25

Momma's for Thanksgiving. She said she called him about coming for turkey day dinner and didn't think much about it when he didn't call her back right away. Seems it wasn't unusual for her to go a month or so without hearing from him. But finally, Thanksgiving was getting close and she wanted to know if he was bringing anyone for dinner, so she tried him a few more times. When he still didn't return her calls, she went by his place. It was locked up tight. She called his best friend; his buddy hadn't seen him or heard from him either for a couple of weeks, maybe longer.

"So then the mom got worried. She got the friend to go with her, went back to her son's place, and jimmied the door. It looked to her like he hadn't been home for a while because all the food in his place, you know fruit and stuff, was rotten and he had a science experiment growing in his fridge. At that point she got really scared. She went to the police and filed an MPR, sorry, missing person report." Dave turned full-faced toward Regan and slowly said, "And she left the name of his dentist."

"So mom said she talked to him last in mid-October and went looking for him mid-November. That puts his murder during that time space."

"Of what year?" Tom asked.

"Oh yeah," Dave replied, "1994."

"Who killed him?" It was Sandy who asked the question.

"All we know is who might have known about the triangle space but didn't kill him," Dave replied. "We know it wasn't Margaret Harper. Her mother-in-law died of cancer three days after Thanksgiving in 1994. That family seemed to have more than its share of cancer deaths in the early nineties." He shook his head and pondered the coincidence for a second or two. "Anyway, the mother-in-law was living with the Harpers from late September until she died. She pretty much needed around-the-clock care and Margaret, her devoted daughter-in-law, had training as a nurse. She was the primary caregiver. Her husband says his wife was a saint, those are the words he used, and rarely left his mother's bedside. No way she came back to California and killed Mr. Rochette without somebody missing her."

Sandy and Regan nodded in agreement.

"Big brother has almost as good a story. He and his brother-in-law opened a sporting goods store in Pennsylvania on October 1st, 1994. They were both working twelve, fifteen hours, twenty-four-seven trying to get it up and running. No vacation, not even a day off, until after the Christmas season that year. Incidentally, he finally found time in his incredibly busy schedule to give Pennsylvania's finest his prints. No match there, either."

"What about the youngest son?" Regan asked. "Have the police been able to talk to him yet?"

"We have. Me personally, as a matter of fact. I bet you didn't know I speak a little German, did you? I got picked to place the call because of that." He chuckled, "Pretty funny as it turns out, because once we tracked down where he was stationed, all I had to do was direct-dial his base and they had him return my call. Deutsch sprechen war nicht notwendig — no German necessary.

"Turns out he knew the Vic."

Regan sat up straighter in her seat. "He knew the victim and could have known where to hide his body? Do you think

27

he killed the man in the triangle?"

"Not a chance. He was on active duty in Korea from September '94 to September '95. And me saying *knew* is overstating a little bit. He said he met the guy once. Seems soldier-brother, who, if you remember, was under booze-buying age then, had a big party to celebrate joining the Army right before he went away to boot camp. Seems he put the word out about the party with everyone he knew and told them to invite friends. The Vic was one of the friends of friends. Junior says there were lots of people at the party he didn't know, but he remembered Rochette because he came with his girlfriend and some of her hot young lady friends in tow and half-a-dozen six packs to share. He made quite an impression on our young about-to-be military man, you know, between the hotness of the girls he brought to the party and all that illicit free beer."

Tom said, "They all seem to have good alibis. Is that what you meant by saying you could tell us who didn't kill Mr. Rochette?"

"You got it," Dave replied.

"What about the key?" Regan asked. "Did the younger son give him a key to the house?"

"You mean like in: Thanks so much for the beer. Here, why don't you feel free to use this nice house any time you want to go to the beach?"

She nodded.

"He says no."

"Then how did he get a key?" Tom asked.

"That's still a mystery. And Regan, don't you go getting any bright ideas. Leave it to us to figure out," Dave commanded.

"I'm sure Regan won't get involved, Dave," Tom said. "Right, sweetheart?"

"Of course." Her smile had never been more innocent or more sincere. Her hazel-eyed gaze had never been more forthright. She meant it. She even almost believed it.

Regan's clients, the Pauralts, were ready to sign the listing agreement and have her sell their house — or at least try to. The median price for houses had dropped precipitously in Santa Cruz County as it had almost everywhere else, although there were some small signs that sales might be improving.

On the lower west side of Santa Cruz, near the ocean where the Pauralt's house was, it wasn't so much that property values had declined significantly, it was that the only houses selling were the less expensive ones. In a recent *San Lorenzo Valley Press Banner* article about local real estate, the expert who interpreted raw data said that sales in the over a million-and-a-half-dollar category had dried up, and the Pauralt's house on West Cliff Drive definitely fell into the over a million-and-a-half category.

It was a sensational house, not one built from the ground up by the Pauralts, but one heavily remodeled by them under the auspices of Santa Cruz' most talented female architect. The home was airy and open, set on a generous lot, which was unusual for houses along West Cliff Drive, and filled with the very-best-quality-of-custom-everything detailing.

By day, the house sported unimpeded views of the bay and ocean. Surfers from nearby Mitchell's Cove were amusing to watch, as were the passing dolphins; and the house was front-row for enjoying the Wednesday night sailboat races out of the Santa Cruz Yacht Harbor. After the sun set, the view was filled with a jewel-like spectacle of lights from Monterey and Pacific Grove on the other side of Monterey Bay. Appreciative artists and photographers often set up easels and tripods across the street from the Pauralt's house to capture the vistas that the homeowners enjoyed every day.

The owners had agreed with Regan about everything for the listing except a lockbox. She wanted one, the Pauralts did not. She explained all the reasons why a lockbox was a helpful tool in getting a house sold. She carefully pointed out statistics that demonstrated how a lockbox cuts down on burglaries. She asked again; the Pauralts declined again.

Regan acquiesced, but on her drive home her mind remained on lockboxes and keys. It wasn't long before the thought of keys turned to the key found in the pants pocket of, as Dave now called him, *their houseguest.*

Regan recalled parts of the first conversation she'd had with Margaret Harper when the woman called her about selling, but their talk had taken place months ago and Margaret had been chatty, relaying so many details about the cottage that Regan couldn't remember them all. She was certain Margaret had said the house was left empty after her younger brother moved out, and that the family all planned to use it for vacation getaways, but none had, so they eventually rented it. Had Margaret said the family considered selling the house before they rented it? Regan thought she might have, but couldn't remember for sure.

By the time she got home, she had an idea how to figure that out. The Santa Cruz Association of Realtors went from paper listing books to computerized listing information at some point in the '90s. After computerization, all listing and sale information remained online and easily accessible. She went to her office, logged onto the Association site, and looked up their cottage's address. No records came up. That probably meant the cottage hadn't been listed before it was rented. Unless …

She quickly entered the address of a memorable listing she had near the end of that year. In 1995 Regan was a new agent excited about her first sale. Her client had tax issues and needed to close escrow before the calendar year ended. An amenable buyer appeared in late November and escrow was on schedule to close in time. But, as Regan saw repeatedly in her career, uneventful escrows rarely happened. The buyer's mortgage broker went on a ski vacation the week between Christmas and New Years and inadvertently took papers critical to the loan with her. The mortgage broker offered to Fed-Ex the documents back to Santa Cruz, but Regan didn't trust the delivery service, overworked as it must be during the holidays, and drove to the ski resort to retrieve them. Escrow squeaked to a just-in-time close on Friday, December 30th.

Her grateful client sent her a celebratory bottle of Dom Perignon with a note telling her it was to be used to ring in 1996. It was hard to forget the date after that much effort and that kind of reward.

Her memorable listing didn't come up on the computer, either. That meant the move to computerization must have happened later than she thought, so it was still possible the cottage had been listed in 1994.

Regan glanced at the clock. It was just before 5:00, before 8:00 back east, early enough for a call. She flipped through her files, found the right one, and opened it to the contact information page. She found Margaret's phone number and entered it. Her phone rang four times and then went to an answering machine. "You've reached the Harper household. You know what to do at the beep," a deep male voice instructed.

She hated answering machines. It was bad enough that she always seemed to fumble her words as soon as she knew they weren't retractable, but she hadn't organized her thoughts before calling — if she left a message, it would no doubt be unsatisfactory. Regan weighed hanging up and calling back the next day, but decided to go forward instead and hope for coherency.

"Hi, Margaret. This is Regan McHenry. You remember, my husband and I bought your family's house in Santa Cruz." *You haven't lost your knack for stating the obvious,* she frowned. "I'm sure the police have already contacted you about … what happened there, but I had a question for you. Did you put the house up for sale before you rented it? Could you call me back and let me know?" She left her phone number in case Margaret had thrown it away. "Oh, and if you did, do you remember who the listing agent was? Thanks, Margaret."

Margaret Harper returned her call within the hour. "We did try to sell the house once," she began. "Let me think when. We had it for sale from late summer until the holidays. I think it was in 1994 — yes, 1994 — I remember because it was the year my mother-in-law died."

"Did you have anything done to the house before you put it up for sale? Maybe you had a new roof put on, or some painting done, or installed a new water heater?"

"No. My parents always took good care of the house. We didn't have to do anything to it. The police asked us if we ever gave a key to any repairmen. Is that what you're wondering, too?"

"Exactly. The murdered man had a key to the house in his pants pocket. How he got the key might give the police a clue to who killed him."

"Oh," there was grave awe in Margaret's voice, "I see."

"Didn't you give a key to your realtor when you put the house up for sale?"

"No." Margaret's emphatic statement was followed by a quick backtrack, "Oh ... well I guess ... kind of. I didn't think of that before." She added defensively, "The police only asked about workmen. But we did give a key to the real estate man, of course we did. Well, not really gave it to him, but told him to get the key from the next-door neighbors, who kept one for us. Mr. and Mrs. Gibson were friends of my parents. They had exchanged spare keys ... you know how neighbors do that sometimes. We exchanged keys with our next-door neighbors here, the Palinskis, just in case we are ever away and there's an emergency. Well, the Gibsons had my parents' key in case they needed to look inside the house for any reason, and to give to any of us who visited ... which we never did.

"But it couldn't be the one you're talking about, though, because I had the real estate man mail it back to me. I remember because I really thought we were going to get to Santa Cruz that winter, take a break after all we'd been through with my mother-in-law, and get out of the snow here for a while. I had him include it with some papers he was sending, and I held onto it. But then we didn't make the trip. When we decided to rent the property, I had to mail the key to the rental company."

Regan made a quick note, "Gibsons — next door neighbors." Given Margaret's confusion, she doubted the woman had told the police about the next-door neighbor having a key. Dave should know; the authorities might want to talk to them.

"Who was your listing agent when you tried to sell the house?"

"It was so long ago. Sorry ... I can't remember. It was a man, though. Oh, I already told you that, didn't I?"

"Do you remember which real estate company he was with?"

"Umm ... no. But it was one of the big ones, I think."

"You mean like Century 21 or Remax?"

"No, no," Margaret hesitated, "not big like that ... big like someone big in Santa Cruz. I remember we found their ads in a magazine — they advertised how many houses they sold. What was the name? It seems like it was a person's name. Oh, I just can't remember. It was so long ago."

"That's OK, Margaret. Now that I know when the house was for sale, I'll be able to figure out who the listing agent was."

"Why does it matter?"

"It probably doesn't, but if he's still around, I'd like to ask the agent if he made any copies of the key."

"Do you think he would remember after all these years?"

"Probably not," Regan laughed. "He's probably long gone, anyway. There's a high attrition rate among realtors — really high — but it's worth a try. Thanks for returning my call so quickly, Margaret."

No point in explaining what agents did with keys to Margaret Harper, but Regan knew the routine. The agent would have made at least one copy of the key for the lockbox before committing the original to the office file. He might have made one for his own use, too. And though the former owner thought her property was fine as it was, she knew a house that had been closed up and essentially abandoned for a few years would need a good cleaning. The listing agent probably hired housecleaners and might have made a spare key for them.

When the listing expired, the agent would have returned the seller's key and destroyed the others. That was the way things worked in a perfect and orderly world, but the real world was sometimes messy. A key might have escaped destruction and found its way into a dead man's pocket.

Regan was at the Santa Cruz Association of Realtors in Soquel the next morning before 9:00 in search of listing books from 1994. If archival copies existed, as she told Margaret, she could find the name of the agent who had listed their cottage.

She had an ulterior motive for her early visit, too. The Association office was a common haunt for realtors and she hoped to run into a knowledgeable one. She was scheduled to testify in an eviction case later in the morning, her first time doing so, and she was a little uneasy about it. Tom volunteered to sit in while she testified, but she told him with great bravado not to bother, that testifying was no big deal. It probably wasn't; she probably had no reason to feel uncomfortable, but she still did.

With luck, she'd find out not only who Margaret Harper's agent was, but she'd run into someone who would explain the court process to her and give her some firsthand reassurance.

Regan nodded hello to the office receptionist as she took a mini-chocolate bar out of the community candy basket on her desk. She slipped it into her pocket, a reward for after her testimony. Then she went to see Nora.

Nora Milano had worked for SCAOR, the Santa Cruz Association of Realtors, for more than twenty-five years. It was widely suspected she knew every bit of scandal that took place in the real estate community during those years; it was certain she'd heard every rumor that came through the office during her career. But while Nora heard everything, she didn't pass anything along. She wasn't a gossip; it would be impossible to find a realtor who could cite any juicy tidbits she had directed their way. Probably that was why she had been so successful at staying employed for all those years.

Nora and Meg Dorsey, an agent who had been around even longer than Nora had and who knew at least as much as she did, were in the midst of a Meg-driven yak. Unlike the discrete Nora, Meg's true calling in life was to act as a clearinghouse for hearsay; she was a woman born to pass along real estate gossip.

Regan caught Meg's last few words: "… cross my heart, that's what she said." Both women burst into uproarious laughter.

Regan knew and liked Meg well enough for hugs. Meg may have been a gabber, but she wasn't a malicious tattletale; she had standards. Her favored gossip, which she shared by speaking rapidly and conspiratorially, included anything realtors did that struck her as humorous, entertaining, bizarre, or inspirational.

"Just the person … people," Regan quickly included Nora, "I wanted to see." She hugged Meg, who returned the gesture and added an air-kiss. "I have a question for each of you. Who's first?"

"Me first," Meg said, "I have an appointment in about twenty minutes. I should be leaving right now to get there on time, so make it fast."

"Have you ever had to testify in court for eviction proceedings?"

"Many times," Meg offered.

"What's it like?"

She tossed her hand dismissively, "There's nothing to it. You just state your name and address ..."

Regan interrupted, "Your address? Aren't you concerned the person being evicted might get angry with you?"

"Not unless you're evicting a crazy. Oh, Regan, are you trying to get rid of a crazy?" Meg put her hand on her cheek, closed her eyes, and gave her head a good shake for added drama.

Regan winced, "Oh yeah, she's crazy all right."

Meg suddenly decided it would be all right to be late for her appointment. She wheeled a chair over from a nearby empty desk, settled into it with a satisfied wiggle, and crossed her legs. She held up her arms and air-pulled Regan toward her. "Tell me all about it — if you can do it in five minutes, that is."

"That depends. Do you want details?"

"Oh, you know how I love details," Meg squealed, "they're the best part of any story! Talk fast."

"I'll try," Regan said. "A couple of years ago I sold a charming little house in Ben Lomond to a client named Maureen. She's an interesting woman ... she'd worked for a Fortune 500 company for years, but said she was ready to change her life completely and pursue her talents as an artist and writer. Buying the house was supposed to be her first step toward a new life. Living in it was going to inspire her to write romantic novels and create pretty botanical paintings. She turned in her resignation at the San Francisco firm where she worked on the same day that escrow closed.

"But as soon as she quit her job, another high-profile company in The City began courting her and eventually convinced her to postpone her plans. Maureen tried commuting, but the daily round trip between Ben Lomond and San Francisco was crushing, so she temporarily abandoned her new cottage in favor of a San Francisco loft.

"She rented her house to an innocuous woman she met in a Santa Cruz art gallery. Things worked out well until recently. Maureen said her neighbors called her late in the summer and complained about some odd things happening at the house. She ignored them at first, but after the second or third time they complained, she called me and asked if I'd go have a look for her."

"And you agreed to? That was your first mistake," Meg snorted.

"Don't judge. I've seen you do helpful things for your clients ... many times." Regan's scolding was softened with a fond smile. "I went by the house and knocked. No one answered, but I heard movement inside so I pounded on the door. The front door finally opened a crack and there stood this ... this creature, with strips of aluminum foil festooning her hair and an aluminum veil partly covering her face."

Nora and Meg tittered and Charles and Preston Alfrey, father and son agents, who had joined the women as Regan told her story, were listening and amused, too.

40

"Maureen swears the woman was normal when she rented to her, but she must have had a psychotic break sometime after that because the poor thing swore Ben Lomond was an extraterrestrial Mecca and that aliens were trying to probe her mind from their nearby spacecraft."

With the mention of alien spacecraft and probes, several agents who had been standing within earshot postponed their business and drifted closer to better hear what Regan was saying.

"The woman said the aluminum made it harder for them to find her and that she'd pulled as much of the electrical wiring out of the walls as she could so they couldn't get to her that way. She'd also smeared feces on the walls to ward them off, and arranged for the toilet to run continuously to flush away tracking beams in the house. The septic system overflowed from the constantly running water and flooded the back yard; that's what caused the neighbors to call Maureen."

"Yep, I'd say she's crazy. Was it human feces?" Meg grimaced.

"We hope it was from her dog, although I don't really know if that makes it any less disgusting. Maureen had me post an eviction notice shortly afterward. The woman is fighting it. Maureen's case goes to court today for an eviction order. The woman will probably be there, too. See why I don't want to give out my address, Meg? Suppose she decides I'm part of an alien conspiracy or that my house needs some doggy-doing? I don't want a tinfoil winky to know where I live."

"Ask your client's attorney to let you use your office address. The judge will allow that if the lawyer asks."

"Really? It's that simple, Meg?"

"Cross my heart," she replied. "You probably don't have anything to worry about even if the tinsel-lady does find out where you live, though. Everyone worries about crazy people coming after them, but crazies don't scare me. It's the people who seem normal you've got to worry about," Meg winked.

"Oh, I'd love to get a look at this loony. Mind if I try to catch the show? My appointment is on May Avenue, just a block from the courthouse, so I'm going to be right in the area anyway. Which courtroom is it?"

Regan fished around in her purse until she found her instructions. "Looks like Courtroom 7."

Once it was apparent that the juicy details of Regan's adventure were over, the listening group broke up; only the Alfreys remained.

Charles Alfrey insinuated himself in front of Regan. "Nora, I need you to ..."

Nora cut him off. "Charles, Regan was here first. Wait your turn, please." Nora thrived for all her twenty-five years by treating agents evenhandedly and in a uniformly courteous manner. Her words to Charles were brusquer than any Regan ever heard her speak, but Charles Alfrey had a reputation: he ran roughshod over anyone who let him, and Nora wasn't about to let him subjugate her.

"Now then, what did you want to ask me?" She turned to Regan with a warm smile.

"I wanted to know if you have old listing books. I'm trying to find out about a house we bought recently. One of the former owners said it was listed in 1994 and I wanted to see who had the listing."

"I heard about your house. It's the one by Schwan Lake where the body was found, isn't it?" Nora asked. "It made the news, you know."

Regan sighed, "I know, I know."

Meg was rolling the borrowed chair back to its rightful desk when Nora's question made her reconsider her move. "Maybe just five more minutes," she said, wheeling the chair back to Nora's desk for a second time. The Alfreys went attentively rigid, and a few nearby agents again stopped what they were doing and unabashedly leaned toward Nora and Regan so they wouldn't miss a word.

"The Association has books going all the way back to when the earth was formed and God created the first real estate agent to sell parcels of it, but we don't have them stored where I can get to them easily. I'll have to get a volunteer to go up into our attic and do a little hunting. I know I can't get anyone to do it today."

Nora lowered her voice and leaned toward Regan. "Have the police figured out who the body belonged to ... I mean who it was in your house?" she stammered with ghoulish delight.

"They have," was all Regan said.

"And?" Meg's query was vigorously asked.

"And, that's it. The remains have been released to his family for burial. It's a very cold case and the police seem to have run out of ideas for now," Regan said.

"Ooh," Nora puckered her lips into a tiny circle as she sucked in air, "so you're looking for clues."

"That's right," Regan laughed. "The police may be stumped, but I'm going to find the murderer singlehandedly.

Nancy Lynn Jarvis

The house address is 102 11th Avenue. I just need any 1994 book with that listing in it. And no rush, Nora; whenever your volunteer gets a chance." She took a quick look at her watch. "Now I've got to go off to my doom. Thanks for the tip, Meg; hope to see you in court as my second."

She nodded to the Alfreys, "Nora's all yours, Charles."

Regan had to walk through a metal detector and submit her purse and eviction packet for inspection before being allowed into the court portion of the County Building. Now that she'd been deemed unarmed and non-threatening, she was free to move along the broad walkway around the centrally located courtrooms in search of where she was to testify.

Benches lined both sides of the passageway inviting people to stop and sit, but most were unoccupied, especially those along the glass exterior wall. The walkway might have been oppressively warm in summer, but in early December there was just enough solar heat transmitted through the two-story glass to make the corridor sunny and pleasantly warm.

She looked at her instructions again to be certain that she had reached the right doorway. Courtroom 7. The numbers matched. The door was open and a few people had already gone inside, but the judge's bench was empty and the bailiff was bent over conversing with the court recorder. Court was clearly not yet in session. She checked her watch. She was early.

Regan decided she would rather wait in the hospitable corridor than in the uninspiring courtroom, so she sat down on the bench next to the doorway and prepared to fill the next few minutes with people-watching.

Individuals moving past her down the hallway made excellent targets for her spectator sport. She assumed those who carried briefcases and were dressed in smart suits or buttoned jackets were lawyers. Male or female, their stride was crisp; they shared the deliberate look of people who had been here before and knew what they were doing.

Most of the people in the corridor, however, looked like she had moments before: they were well-dressed but their progress was uncertain. They moved slowly, clutching documents similar to the one she held, going from doorway to doorway with confusion or trepidation in their eyes, looking for courtroom numbers and reading the names of the presiding judges posted there.

A man with longish sandy-colored hair that Regan guessed was in his early twenties caught her eye. He was moving through the meanderers as quickly as members of the legal profession, but his torn jeans and tee-shirt worn under a baggy jacket made him an anomaly — he clearly wasn't dressed to impress a judge — and he was scanning people instead of courtrooms. He spotted Regan and approached her with purpose.

"You the reel-a-ter?" he asked. "You the one who's been hassling my mom?"

Regan was startled by his question, "I'm a realtor, but I haven't been ..."

He cut her off and leaned down toward her so his face was

close to hers. "I thought you looked like the bitch my mom told me about. She never did anything to you — why are you trying to get her tossed out of her house?"

Regan was filled with indignation by the way she'd been spoken to and answered back sharply, "It's not your mother's house. The house belongs to my client. She asked me to serve a notice to vacate on your mother. That's what I did. I'm here today to testify that I did everything correctly. The court will decide whether or not your mother has to leave."

For a few moments he continued to lean close and scowl, going for intimidation by hovering over her. She returned his stare unflinchingly. Finally, he sat down on the bench next to her, jammed his hands into his jean pockets, and slouched against the wall behind him.

"I'm sorry, ma'am," he said with newfound softness, "but you gotta' understand, my mom's not well. You go in there and tell the judge you did everything right and he's gonna kick her out. She doesn't have anywhere to go and she's feeling real scared. Can't you just not show up or else go in there and say you forgot to give her the papers?"

Regan answered sympathetically, "I'm sorry about your mother, but I can't do either of those things."

His temper flared again, "Then understand this real good," he hissed. His right hand came out of his pocket in a flash and formed into a fist which he shook so close to her face it almost brushed her cheek. "I'll be watching you. You hurt my mom and I'll make sure you regret it." He straightened up slowly, keeping his fist in front of her eyes as he stood, and then turned and swaggered into the courtroom.

From the witness stand, Regan looked over the people seated in the courtroom. She saw Meg, who had arrived in time to walk in with her, smiling and clutching the purse she'd been entrusted to hold while Regan testified. She carefully scanned the courtroom looking for the alien-evader tenant. None of the women in the courtroom appeared to be her, even sans tinfoil.

The proceedings went as easily as Meg said they would. Regan's eviction packet was submitted to the judge for review, her testimony took only a few minutes, and then she was told she was free to leave. Meg got up as Regan reached her, returned her purse, and followed her down the aisle toward the courtroom door.

The next witness was being sworn in by the time they reached the back of the courtroom where the tenant's son was sitting next to the aisle. Regan intended to ignore him, but as she passed him, he reached out and touched her arm. With his other hand, he silently drew his index finger across his throat.

When the courtroom door closed behind them, a wide-eyed Meg gasped, "My God, Regan, did you see that?"

"It was hard to miss. Thanks for your moral support, Meg, and especially for the tip about using my office address." She raised her shoulders and effected a shiver, "I'm glad no one in that family knows where I live."

Regan was almost home when she realized the black truck was still behind her. She had first noticed it at the long straightaway where trails from the University of California at Santa Cruz crossed Empire Grade Road. She was exceeding the posted 40 mile-per-hour speed limit as she usually did, especially there, where the road was straight, flat, and open. The truck had gotten very close to her, tailgating. The straight stretch had a passing area with wide paved shoulders on either side. When the truck got uncomfortably close, she assumed he was getting ready to pass and politely moved to the paved shoulder and slowed to make it easier for him to go around. But the truck slowed, too, and didn't pass.

She lost the truck as the road began its twisting ascent and her familiarity with the route and her uphill driving assertiveness kicked in. When she didn't see the truck behind her where the road straightened again, she assumed it had turned off, but as she neared the turn to her house, she saw the truck was still behind her and getting closer again. Too close.

Regan peered into her rear-view mirror — she couldn't see the driver's face, but she could tell the driver had longish light-colored hair. *Could it be him?* She gave her office address in court instead of her home address — the tenant's son didn't know where she lived. *You realize how paranoid you're being?*

She turned off Empire Grade in the direction of home and drove slowly, looking in her rear-view mirror again. *Don't turn, keep going, don't turn, keep going.* She repeated the incantation silently as if that repetition might magically keep him aimed up Empire Grade Road. But the black truck turned as well. *He could have followed me from the courthouse.* The realization hit her hard.

She quickly formulated a plan. She wasn't going to risk leading the truck driver to her home. Rather than making the next turn onto her street, she went straight. The road she was on would come to a dead-end after all the other streets in the area branched off of it. If the truck was still behind her when she reached the end, she would know for sure she was being followed and not turning an innocent neighbor into a boogie man.

The black truck followed her past each diverging street. As Regan neared the end of the road, she saw a couple she knew working in their front garden. She turned sharply into their driveway, stopped, and got out of her car, very glad for their presence.

As soon as her feet hit the pavement, the truck stopped abruptly in the roadway, did a rushed three-point turn, and sped back down the road. She ran to the middle of the street and managed to catch the Chevy insignia and the first four figures on the license plate, 2BCF, before the truck disappeared around a curve.

🏠🏠🏠🏠🏠🏠🏠🏠🏠🏠🏠

As she finished telling Tom about her pursuer's gunned-engine rush back toward Empire Grade, Regan grew more and more certain she'd seen the last of the tenant's son. "When he saw the Melvilles and realized I wasn't going to be alone, he took off like a dog with his tail between his legs. Isn't it amazing how quickly a bully can fold when someone doesn't go along with his intimidation?" she blustered.

She was confident. Tom was not. "I don't like this at all. That guy stalked you. He may be a true threat."

"No," she tried to soothe, "he's made his point. I'm sure he won't do anything else, especially not after being so public about his threats. He knows he was seen harassing me. If anything happened to me, he'd be suspect number one. He wouldn't take that chance. Besides, if he's truly angry with anyone about his mother's eviction, he'll be angry with Maureen. She's the one he'll target."

"His mother is nuts — he shares her genes. Maybe his reasoning isn't as judicious as yours. Your client didn't come to court. You live close by and you're visible; you're the one he saw testify. Call Dave and see if he thinks we need to be concerned." Tom poured more wine into her glass, "Do it now, before dinner."

Regan rolled her eyes, but she made the call.

Dave listened in relative silence as she told him what had happened, only interrupting to have her confirm the license plate numbers and for the last name of the woman being evicted.

"What did the truck look like?" Dave asked as she finished her story.

"It was black and had one of those cow catcher things on the front of it. And it looked like it had seen better days. Can you find out who it belongs to?"

"Of course I can, Regan. If you want to know tonight, I can call the night shift and have them trace it right now. Why don't I do that. I'll call you back in a bit."

Regan and Tom were just finishing dinner when Dave got back to them. "How's this. A Seth Cooper, same last name as your tinfoil gal, owns a 1994 Chevy Silverado, license plate 2BCF945. Guy lives in Santa Cruz near 17th Avenue. A deputy sheriff friend of mine is going to do a little drive-by and see if his truck is black and has a brush guard, or what you so adorably call it," he dripped sarcasm, "a cow catcher, on it.

"This has been quite a holiday season for you, Regan. A body and a stalker, and we're not even half way through December. What are you planning for a year-end grand finale?"

She ignored Dave's question. "If it is the man from court, what happens next?"

"You could go the formal route and get a restraining order. But I have a feeling he'll be impressed once he understands how unhappy he's made some of your friends-in-uniform. I think you're right about him being a bully, and bullies usually don't make waves once they run into bigger, badder dogs." Dave's metaphor was mixed, but his meaning was clear. "I wouldn't lose sleep over tinfoil momma's baby boy."

"Thanks, Dave, you're marvelous; I mean all of you are, taking care of my shadower so quickly. I bet you'll solve the murder of the man in our house quickly as well, won't you?"

"Murders are harder, Regan. And, if you really want to make us feel like you appreciate us, you won't go getting all agitated when I tell you we're backing off a bit on your murder."

"What do you mean?"

"What I mean is the budget's tight; we don't have enough officers working current crimes. Your houseguest has been dead a long time and so are clues about who killed him. We figured out who he was and when he was killed. Figuring out who killed him is a lot more difficult and will take time.

"Your murder has been assigned to Detective Harrison. He's not real happy to have it. The poor guy's already overworked — with Rochette, he's got four unsolveds, two moving through the courts, and two more getting ready to. Realistically — and I know this sounds harsh, Regan — your houseguest just can't be a top priority."

"But he was murdered," she squeaked.

"See now, there you go. I'm not saying your guy's getting filed; we'll find his killer. I'm just saying he's getting moved off the priority list. Be patient. At least try to be patient.

"I know how hard that is for you," he added as a final jab.

"Would some new information up your level of investigation?"

"It might. What kind of new information would we be talking about, here?"

"I talked to Margaret Harper. She told me the house was for sale during the last half of 1994."

"I'll have to check with Harrison, but I don't think she ever mentioned that before."

"She said she wasn't asked about putting the house up for sale when the police talked to her, so she didn't mention it. The listing agent probably put a lockbox on it; any realtor with a lockbox key would have had access to the house."

"So … are you suggesting we check out every realtor working in 1994 as a suspect in your murder?"

"Of course not."

"Then how does what you're telling me about realtors having access help us?"

"Well, I'm not sure … exactly," she faltered. "But I'm trying to find out who the listing agent was. It's a starting point."

"Good plan, Regan." He sounded like a Little League

coach offering a *good job* to his losing team. "Maybe that will keep you out of trouble for a while. Give me a call when you narrow the field. In the meantime, from Detective Harrison's mouth, through me to you — your murder is off our priority list."

Nora Milano was still promising to get someone at the Santa Cruz Association of Realtors to go look in the office attic for 1994 listing books when Regan got a call from Margaret Harper about a discovery she had made in her attic.

"I was looking for Christmas decorations yesterday and came across a box with old tax returns that went all the way back to the eighties. I decided to sort through them, keep what we needed, and burn the rest. When I was going through the big manila envelopes we used for individual years, I found some papers from when we listed the house in Santa Cruz. We don't need them any longer. Would you like me to send them to you?"

"Yes, I would. But before you do, could you look at the papers and tell me the name of the listing agent?" Regan asked.

"I knew you'd want to know that so I've got it right here. It was Bradley Real Estate," Margaret announced proudly.

"That's the listing company. Who was the agent who signed the papers? The signature should be right under the company name."

"Oh, umm, just a minute, let me look. Well ... the signature's hard to read ... it looks like ... I can't read the first name, but I can tell it starts with a C. Unless it's an open sort of O. The last name looks like it's A something, and then F, or a sloppy L, and then some squiggles. I can't tell, but I'm sure the last letter is a Y, unless it's a Z. That's the best I can do. I guess you'll have to wait 'til you get the papers and see if you can make it out. I'll send them to you first thing tomorrow."

Kathy Valdez, one of the agents at their company, opened the door to Regan's office just as she was thanking Margaret for the call and animatedly waved some papers in the air.

"Fax delivery," she sang out. "I'm being so helpful today. These were in the bin; they're for you."

Kathy handed her two papers from Nora at SCAOR: a fax cover page and a badly copied page from a listing book. Nora must have felt guilty after Regan's last call and forced someone to volunteer for attic duty right after they talked.

The book page was sloppily copied — books, even softcover ones, could never be made to lie flat — but the agent's name for their house was completely legible: Charles Alfrey. Starts with a C ... last name starts with an A ... ends in a Y. No interpretation needed.

Regan's memory flashed on Preston and Charles Alfrey listening in as she asked Nora for a 1994 listing book. They overheard her say she wanted to know who the listing agent for her cottage was. She remembered both men listening with rapt attention as Nora led the conversation to the murder victim found in the house. Preston would have been little more than a child in 1994; the property address wouldn't have meant anything to him. He would only have been listening for titillating details. But what about Charles?

As Nora said, the discovery of a body in a house on Schwan Lake made the news. Unless Charles was one of the most obtuse realtors in Santa Cruz, he would have heard about it. And since there were only a handful of houses on Schwan Lake, when the discussion turned to a newsworthy murder in one of them, surely Charles would have remembered listing such a now infamous property. How odd that he hadn't said anything to her.

🏠🏠🏠🏠🏠🏠🏠🏠🏠🏠🏠

Regan didn't like Charles Alfrey. She wasn't the only person who found him an abrasive and difficult man, either. Several years ago, she'd listed a house in The Circles, an area on the lower west side of Santa Cruz where the streets were laid out like target rings around a central church.

The house she listed — a white clapboard bungalow with cobalt blue trim on a double lot behind a privacy fence — belonged to a world renown British guitarist who had spent the last two years off the tour circuit resting, enjoying the laid-back charm of a Santa Cruz lifestyle, and composing.

The musician hadn't been completely reclusive. He had occasionally played at clubs like Kuumba and the Catalyst during his residency, but he had kept a low enough profile that few people knew where he lived. Still, celebrity, even cosseted, did attract some attention. When he was ready to sell and move on, word got out that the house was *his* and had acquired *good energy* because of his ownership. Six offers all over the asking price arrived within two days of the house being put on the market. Charles Alfrey brought one of the bids.

All six offers were countered to match the highest price proposed. They all came back with the upped ante of a genuine bidding war.

The seller was a sensitive artist. He was overwhelmed when the even higher bids came back accompanied by gifts of cookies purportedly made with secret family recipes, bouquets of home-grown flowers, and even the promise by a young pregnant couple who offered, tongue in cheek he and Regan sincerely hoped, to name their firstborn after the owner: Martin if it was a boy, Martina if it was a girl, if only the musician would sell to them.

The musician suffered dreadfully and genuinely, steeped in remorse that he had only one house to sell and six buyers who said they were desperate to own it. Regan suggested the musician let her number the offers one thru six and refer to them in that way to take buyer personalities out of his decision making. He refused. Instead, he made things more difficult for himself by dubbing five of the buyers' laudable potential owners and using charming titles to describe them: the sweet young couple, the soon-to-be-parents, the deserving one-legged man, the talented artist, and the dear older lady.

The only buyer he excepted from earning a warm title, and the only one whose counter offer he quickly rejected, was the one he christened the couple with the loathsome agent — the couple represented by Charles Alfrey.

Bidding wars can make people crazy. When the deserving one-legged man found out his wasn't the winning offer, he picketed in front of the house and consulted an attorney to find out if his handicap might enable him to sue for discrimination.

On hearing her client didn't get the house, the dear older lady's agent, an older woman herself, came to Regan's office to confront her, and when she was told Regan wasn't in, slapped the receptionist.

And, according to the whispered tale their agent told Regan months later, one night soon after the sweet young couple who succeeded in buying the house moved in, Charles Alfrey knocked on their front door, grabbed the husband by his shirt-front, and while yelling at him and accusing him of using devious means to gain the musician's sympathy, pushed the new homeowner all the way across his own living room and into the next room.

That story shocked her, but it didn't surprise her. Charles Alfrey had earned a reputation for being snappy and mean-spirited. There was even quiet speculation in the real estate community about what he might be capable of were it not for the influence of his second wife, Corinne, a woman as universally liked by all who knew her, Regan included, as Charles was disliked.

Regan parked by the house with the Bradley Real Estate open house sign about fifteen minutes before noon. According to the broker tour schedule, Charles Alfrey would be holding the house open as part of the nine-to-noon morning tour. Realtors were notoriously slow starters on morning tour; during the first hour open houses were sparsely attended. The reverse was true during the last hour as agents tried to make up for their late starts by rushing to as many houses as they could. She wanted to talk to Charles but wasn't anxious to be alone with the infamous Mr. Alfrey. Safety in numbers couldn't hurt, so she decided to use tour behavior to her advantage.

Regan took a cursory look at the house as she would have had she truly been on broker tour. She did it, however, not to see the house's features but to confirm the presence of other realtors. Then she went to the kitchen where Charles Alfrey was reviewing a parcel map with an agent. She bided her time.

"Does that answer your question?" Charles asked, projecting affected warmth toward the questioning agent through a shallow smile. "Are you going to be bringing me an offer soon?"

"Well, let's say I'll be showing the house soon," the agent equivocated.

"I'm sure once your clients see the house and you explain what a great value it is, I'll be hearing from you." His smile became even less genuine.

"Nice to see you," Charles waved an exaggeratedly sociable acknowledgement to a couple of agents who dropped their business cards on the kitchen counter before they began their tour. Regan and Charles were momentarily alone.

"Regan, do you have a buyer for me?" he aimed a professionally genial smile at her.

"It's a nice house, but I'm not working with anyone looking in this location and price range right now." She decided to be direct, "I came to talk to you; that's my real purpose in coming here today."

"A personal visit? Just to chat with me?" He opened his eyes wide in a disingenuous dig. "How flattering." He spoke petulantly but her ears picked up a bit of something else in his voice — wariness possibly.

"You and your son were at SCAOR the other day waiting to talk to Nora — I'm sure you remember — when she recapped the story about a murder victim being found in the house Tom and I just bought. It seems our property was listed during the last half of 1994, that's when the police think the murder took place, and I was trying to find out who the listing agent was. I know you heard that part of our conversation. So what I'm wondering, Charles, is why you didn't mention that you were the person I was looking for?"

His practiced smile remained unwavering and he said nothing for a moment. To Regan's trained eye, he seemed to be buying time, holding a pose while he tried to decide if her question was a bluff or an attempt to trap him into admitting his involvement.

"It was the one on 11ᵗʰ Avenue, wasn't it?"

"Yes," she nodded.

"I did have that house listed. I sell so many houses," he shrugged indifferently. "I realized it later. I thought about calling you, but I'm a very busy man. Anyway, between you and Nora, I assumed you'd figure it out … eventually."

Good old Charles — always so thoughtful and humble, she bristled. She was immediately annoyed at herself. He was good, all right. With just a few dismissive words he had derailed what was supposed to be her controlled interview.

The two card-dropping agents poked their heads into the kitchen. "Thanks," one of them said before they left.

"You're right. We did figure it out," she said evenly, pulling herself back on track. "And now that we both know you were the listing agent, I have some questions for you." She hoped her overly bountiful smile conveyed that she was his equal in controlling the situation and getting answers. She didn't mind if it insinuated the "you jerk" she left unsaid as well.

"I can hardly wait to hear them." Charles signaled another departing agent with a nod of his head.

"The murder victim's name was Julien Rochette. Did you know him?"

His eyes narrowed reflexively, but his overall expression didn't change. "Why would I know him?"

"He had a key to the house in his pants pocket. The police wonder how he got it. Did you give it to him?"

"Why would I give him a key?"

"I thought he might have been a workman, or a handyman you hired, something like that. Do you remember him now?"

"How much do you remember from 1994?" His practiced smile returned. He was parrying her questions with questions, telling her nothing, handling her.

"Is anyone still left upstairs?" Charles called out to a departing agent.

"I didn't see anyone."

"It's after noon, time for me to cut this thing off. Could you twist the front door lock closed on your way out?" Charles asked.

"Sure thing."

"Thanks." He offered the agent an oily smile.

Charles froze his expression of geniality for a few seconds

while he waited for the departing agent to reach the front door. When enough time had passed for the agent to be outside and out of earshot, he turned on Regan.

"I don't much like your questions. What are you implying here? You think I'm somehow responsible for the guy's death? Do you think that's why I didn't tell you I had the house listed?"

He grew more agitated and moved closer to her, jabbing his index finger at the air after each query. She began to think she might be his next target for collar-grabbing and wall-banging and wished she had come to the open house earlier when other agents were still coming and going.

"No ... no ... not at all," she stammered, "I thought maybe you'd remember ..." She took an involuntary step backward.

"I don't like being quizzed, especially not by you. You don't have any authority to ask me anything. I don't want you bothering my family, either, with your stupid questions. Bad things have been known to happen to people who ask annoying questions."

"Oh Charles, you can get so worked up over nothing," Corinne Alfrey, Charles' wife, scolded as she walked into the kitchen, pocketed the key she had just used to unlock the front door, and gave him a little peck on the cheek. "Regan's a friend. She doesn't suspect you of anything, do you? Of course not," Corinne answered for her. "She just wants to solve a mystery." The provocative tone in which she framed her next question made Corinne seem like she was introducing the latest Masterpiece Theater mystery. "Wouldn't you want a murder solved if you just bought a house and discovered a body in it?"

"I'm sorry, Regan," she snickered, "He gets so grumpy when he has to hold an open house. Everything annoys him. Preston and I try to spare him and the public as often as possible, but we both had appointments this morning. Come on, Mon Cher, say you're sorry for being so unpleasant and then let's go get some lunch into you," Corinne charmed.

The change in him was astounding. The churlish Charles was instantly transformed into a wrapped-around-her-little-finger pushover, who looked first down at his feet in embarrassment and then up adoringly at his wife.

"She's right, of course. I'm sorry," he shuffled his feet like a little boy being made to apologize to a grown-up.

One mystery at least was solved in Regan's mind — how Corinne managed to put up with Charles. With everyone else he might be harsh and ill-tempered, but when he was with his wife, he was an adoring softy who obeyed her every command.

"Come on all," Corinne cooed. "Regan, we'll walk you to your car on our way out."

She responded to Corinne's suggestion with a tight, relieved smile and made sure her rescuer was between her and Charles until she got to her car. Once inside, she hit the door lock button, something she usually did only when she was driving alone through a seedy area of Santa Cruz on a dark night, relieved to trade the hostility of the open house for the security of her car.

Regan wondered if Corinne's arrival hadn't been so timely, would Charles have pushed her with more than words. What was it about her simple questions that upset Charles Alfrey so much? She had hit a nerve. He had warned her —

no, he had gone farther than that — he had threatened her as surely as Seth Cooper had. But unlike Seth Cooper, Charles Alfrey cared about witnesses. He was a calculator, not an impulsive boy; he had saved his threat until they were alone.

Why did he care about her amateurish investigation? He was behaving like a man with something to hide. A little shiver went up her spine. Had she stumbled onto something important? In 1994 Charles Alfrey had more access to where Julien Rochette's body was hidden than any other real estate agent; now he was acting like a man with a guilty secret.

She rolled that information around in her mind, growing more and more uneasy as she did. Was it possible she had just been threatened by a murderer?

"Do you think it's possible, Tom?" Regan took a sip of wine and gave the stir-fried green beans and shallots a final swirl around the pan. "Charles was the listing agent. He could have put the body in the house late one night knowing no one lived there, couldn't he?"

"Anything's possible, but why would he? What was his motive? Did he even know the victim? Why bring a body to the house to hide it; wouldn't there have been better places to put it? Details, sweetheart," Tom grinned. "Tame your over-active imagination. My guess? His wife was probably right about him being in a bad mood. Charles Alfrey was most likely just being gruff and provocative because he could be, because that's who he is."

Their speculation was interrupted by their business line ringing in the office. Tom held his thumb up, raised his eyebrows, and then turned his thumb down. "It's dinner time. Hunger trumps curiosity for me. Besides, whatever is in the oven smells really good."

The phone sounded again. "Then you put everything on the table and I'll see who it is. You know me, I can't let a ringing phone go unanswered, but I'll make quick work of our dinner-hour caller."

Regan caught the phone just after the fourth ring and greeted the caller with a businesslike, "Kiley and Associates Real Estate. This is Regan."

"Oh, hi. You must be the," people were talking loudly in the background on the caller's end and Regan had to listen carefully to understand the woman on the line, "listing agent. This is Linda Ku ..." loud laughter drowned out the caller's voice. Regan missed most of the woman's name. "I'm with Coldwell Banker in San Jose. I'm in Santa Cruz for a party and I just met the *nicest* couple."

Regan imagined the caller smiling at her new clients for effect.

"We started talking real estate, you know how that is, and it turns out they've been meaning to see your listing on West Cliff. Well, I suggested we do it tonight. I didn't bring my lockbox key with me to the party; I never expected to run into anyone interested in real estate," she giggled.

Regan rolled her eyes. She knew Linda even though she had never met her. Linda was a room worker. She may not have brought her lockbox key, but Regan was certain the woman's outfit had a pocket, and that the pocket was stuffed with business cards.

"Can you help us out here? I know it's awfully short notice, but could you set it up with your clients so we can see the house tonight?"

"The sellers are out of town. I'd have to open the house for you in any case because it doesn't have a lockbox."

"Oh, how *nice* of you to volunteer," Linda gushed.

Regan shook her head. It was the Pauralt's house that Linda and her new clients wanted to see. The Pauralts — the only clients she had in at least three years who refused to have a lockbox; the clients who had assured her they didn't need a lockbox because they were such homebodies they would always be available to let people in at any time; the clients who were out of town for the next three weeks. They were also the clients who were getting restive because their house had only had one showing since it was listed.

Regan sighed. "We were just sitting down to dinner. I could meet you there in an hour — better make it an hour and fifteen."

"Perfect," Linda burbled. "We'll just have a little more bubbly. We're so close by," she laughed, "we can walk, so we don't need to worry if we get a little tipsy," she said, singing out the word tipsy until it became inebriated.

"I've got to go show the Pauralt's house after dinner," Regan complained when she returned to the kitchen. "I was looking forward to an at-home evening."

"I'll give you a choice," Tom offered. "I'll make the drive into town and show the house for you, or I'll stay here and clean up the dishes."

Regan had been in a cooking and experimenting mood that night and had created a complicated meal that required almost as many bowls and pans for preparation as a Thanksgiving dinner. "Oh, what an easy choice. It's my listing; I'll make the drive. Twenty minutes down, twenty for the party-goers to scope out the house, twenty home. I'll be back in time to have dessert with you but too late to help with the dishes." She feigned sadness, "What a shame."

Winter weather had been late arriving. There was a fierce rain storm in early October that everyone assumed was a harbinger of an early winter, but then the air warmed and dried again and tenaciously clung to Indian summer. There were only a few light rains that came through the Monterey Bay area the rest of October and into November. Now that they were in December, though, daytime temperatures had finally dropped below fifty, nighttimes dipped into the high thirties, and rain was coming with increasing regularity and intensity.

People who hadn't lived all their lives in mild California would have considered the night temperate, but Regan was California spoiled, fifth generation San Francisco Irish on her mother's side, fourth generation on her father's. She considered the night a nippy one.

She pulled a thick, well-worn and comfortable jacket over her sweater before opening the garage door to the chill. No need to be fashionable tonight. Her sole job was going to be door monitor and question answerer for Linda and her newfound clients.

The pounding storm that passed through in the afternoon scouring the Santa Cruz Mountains with rain had mostly cleared even in the high elevation of Bonny Doon where they lived. The driving rain had dwindled to a light drizzle that only required her windshield wipers to be on an intermittent setting. Her car was steady; the day's blustery wind gusts that scattered dozens of small tree limbs on the road were long-gone, and the downed branches had been driven over enough to be reduced to hazardless piles of roadside debris.

The road into Santa Cruz was fairly deserted at this time of night. Residents had already made it home after work, or if they were out like Linda, arrived at their holiday parties where they would remain for at least another hour if they didn't want to risk offending their hosts.

Regan was a confident driver. She knew every curve in the road and drove slightly faster than the speed limit and faster than she should have, given the possibility that something bigger than mulchable branches had been brought down by the storm. Even with her speed, however, the set of headlights that appeared behind her right after she turned onto Empire Grade grew brighter and closer with each turn. Someone was in a rush.

Regan was already going at the uppermost limit of her driving abilities and didn't feel comfortable going any faster, so she looked for a good place to pull over to let the speeder go past. The road was steep in the stretch where she was and the unpaved shoulders were deeply rutted by downhill runoff. She passed several places wide enough for her to pull over but decided her car's suspension would take a beating if she went off the pavement.

The vehicle behind her drew close enough that the driver should have lowered his high beams. They reflected annoyingly in her rear-view mirror and glared into her eyes. She used the night setting on her mirror, but it didn't help for long. The vehicle behind her was big, probably an SUV or a pickup truck, with high-set headlights; her mirror change only reduced the bright glare minimally and momentarily until the vehicle came closer and overcame the improvement.

Didn't the driver realize he was blinding her? Regan held

her hand up in front of the mirror, trying to signal him to turn off his high beams. The driver was either in a very big hurry or had celebrated the coming holidays a bit too much to pick up on her signal. The vehicle came even closer, its high beams unrelenting.

She grew increasingly anxious for him to go around her. She knew there was a straight section coming up after the next curve. Even if she couldn't get completely off the road, she could slow and get over enough that hopefully he would understand her intent, see that there weren't on-coming headlights, and swing over the double yellow line and pass. When she reached the straightaway, she maneuvered her car as far to the right as she could.

Rather than passing, her hasty follower slowed, too. He must have finally realized his driving was annoying and dangerous. Regan moved back into the center of the lane and regained speed.

Within seconds he was tailgating again. She squinted to minimize his high beams and peered into her rear-view mirror, trying to make out her reckless tormenter. All she could see was that the vehicle was indeed large and dark in color.

That's when she felt the first hit. It was brief and hesitant, barely contact, but it was terrifying. She gripped her steering wheel tighter and instinctively braked her car.

The second hit was more deliberate, more certain, and more assertive. The looming vehicle locked against her rear bumper and pushed her while they sped through a narrow high-walled cut in the mountain. Regan floored her brake pedal. Her brakes rasped and screeched but her speed

71

continued to increase.

 Her attacker eased off as they rounded a right curve, the beginning of a series of increasingly tight turns where the road came out of the mountain cut and opened again to trees growing along a cliff edge.

As Regan maneuvered around the first curve, her heart pounding, she was suddenly doubly blinded. Headlights came at her from the front as well as the back. The approaching car passed in a second — before she could flash her lights or in any way try to communicate her terror.

The dark vehicle stayed back through the first left curve, but as they began the swing into a right turn, it pressed forward again and smashed into her sharply, this time not directly from behind but near her left rear wheel.

What happened after that ticked by in unnaturally slow motion. She saw her rear passenger window glass explode. She felt her car lurch to the right. She knew when her front wheels left the road and the precise moment her rear wheels followed. She experienced a momentary sensation of weightlessness as her car cleared the edge of the road and dove into the night sky toward the litter of trees growing on the slope beneath her. She sensed the angle of her seat change as the weight of the engine tilted her car downward.

She became preternaturally calm and detached as her car began its plunge down the steep mountainside, saddened by her fate, but no longer afraid.

I love my life. And now I'm going to die.

Voices? Maybe. Yes, voices. The understanding of what she was hearing came to her gradually. At first, she just heard organic noise. Then a sound or two became significant and formed into a string of meaningful utterances: words. Finally, she understood the words and recognized the voices … Tom and Dave.

She opened her eyes slowly and asked feebly. "Am I alive? I hurt everywhere."

"You're still with us, sweetheart. You're bruised and banged up. They don't think anything's broken or seriously dented but you may have a slight concussion. They want to keep you overnight for observation.

"You had a close call." Tom took her hand as he continued, "People in a house on Empire Grade heard you crash and called the Bonny Doon Volunteer Fire and Rescue Team. The Volunteers got you out of your car and back up the mountainside. They said if that tree hadn't pierced your front window and held your car up, you would have gone to the canyon floor. One of the recue team also said if that tree was about two feet to the left, it would have gone through

73

you. Remember, that happened to a girl in a catering truck a few years ago?"

Regan pressed her lips together, took a quick shallow breath, and nodded slightly. A young woman had died when the vehicle she was in went off Empire Grade Road. It hadn't been a serious accident, no one else in the truck was hurt, but she'd been impaled by a small redwood tree.

"You don't even look like a raccoon," Dave chimed in. "Airbags break short women's noses sometimes or give them a good sock in the eyes. They wind up looking like raccoons. You're tall enough the bag didn't hit you like that."

"I bet you're disappointed," Regan said.

"A bit, yeah," Dave laughed. "I brought my cell phone to take your picture. I planned to post it on Facebook, maybe YouTube, too."

Tom could reassure her endlessly, but Dave's taunting meant she really was fine; he would never tease if she weren't.

"I wasn't speeding or anything like that; I didn't lose control of my car," Regan asserted.

"Sure you were speeding," Dave insisted. "I know how you drive."

"No, I wasn't. Well, I may have been going faster than I should have been, but barely. I didn't lose control of my car, I was attacked," she stated emphatically.

Regan immediately regretted her vigor. The deploying airbag may not have left her visibly bruised, but something had hit her in the face hard enough that the movement needed for animated arguing was painful.

"Yeah, we know that, too," Dave replied, finally serious.

"We got multiple reports. A couple you passed on your way down called in that a big dark vehicle might have lost its brakes and bumped a car. Then your buddies on the fire team said your car has crumpled bumpers front and back, and there's lots of damage to the back end, but the roof is clean, so you didn't end-over-end. Since your car was aimed downhill and you were dangling by your seatbelt when they got to you, they thought that damage pattern was strange. Your back bumper shouldn't have been crumpled, considering how you landed.

"We'll pull your car up in the morning once we get some daylight and take a closer look. Could be interesting. In the meantime, you want to tell me your version of what happened, or are you too addled?"

Tom held up a hand. "Dave, Regan needs some sleep. Can't this wait for daylight, too?"

"Really, I'm OK. I'll sleep better if I talk first, anyway. And I don't want to risk forgetting any details."

"Good gal," Dave beamed.

"What happened is I noticed someone behind me shortly after I got on Empire Grade. They were moving faster than I was, so I tried to let them pass, but they wouldn't. Then they hit me from behind and kept doing it until they finally forced me off the road."

"Can you tell me anything about the vehicle and the driver?" Dave asked.

"Not much. I couldn't see the driver at all, and with the dark night and the headlights in my eyes, I couldn't tell much about the vehicle either, except it was big, and possibly a dark color."

"Big, huh? Why do you think it was big?"

"Because of the headlights. They were high; the light from them came right through my back window when it got close. And it seemed more powerful than my car because it pushed me one of the times it hit. I was braking hard and it could still push me. So, big and heavy, like a large SUV or a truck. Oh Dave, one other thing I remember about the lights — they were weird. They were round and clear when they started following me, but they had stripes on them when they were up close."

"Stripes?" Dave frowned. "You mean like jail bars?"

"No. Horizontal stripes."

Dave clamped his upper teeth over his lower lip and twisted his face into a smile. "You said the vehicle caught up with you real quick after you got on the main road? Like it was waiting for you to come out?"

"I don't know." Regan visualized looking in her rear-view mirror and seeing her pursuer for the first time. "I guess … yes, I guess that's possible."

"I told you about the call from the real estate agent, Dave," Tom said. "It just occurred to me no one called to complain that Regan didn't show up. I sure would have. I think any agent would have to save face in front of their clients. Are you thinking some kind of set-up?"

"Yeah." Dave turned to Regan, "We'll see if we can back track and find out who the caller was. I'm thinkin' the crazy woman you testified against made like a real estate agent and set you up so her son, who threatened you and tried to follow you home, could wait for you at the first place he was sure you'd pass. They had it planned; he'd wait in his black truck

76

with the brush guard and whack you when you started into town."

"Dave, I've got a gut feeling it wasn't him."

"Oh great, she's got a gut feeling," Dave looked to the ceiling and wagged his head from side to side.

"Well, maybe it's more than that. I do think you two are right about the realtor call being a set-up; it seems like too big a coincidence that someone was waiting for me at precisely the right time unless it was, but the woman who called sounded real, like she had real estate experience. I don't think that poor unstable woman would know enough about the business to speak so convincingly. I'm not even sure she could keep it together enough to make the call. This is a woman who wears tinfoil to protect herself from alien mind control, you know."

"Maybe her aliens told her what to say about real estate. I think we'll be wanting to ask your Seth Cooper where he was tonight between six-thirty and eight and have a look at his truck to see if he's put any new dings in its pristine paint job."

Dave headed for the hospital room doorway. "I'll give you a call at home tomorrow. In the meantime, you take care."

Tom called after him, held up his cell phone and wiggled it, "Dave, how about a heads-up when he's in custody?"

"Will do."

Regan took a deep breath, regretted it immediately, and winced.

"You act like you could use a little more help in the pain department. I'll buzz for a nurse," Tom said. "Do you need something to help you sleep, too?"

"No, don't bother. I'm fine as long as I don't move, and I'm dead tired. I'll be asleep in no time."

Tom moved his cushioned chair so it was perpendicular to her bed. "Mind if I borrow one of your pillows?" he asked as he kicked off his shoes. He carefully removed one of the pillows from behind her back, watching her face closely to be sure he wasn't causing her any discomfort. He sat down, arranged the pillow as best he could behind his back, and put his feet up on her bed. His long frame meant he couldn't get proper support for his head regardless of what he did with the pillow or how far down he slouched in the chair.

"What are you doing?"

"Settling in for a romantic night with my wife," he grinned.

"There's no need. You don't have to."

"I want to — at least until I hear from Dave. I'll feel better being here just in case that Cooper kid eludes the police. He may want another crack at you."

"You don't have to protect me from him. He sounded tough, but I think he's harmless — like I told Dave — gut reaction. Seth Cooper tried to scare me out of testifying. When that didn't work, his fallback plan was pleading and then posturing, not real aggression."

"What do you call following you home?"

"He couldn't stop his mom from being evicted. I'd call that spur-of-the-moment anger that came from feeling helpless. But as soon as I confronted him, he ran.

"What happened tonight took serious thought, planning, and violence. I don't think Seth Cooper has all that in him. I bet Seth has an alibi."

Tom started to shake his head.

"Please, don't you dismiss my hunch like Dave did, especially when there's logic behind it. Besides, I do have an idea about who could come up with the plan and is aggressive enough to hit me."

"And who would that be?"

Regan paused and took another breath, carefully testing the limits of how deeply she could inhale without it hurting. "Charles Alfrey."

Tom put Dave on speaker-phone when he called the next morning so both he and Regan could hear his report.

"Your Seth Cooper was sleeping like a guy with a clear conscience last night when one of our finest knocked on his door, or at least that was the way he played it. He was in his jammies and acting all sleepy-like when he answered the door. According to him, he came right home after work, had dinner, and then hoisted a few with a buddy before going to bed by ten-thirty like a good little boy 'cause he had an early morning coming up at work. All he left out of his story was how he and his pal watched a Christmas special on TV and said *awh* when Rudolf saved Christmas."

Regan sounded just a little triumphant as she said, "So he has an alibi."

"Let's say he *may* have an alibi, but it's hardly an airtight one. His buddy backs up his story, but that guy's a musician with a long drug record. Let's just say he isn't the most reliable little drummer boy."

"Regan has another theory," Tom said.

"Your gut again, Regan? Maybe you should get a doc to

check that out for you."

"I had a second threat recently."

"I thought you were the likeable type; now you're saying you got guys lining up, wanting to take you down? And why didn't you tell me about a second threat?"

"It's my fault," Tom said. "The man who made it has a reputation for being abrupt and grating; I thought he was just behaving like he so often does. I didn't think he was serious."

"Can I decide that? Spill."

"His name is Charles Alfrey," Regan offered. "He's fifty-ish, a top producer at Bradley Real Estate, and not the most popular man in the real estate community."

"Why is that?" Dave asked quietly. He was in professional mode; his voice didn't contain a trace of teasing or mockery. "Cheats and backstabs and does underhanded business?"

"No," Regan considered, "no, I've never heard anyone complain about his ethics. But, remember I was trying to track down who the listing agent was for our new bungalow when it was for sale in 1994? Well, it turns out he was the agent, and when I asked him a couple of questions about it, he told me to back off, and said if I didn't, something bad might happen to me."

Except for the loud sigh he emitted, Dave was silent for several seconds. "We'll take a look at him," was all he said before ending the conversation.

Regan guessed Dave was smiling as he talked to her early the next day. "Yeah, I'm checkin' up on you, but this is an

FYI call, too. We dead-ended on the phone caller; the number was a pre-paid cell. However, we got what was left of your car off the mountainside. There's definitely some black paint on the bumper and the left rear side. We'll be taking a real good look at your Mr. Cooper's truck, especially the brush guard part to see if it's the same color and to see if there's any of your car's red paint on it. I think we'll get him."

"What about Charles Alfrey? Weren't the authorities going to look into where he was night before last?"

"Been there. Done that. And all so discreetly he doesn't even realize we took a peek at him. He does have a big vehicle, a Land Rover, black one, too, but it doesn't have a brush guard or any scuff marks anywhere on it. That sucker's as smooth and shiny as the day it came out of the factory.

"The kicker is he was at his company's holiday office party the night you went airborne. He left his Rover at their Santa Cruz office and a little before six hitched a ride with his broker to Michael's on Main in Soquel where the party was held. He didn't leave 'til almost midnight. His whole company saw him enjoying the party.

"It seems he had a little too much holiday cheer, and being a responsible citizen," Dave chuckled, "let his wife drive them home. She'd been showing a house, isn't that what you real-a-ters call it," Dave deliberately mispronounced her profession, "up in your neck 'o the woods, in Bonny Doon, so she came to the party late and had her own car. They left his Rover in the Bradley parking lot overnight and she drove him to work the next day.

"Hey Regan, how's your gut feelin'?" If he hadn't been smiling before, Regan was certain he was now.

12

Terrance, their regular UPS driver, dropped off the packet from Margaret Harper just after 9:00 on Tuesday morning. Regan had been treating her body gently — she was still sore especially where her seatbelt restrained her after the airbags deflated — and letting herself recover from the effects of her too-abrupt stop on the mountainside by spending her days doing no more than the annual deploying of her Santa Claus figures.

There must have been a time in her past when she told someone she was a fan of Old Saint Nick. If that was how her collection started, it was so long ago she no longer remembered who gave her the first one. She didn't actively collect them, but Santas found her. She had a cowboy Santa, a surfer Santa, a skier, a hand-sewn patchwork model, and Santas in traditional garb from Scotland, the Ukraine, Switzerland, and an Uncle Sam version with a stars-and-stripes top hat and a flag. There were musical versions and Santas dressed in blue velvet or snowy white robes to be crowded onto the mantel as well.

The UPS delivery put a halt to her Santa arranging. Regan

ripped the packet open and dumped the contents onto a kitchen counter. The listing contract landed on top and was the first document she picked up. Regan flipped to the last page. Not that she had any doubt about what she would see, but she confirmed Charles Alfrey's signature. Regan didn't bother looking at most of the packet contents: the preliminary title report, old deeds, parcel maps, and the conditions, covenants and restrictions on the property.

The final document was the largest — a pest inspection report. She scanned the cover page. Charles Alfrey had ordered the report. Once generated, it would have come to him. He would have sent a copy to the sellers and kept a copy for his files, and he would likely have reviewed it before filing it. If the house had issues that might concern a buyer, he would need to be prepared and possibly have repair bids ready. If the report was clean, he could use that as a selling feature for the house.

Regan read the narrative portion of the report carefully, looking for any mention of the triangular space where Julien Rochette's body had been hidden. She reached the end without seeing any reference to it.

The final page was a house diagram drawn by the inspector. The house was outlined and a fairly accurate demarcation of the walls and basic features like the kitchen and the bathroom was provided. The fireplace and the oddly angled wall that formed the front of the triangle were also shown, although there was no mention of it being hollow or accessible from above the ceiling.

Tom came into the kitchen in search of coffee and spotted the open UPS packet. "You better not be opening anything from …" he caught himself in time, "well, I better not say where a package might be coming from," he laughed. "Just the store name could give away the contents and blow my Christmas surprise for you."

"Umm, so it could fit in something this size," her lips curled up as she tapped them. She picked up the empty mailing envelope and turned it over a couple of times. "Let's see. Jewelry would fit, or tickets to something … or some-where. A book would fit. No — I know — a gift certificate and a catalog from a nursery that has exotic plants," she added enthusiastically.

"Thanks for all the ideas," he chuckled.

"Were you really expecting something?" She tilted up her chin and looked at him suspiciously, "Awh, you're conning me, aren't you? I will be on the lookout for Terrance between now and Christmas though, just in case you're not," she grinned.

"This packet is from Margaret Harper. It's the listing documents she received when the family tried to sell our little house in 1994. Charles Alfrey was the listing agent, but we already knew that. There's a termite inspection in the packet. The schematic does show an angled wall. If Charles attended the inspection, the termite inspector could have told him all about the space it created. He could have known and planned — the house would have been vacant and he would have had a key."

"But would he have known?" Tom asked. "If the house was vacant, would he have bothered attending the inspection? 'Busy man like me,'" Regan laughed as Tom imitated Charles' smug pomposity, "'I don't have time to spend a couple of hours with an inspector.'"

"He might have called the inspector after he looked at the report," Regan suggested.

"Is there anything about the triangular space mentioned in the report body?"

"No, there isn't."

"Then if it's just a line in the schematic, I bet he wouldn't even have picked up on it. That drawing doesn't prove knowledge." Tom's statement was definitive. He dropped the report to the counter with the other documents.

Regan picked up the report again and looked for the inspector's name on the introductory page. "Jessie Bolten did the report. I know he retired a couple of years ago, but I can probably track him down and ask him a few questions. You remember what a talker Jessie is. Maybe he'll remember talking to Charles Alfrey."

"Jessie didn't talk to me that much. What I remember about him is that he was always loquacious in front of *female* audiences. The younger and prettier the woman, the more he talked, the wilder his hunting stories became, and the more heroic his role was in those tales. I always suspected if an attractive female agent listened to his stories with rapt attention, her clients got a more favorable report than they would have otherwise.

"With men, especially irritating men like Charles Alfrey, I bet Jessie was completely mum," Tom snickered. "Even if Jessie did mention the triangle to Charles, it was such a long time ago he probably wouldn't remember the conversation. And now that he's retired, what's your plan for contacting him? For all we know, he could be living in Florida now, wrestling alligators for a hobby — or at least telling good looking widows that's what he's doing."

"He's probably still around. Jessie had family here. He was always bragging about his daughter and he owned a house near Salinas, a ranch he called it, that he loved. Some of the hunting stories he told me happened on his property. I vividly remember him saying how he dropped a wild boar at his feet with his last bullet and how he shot a coyote that was menacing his livestock and hung its carcass on a fence as a keep-away warning to other coyotes."

Tom's smile grew bigger and bigger as Regan reminisced. "Got a lot of favorable termite reports, didn't you?" he winked.

🏠🏠🏠🏠🏠🏠🏠🏠🏠🏠🏠

It wasn't difficult to find Jessie Bolton. He still lived outside Salinas, just as Regan remembered, and he still had a listed phone number. When Regan called, Jessie boasted he had just come in from a ride on his back forty.

"Yep," he said, "been out lookin' for a renegade cougar that's been leave'n tracks nearby."

Same old Jessie. "I was hoping to talk to you in person, but I cracked up my car and I'm still too sore for the drive to your place."

"Sorry to hear it, Regan. It would have been good seein' you. So, what can I do ya for?"

"How's your memory?"

"Depends. If it's a problem you think I caused, it's pretty faulty. If you figure you owe me money, it's awful good."

Regan laughed, "It's not a problem and I know I don't owe you money, but it is sort of work related. Tom and I bought a little house a couple of months ago. You did a termite inspection on it in 1994. I had a question for you about that report."

"A report from 1994? Let me think back. That's three reports a day, times five days a week, times forty-eight weeks a year — I'm takin' off four weeks for vacations and holidays — times all those years, that's ... oh hell, Regan ... that's too much for anybody's memory. Can you give me anything else to work with?"

She laughed again. "I can fax or email you a copy of the report. Maybe you'll recall more if you look at it. The house had this weird little triangle space near a fireplace. It may not mean anything to you when you see the report, but that space has certainly created a lot of drama in our lives ... a body was found in it."

"Woo!" Jessie exclaimed. "I'm sure I would have remembered a house with a skeleton in it."

"Oh, you would have remembered him, all right. There was a little bit more to him than a skeleton, but based on the date on your report and when the man went missing, we know he went into the triangle after your inspection. What I'm trying to find out is if you noticed the space or mentioned it to anyone."

"You mean like in 'Hey, if you ever want to kill someone, here's a great place to hide a body.'"

"Exactly like that, yes." Regan's laugh was becoming a regular response to each of Jessie's questions.

"Sounds like you know who he was. Wouldn't it be easier

to start from that direction than from workin' from me backwards?"

"You'd think so, but I have a suspect in mind for who killed Julien Rochette, that was the murdered man's name, and I'm trying to connect him to some prior knowledge of the place where the body was hidden."

There were no more questions from Jessie. His next statement, which was slow in coming, was a stunner: "When you find out who killed that worm, let me know. I want to send him some prime steaks from one of my best steers. You said you can't drive out here — can you make it to the house I did the report on? I'll meet you there, take a look, and see if it jogs my memory. I want to see where Rochette died."

"Uh ... well ... OK." Regan gave Jessie the address and agreed to meet him at the bungalow the next day at 11:00. Then she hung up and put her hand over her mouth and leaned back in her seat. *Wow*.

Regan was early. It was the first time she'd driven Empire Grade Road since her attack and she knew she'd drive cautiously so she gave herself extra time, more it turned out than she needed.

Even so, Jessie was already parked in front of the house and waiting for her. He climbed out of his truck as soon as she turned her rental car into the driveway, not even waiting for her to park. He walked to the front door and stared at it, his back to her, waiting for her to catch up and unlock the door. From the back, he looked stronger now than he had before his retirement, as if time spent on horseback and doing ranch chores had fortified him.

"Hello, Jessie. It's good to see you."

In the past his greetings were warm and effusive, often involving a hug; today he merely nodded an acknowledgement. "This is the place, is it?" She noticed his jaw work and his teeth clench.

Regan opened the door and preceded Jessie into the house. "The triangle where the body was found is gone. The authorities took it apart the day they removed the remains and cleared away all the pieces of construction that formed it — forensic evidence they said — so the house looked a little different when you inspected it."

"Doesn't matter. I remember this place." Jessie walked to where the triangle had been. He put his hands on his hips and smirked. "Serves you right, you little punk," he said to the emptiness that had held Julien's body.

Regan's mind was full of questions — why Jessie hated Julien Rochette was the foremost one. She wanted answers but didn't want to lead him. She waited for him to fill the vacuum her silence created. It wasn't a long wait; he was eager to unload.

"Yeah, I remember this inspection all right. Corinne Alfrey let me in. I don't know if she had her license yet or not; she was Charles Alfrey's assistant before they got married, you know. But even after she was licensed, she was always the one who handled their inspections, which was fine with me 'cause she was nicer to look at than he was." Jessie's mouth formed a sour smile as he mentioned Corinne's looks. His expression seemed like an unkind commentary about her and negated his appreciative words.

"I was up in the attic space finishin' up, lookin' for termite droppings below the rafters. I was at the back of the house and Corinne was quiet, workin' on some paperwork or somethin'. I heard a voice at the front of the house call her name — thought it sounded like a man. She went up front and they started talkin'. I was movin' in that direction anyway," he shrugged, "and got close enough to more or less hear what they were sayin'.

"You know how you can tell when people are cozy, even

91

if you don't exactly catch their every word? Well, I could tell they were cozy. Corinne was gigglin' and shushin' him. I heard her say something like, 'Stop it, we're not alone' and giggle some more.

"I finished up and dropped back down through the ceiling hatch. I figured the man was Charles Alfrey and I wanted to say Hi to him. He threw a lot of business my way so I never wanted to miss a chance to say thanks for that. But the guy wasn't Alfrey. It was Julien Rochette," Jessie's voice oozed contempt as he said the name, "the same guy'd been hounddoggin' my daughter, Isabel.

"I didn't like that guy one bit. He was way too old for Isabel. She was eighteen, just out of high school, and he was in his twenties, but old for his age — wild, tough, swaggery — too experienced. I knew his kind. Hell, I *was* his kind comin' up. Man like that'll suck the life and joy out of a woman who loves him. Isabel was such a beauty and did good in school, too. She was accepted at Carnegie Mellon in their drama department; she was gonna study acting. She had the looks to be a movie star, but she started sayin' she didn't want to go so far away and leave Julien. She deserved better'n that kind of man.

"Yeah, you could say I was pre-loaded to dislike the guy. And now here he was makin' moves on Corinne Alfrey, a married woman, to boot. Pissed me off. Pissed me off, big time.

"They practically pushed each other across the room when they saw me. Corinne tried to introduce us and say he was her cousin. Julien looked at his feet and said we'd already met. Then he backed out of there about as fast as a man could move butt-first.

"Just before she was supposed to leave for college, my Isabel came in wearing a ring and said she and Julien were engaged. She cancelled out of Carnegie Mellon, wouldn't listen to any kind 'a reason, and said they were gettin' married in June."

Jessie clenched his fists, "Then that jerk just stopped calling her and cleared out of town. I think once he had her, that was all he wanted. She was just a challenge to him. He wanted to see if he could make a girl like her love his worthless ass. He broke her heart and ruined her future. If I ever ran into him, I planned to choke the life out of him for what he did to her."

Regan didn't doubt for a minute Jessie meant what he said.

He'd worked himself into a seething rage explaining how he couldn't protect the daughter he loved from being used and discarded by Julien Rochette. Regan put her hand on his arm and said gently, "He didn't abandon your daughter, Jessie. He was murdered."

Regan grasped what Julien's murder meant, but Jessie had to roll it around in his mind for a few moments before he genuinely understood. After such a long time, the truth was too jarring for him to accept immediately. His eyes darted around the room as he tried to reconcile what really happened to Julien with what he had believed for so many years. His body seemed to shrink along with his fury.

"He was still no good for my daughter," he said finally, in the weak voice of an old man.

Regan tended toward lead-footed driving, especially when she was excited. If not for her unfamiliarity with her rented Ford, she would have made the twenty-minute trip from the cottage on 11ᵗʰ Avenue to their across-town office on Swift Street in less than fifteen.

Their office lot was mostly deserted, but Tom's car was there, and that was all she really cared about at the moment. She parked her car next to his and hurried to the front entrance. Her aggressive driving, her twisting to get out of the car, and her hurried close-to-running stride hadn't produced even a twinge of post-accident discomfort, but when she pulled on the heavy glass office door, she got a sharp reminder that her accident had happened only days before. The sudden jolt of pain faded immediately, though, and she congratulated herself for not groaning in public and for mending quickly.

She offered a smile and a raised-hand finger-wiggle by way of greeting to Amanda, their receptionist, and then hurried down the hall to Tom's office. The upturned sides of her mouth sagged when she discovered he wasn't there.

Regan went back to the reception area, "Any idea where Tom went?" she asked Amanda.

"Not exactly. He left not more than five minutes ago with that policeman friend of yours. He said they were going to get some 'guy food' for lunch and he'd be back in about an hour. You could call him," Amanda offered, "and ask him where he is."

"I can guess. When those two get together, I know what 'guy food' means."

🏠🏠🏠🏠🏠🏠🏠🏠🏠🏠🏠

She spotted Tom and Dave in a booth as soon as she walked into 99 Bottles of Beer on the Wall, a popular eatery on Walnut Street that was a distinctively Santa Cruz blend of pub and sports bar. Restaurant patrons could earn a plastic wall plaque inscribed with their name and a quotation, often thought of under the influence of a final beer drinking push judging from some of the sayings, once they had tried all 99 beers on the menu. Both Tom and Dave carried punch cards and were working on their plaques, although neither had earned one yet.

Regan caught Tom's eye and directed a radiant smile at him just as he took a big bite of his California burger. When she reached the booth, his mouth was still too full for him to speak. He silently slid over to make room for her.

A waitress appeared with a menu. "No need, thank you. I know what I want. I'd like a black bean quesadilla and coffee."

"No beer for you today?" the server quizzed.

"No. Thank you. I don't like beer."

The server gave her a befuddled look and was still at the table writing the order when Regan announced, "I've got news and maybe a motive for murder."

"Oooh," Dave said, stretching out his pronouncement, "this ought to be interesting." The waitress stretched, too, writing her order much more slowly than was necessary, hoping to overhear more.

Tom finished chewing and swallowed. "Did Jessie say Charles knew about the triangle?"

"He couldn't remember ever telling him about it directly, but he had some other even more interesting things to say." Regan looked up at the waitress who was no longer pretending to write, "That's all for me, thank you."

The server heaved a disappointed sigh and slowly left to place the order.

"He said Corinne — she's Charles' wife, Dave — was there for the inspection and that Julien Rochette came into the house and started making kissy noises at her before he realized Jessie was there climbing around in the attic and could hear him."

"Was Mrs. Alfrey — don't you love the way she phrases things, Tom — making kissy noises back?"

"Jessie wasn't sure, but I don't think it matters, really. If she was, Charles might have killed Julien Rochette because he was jealous. If she wasn't, and Julien was making unwelcome advances, Corinne might have complained to Charles, who could have killed him to protect her. Both circumstances would explain why Charles said to leave his family alone — he wouldn't want me asking questions that might get Corinne wondering if he was responsible for Julien's death."

"You're leaving out who this Jessie guy is," Dave interjected.

"He's a pest inspector," Tom illuminated. "He did a report on the house in August of 1994. He would have discovered the triangular space and how to access it when he did his report, just like our home inspector did when he discovered the body."

Dave nodded as Tom asked Regan, "Do you think he read the situation correctly, and if he did, would he have told Charles?"

"He might have. He thought he was hearing Corinne and Charles and wrapped up his inspection so he could come down and thank Charles for his business. I guess whether or not he would have told Charles would depend on whether he thought telling would produce more or fewer referrals.

"Jessie seemed to think Corinne and Julien acted suspiciously and looked guilty when he walked in, like he caught them in the act. He was livid when he recognized Julien. Jessie has a daughter, Isabel, whom he thinks the world of," Regan explained. "It seems when this all happened, she had just graduated from high school, and Julien, who would have been twenty-four — that's how old he was when he was killed, right — was dating her, much to Jessie's disgust. He may have read more into what was going on than he should have because of how he felt about Julien.

"You know, the more I think about it, the more I think he would have told Charles, and probably everyone else who'd listen, about what he overheard just to expend vitriol against Julien, never mind how it might make Corinne look."

"That, and because he's such a purveyor of gossip," Tom derided.

"You're back to working Julien Rochette's murder, Regan. You keep concentrating on that when I keep telling you we need to figure out who helped you off Empire Grade Road. You got to keep your priorities straight." Dave wasn't teasing; he seemed genuinely annoyed at her.

"Don't you see, Dave? The two are related."

"No, I don't see that. I see you *wanting* them to be related 'cause you like the Alfrey guy for the one who bumped you, but I don't see the connection just because he mouthed off at you. He's got a reputation for doing that sort of thing. And you know his wife's reputation is squeaky clean; nobody we talked to, nobody other than your Jessie guy, ever said anything negative about her, especially not vis-à-vis her maybe fooling around on the side."

"Dave, you actually took a more serious look at the Alfreys than you were letting on. How sweet." She thought she hit the perfect note halfway between credulous and sardonic.

"You know we want to get whoever knocked you off Empire Grade, so yeah, I took your gut feeling seriously," he squirmed at his admission. "We looked," he said softly. "And after we did, my money's still on the Cooper family for ramming you, even though Seth's alibi is looking a little stronger."

"When were you going to tell us his alibi is looking good?" Regan challenged.

"As soon as you stopped yammering and started eating. Oh look, here's your quesadilla," he grinned at the waitress as she put Regan's order in front of her. "I might have a fighting chance right about now.

"Seth Cooper's alibi got a little stronger 'cause a neighbor of his says she saw him come home when he says he did and that he stayed home even though his truck didn't.

"That looks good; you should eat it before it gets cold," Dave smiled broadly and gestured toward Regan's plate.

"What do you mean, 'he stayed home but his truck didn't?'" Tom asked.

"It seems Seth's crazy mother borrowed his truck that night. The neighbor remembers that part real well because she watched the nutcase mom walk around the truck three or four times, kind of chanting something before she got in and drove away.

"We even got the time for that. The neighbor says she was watching the local news but decided the tinfoil lady was more entertaining than the TV. Neighbor says she wouldn't give up national news for peeping, though, so that puts the crazy lady in Seth's truck before 5:30 with plenty of time for her to call you and then get in position on Empire Grade before you started for town."

"Were there any paint bits from my car on his truck?"

"Funny thing about that. Your Mr. Cooper is a real good boy, isn't he? He does his best to take care of his momma, like when he threatened you for testifying at her eviction hearing. Well, it seems your Mister Cooper's been a scrub-bing fool. Truck's freshly washed and waxed. There's even some new black Rust-Oleum on the brush guard. He didn't do stellar work — it looks more like a haphazard clean-up than a nice detailing job — but it makes us think he wanted to get rid of some evidence.

"Hey, Regan, I got another question for you. The woman who called to set you up — remind me what she said her name was."

"I didn't catch all of it; there was a lot of background noise."

"Tell me the part you heard," Dave pressed.

"Linda … something."

"Linda something," he repeated. "Isn't Linda Cooper the tinfoil queen's name? Come on, Regan, admit it. Crazy Momma, especially with some afterwards help from her son, is a better fit for booting you than good ole Chuck is," Dave raised his eyebrows and nodded as he cajoled. "And if we get your ramming situation settled, we might just find a nickel's worth of time to spend on your murder."

"You at least think Charles Alfrey may have been involved in that?" Regan asked, hopefully.

"Did I say that? Tom, did you hear me say that? For your murder, Regan, I want you to tell me a little more about your Jessie guy."

"Jessie Bolton?" Regan frowned. "Why do you want to know about him?"

"OK," Dave exhaled dramatically, "I'm about to share how serious investigating works. You'll want to take notes. First point: you said your pest guy didn't like the Vic putting moves on his daughter, his special little girl, who was younger than the legal age of consent, I'd guess, when she first caught Mr. Rochette's eye. I'd be a mad daddy right there.

"Next, you said … no … Tom, it was you who said this

guy Bolton knew about the triangle space."

"That's right. He drew it as part of the schematic on his report," Tom said.

Dave uttered a meaningful, "Uh-huh."

"No, no, no," Regan shook her head. "I see where you're going, Dave, but you're wrong. He was dazed when he realized Julien Rochette had been murdered. Until then, Jessie always thought Julien dumped his daughter and broke her heart. If he killed him, he wouldn't have reacted the way he did."

"Regan, you impress me sometimes at how good you are reading people. Then other times, like right now, I can't believe what you miss." There was no disparagement in Dave's tone, only disappointment. "If he did kill Rochette, he had years to plan how he'd play it if the guy's body was found."

"If that's true, why would he want to meet me at the house? Why wouldn't he just say he didn't remember the inspection? I wouldn't have questioned that. Why would he even admit to knowing who Julien Rochette was?"

"She has some excellent points there, Dave."

"Perps love to return to the scene of the crime. You'd be amazed how many killers go to their Vic's funeral. We like to stake out crime scenes, too, just waiting to see who drives by. It's practically routine procedure. Maybe your termite guy wanted another chance to admire his handiwork. The way I see it, your Jessie guy wanting to go back to the scene makes him a stronger suspect, not a weaker one.

"Then he came up with the story connecting the Vic with Corinne Alfrey. I bet that story was a surprise to you, wasn't it? Not consistent with what you know about her, was it?"

"No, it wasn't."

"Good attempt to throw you off thinking about him, I'd say. Can you think of a way the pest guy could get easy access to the house for a private visit? Would he have been given a key for his inspection that he could have copied?"

"Probably not for the inspection," Tom said. "Corinne would have let him in, but I did note a payment slip for termite fumigation attached to the inspection report. Realtors don't go to tentings. With a vacant house like that, the usual procedure is to leave a key somewhere, like in the electric meter box, for the pest inspector to pick up."

Dave looked first at Regan, then at Tom, "We've got potential motive, knowledge of the triangle space where the body was hidden, and now it sounds like we've got access. Our news is worthy of a mention to Detective Harrison, the officer in charge of the Rochette murder investigation. I'm guessing he'll want to talk to your termite inspector pal.

"Your Jessie Bolton say anything else to you that we might find interesting, Regan?"

Regan bit her bottom lip and considered, then nodded slowly. "He said if he ever ran into Julien Rochette he planned to choke the life out of him."

15

Regan didn't feel vulnerable right after the attempt on her life. The distressing realization that someone had tried to kill her and almost succeeded crept up on her gradually. Once that comprehension awakened in her though, she wanted to curl up in a ball and stay in bed.

As appealing as that idea seemed, she knew she couldn't give in to it. Instead of hiding from reality by cocooning in her bed, she settled for hiding elsewhere. Her lead foot and assertive driving style were replaced by caution and going to and from town huddled in the midst of forty-mile-per-hour convoys of speed limit abiding Empire Grade Road drivers.

She gave up passing, even when it was safe, in order to remain nestled among other motorists, and tried to assure herself that these new precautions would preclude another attempt on her life.

Dave called as she was preparing to leave home for a mid-day cozied-up drive to Capitola Village for a final pre-holiday shopping trip. He told her the police still didn't have enough evidence to charge either Linda or Seth Cooper, but that both had been warned they were being closely watched.

Dave said Seth insisted his mother washed and waxed his truck, at least where she could reach, innocently, to remove all traces of alien fingerprints which she believed began appearing the day of Regan's attack.

He snickered as he told her that Linda Cooper said the fingerprints were proof that aliens were trying to attach a tracking beam to her son's truck and proudly admitted she had cleaned and polished the truck and spray-painted the brush guard because wax and fresh paint made the vehicle slippery and thwarted extraterrestrial plans. She said she intended to follow the waxing and painting ritual every fifty-two days until the world ended along with the Mayan calendar in December of 2012.

Regan decided to abandon her mousy driving after her phone call with Dave. If someone wanted to harm her, driving in slow moving caravans offered her no more real protection than Linda Cooper's cleanliness rituals. Her best protection against a second try on her life was to figure out who was responsible for the failed attempt. For that, she needed to think — something she did better with an open road in front of her.

When an empty straightaway appeared, Regan swung into the oncoming lane and resurrected her spirited driving style in a two-car-passing burst of speed. The rented Ford's pick-up wasn't as quick as her destroyed car's had been, but it was good enough. Out in front of the pack, she returned to her lane and the caravan of drivers disappeared in her rear-view mirror.

She might call it a gut reaction, but what caused her intuitive perceptions was more complicated than a feeling in the pit of her stomach. She spent much of her time reading people, watching them, and picking up as much meaning from what they didn't say as from what they did. That process gave her insight into the way people thought, the way they dealt with the world when it didn't work the way they wanted it to. Facts alone didn't always offer a complete picture of what was going on, but the police seemed to rely on them exclusively. Why did the authorities seem so reluctant to consider suspects the way she did as part of their crime solving work?

The Coopers, Dave? Really? Let the authorities watch them if they wanted; her gut still told her she read Seth Cooper correctly. He was an angry young man but he was no plotter.

And as sure as she was that Seth hadn't attacked her, she was even more certain his mother hadn't either. There was an elegant if demented logic in the reason the pathetic woman gave for tinkering with Seth's truck. "Crazy Momma," as Dave dubbed her, focused on thwarting her other-worldly demons. Regan doubted Linda Cooper even remembered who she was or what grudge she might hold against her.

Dave's delight that the set-up caller said her name was Linda was misplaced. Linda was a common name, one that might pop into the mind of a woman thinking up an alias. Linda Cooper didn't know any realtor jargon and the woman on the phone did. Besides, Regan was sure Linda Cooper wouldn't be able to keep herself together long enough to put together a plan, make a clever call, and carry out an attack. She was too unstable to execute that kind of linear strategy while battling aliens.

Regan put the Coopers into her *no way* mind file and moved to considering Jessie Bolton.

Yes, she could see him as a righteous killer if he thought someone hurt his daughter. But Jessie was a braggart; he couldn't have remained quiet about what he had done for sixteen years. He would have hung Julien Rochette's carcass on a fencepost like he had another coyote's — consequences be damned. And on the day she was attacked, Jessie didn't even know she was playing private detective; he had no connection with her. He quickly became another *no way* in her mind.

She moved to thoughts of Charles Alfrey. When he threatened her at his open house, she felt truly menaced. He certainly had the ability to quietly construct a plan and follow it through to a desired result. His job required that of him every day.

Dave insisted Charles Alfrey had a rock-solid alibi. That was a game ender for the authorities; it wasn't necessarily for her. *If I wanted to harm someone without getting caught, the first thing I'd do would be to create a perfect alibi,* she reasoned.

Realtors coordinated events and managed contractors; their job description was heavy on those activities and skills. She played with just how Charles could have orchestrated her attack. The phone call came first. He could have given a script to a woman and had her make the call, but Regan thought her caller was too flexible and fast on her feet for scripted words. Regan's question became: How could Charles have convinced a realtor to make the call without letting her know what she was doing?

He might have enlisted someone at his office holiday party, someone who'd had enough to drink to go along, to make the call by telling her she was participating in a practical joke. Regan smiled slowly. Better yet, he might have told the innocent agent she was getting Regan to a surprise party being held in her honor. She nodded to herself. *Yes, there were plausible surreptitious ways to get the phone call made.*

What about the physical attack? How would he get someone to do it? Would Charles Alfrey have paid someone to ram her car while he partied in front of witnesses? Surely it was possible, and maybe that was what he did, but hiring an accomplice seemed risky. She didn't like that idea. Figuring out how he got someone to attack her was going to take more thought.

In the meantime, she considered what Charles knew and when he knew it. He overheard her telling Meg and Nora that she was *personally* going to solve a long-ago murder the police had back-burnered. He warned her not to ask his family about Julien Rochette and threatened her as soon as he thought her investigation was turning in his direction. The attempt on her life happened right after that. Her gut said all of that was connected.

She channeled Tom's logic. Why would Charles have taken any action so soon after making his threat? Wouldn't he have waited to see if he scared her off? Between that question and the issue of who carried out the actual attack on her, she was stuck. She must be missing something. Something important.

Regan's speculating had carried her all the way down Empire Grade, through the west side of town, and onto Highway 1 and the freeway. She zipped past the backed up 41st Avenue off-ramp to the Capitola Mall, gleeful to be avoiding the holiday shopping throngs. She was headed for the Craft Gallery in the Capitola Village and could take the next exit, which was nearly deserted.

Her joy disappeared as soon as she reached the Village and realized that parking, limited and difficult on a good day, was impossible this close to Christmas. She briefly flirted with the idea of giving up on the store where she knew she'd find the special little gift she wanted for Ben, her oldest son, but quickly realized that facing the shopping hordes at the mall would be daunting, too, and that in the end, she'd leave with only a settled-for gift.

Ben, a nightfall actor like so many others in L.A., had secured a surprisingly well-paying day job. With the income and job security it presented, the depressed real estate market, and some help from Tom and her, he had managed to buy a modest house in the San Fernando Valley. Now he wanted a Christmas present for his house that reminded him of Santa Cruz, the place he would always consider home.

Regan had discovered that the Craft Gallery sold enchanted sandcastles, foot-tall turreted lanterns that held a candle within to cast light out their many windows. They were handmade by a local woman using Seabright Beach sand — you couldn't get more Santa Cruz and whimsical than that — so she circled the Capitola Village another time.

On her third loop, she got stuck in a slow-moving line of cars working their way through the stop sign near Capitola's

Bradley Real Estate office. She noticed the office's small parking area was deserted except for a lone car. The office was just a few stores from the Craft Gallery, tantalizingly convenient for a quick stop. She impulsively decided to ignore the warning posted at the parking lot entrance: "This lot is reserved for Bradley clients and real estate agents only. All other cars will be towed at the owner's expense." She was a real estate agent after all, and the sign didn't say anything that prohibited shopping real estate agents from parking there, now did it? Besides, it wasn't like one more car would fill the lot, she rationalized.

As soon as she turned off her engine, she began to worry. How would she go about retrieving a towed rental car? Normally she was a great believer in the idiom, "It's easier to ask forgiveness than permission," but today, since her car was rented, she decided she'd better play it safe. Regan opened the door of Bradley Real Estate and stuck her head inside.

"Hey, Regan," Meg Dorsey saw her and sang out her name from across the office. "How did you know I was here alone stuck doing floor-time with no walk-in business and a non-ringing phone? I'm bored to tears and just desperate for company. Come on in and talk to me."

"I'll do better than that if you let me use the parking lot. I'm going to run to a store, make a quick purchase, and then I'll be back with good coffee and ready to chat for the rest of your shift."

Regan was delighted at her good fortune. She'd found parking and Meg, a repository of gossip sufficient to fill a thousand-page tome, in a talkative mood. She smiled to herself. Meg was always in a talkative mood; her real good fortune was in finding parking and Meg alone, where delicate questions could be privately asked and answered.

She was back in less than ten minutes, her purchase safely out of sight in the rental car trunk and a cup of coffee from Sea Side Coffee in each hand, pushing the Bradley Real Estate door open with her backside. As she swung through the door, turned and walked toward Meg, Regan's eyes widened. Since she'd seen Meg in Courtroom 7 a few weeks before, Meg had had some work done. More work done.

Meg often joked she became a real estate agent before California became a state, but she was touchy about her actual age, and aided by numerous trips to the cosmetic surgeon for various facial procedures, managed to keep it a secret. Meg favored conservative clothing with long sleeves and high necklines topped by her trademark scarves held taut against her neck by an emerald frog pin. She said her clothing was part of her professional image. Many agents, Regan included, suspected the sleeves and scarves camouflaged crepey skin that remained untouched during her nips and lifts.

Meg's latest procedure must have been a doozy. Her current expression could only be described as sleek and startled. Her greeting smile for Regan was warm like it always was, but it appeared to be the only part of her face that still moved.

"Sit, sit. Talk, talk," Meg commanded happily through lips that reminded Regan of Conan O'Brien's skits where he interviewed celebrity still photos with superimposed moving mouths. Meg took her coffee and enthusiastically slurped some of it. "Rumor has it you were in an accident, but you look OK to me. Nothing broken?"

"Right on both counts."

"Rumor is it happened after that nasty little man threatened you for testifying," Meg fished. "I know you may not be at liberty to talk about it, but just between us, what do the police think?"

"You're right; I'm not supposed to talk about it."

"Oh," Meg intoned with disappointment. Then she gasped, "Oh!"

Regan let her friend read whatever she wanted into her statement, amused at how much she imagined that would be, and then maneuvered toward the questions she wanted to ask. "Did I ever tell you the name of the man whose body was found in our house? You wanted to know, didn't you?"

"Oh, yes I did, and no, you didn't." Meg pulled her mouth into a perfect circle and sounded thrilled at the prospect of finding out, but she couldn't raise her eyebrows to demonstrate her excitement.

"His name was Julien Rochette. Rumor has it," Regan used Meg's favorite phrase to introduce her test statement, "he knew your officemates, the Alfreys."

"Julien Rochette? Get out! *I* knew him! He kind of worked here, you know. He was sort of a paid-under-the-table handyman. He was never on the office payroll, but he did things for some of the agents who were here at the time. It was years ago, not many of us originals are left in the office," she chuckled. "Semi-officially I think he worked for Charles, though."

Regan tried to keep her own expression as unmoving as Meg's while her heart thumped a little harder in her chest. A direct connection between Charles Alfrey and the murdered man, a connection she had so far only been able to make by creating suppositions out of Charles' threat and Jessie Bolton's words was being confirmed by someone reliable, someone without any possible interest or agenda that might influence her statement.

"So he and Charles were friendly?" she asked with careful casualness.

"Well, I wouldn't say friendly exactly. They had more of a boss employee relationship. Charles didn't keep him around very long." She leaned forward and put the fingers of her hand against the side of her mouth to make her stage whisper more conspiratorial, "Rumor has it there were problems with keys and things disappearing from houses Julien repaired."

Her whispered speaking-ill-of-the-dead concluded, Meg leaned back in her chair, "Of course, there were never any charges filed … I think Corinne saw to that. Julien and Corinne, they were the ones who were close — he was a friend of hers or a relative, something like that — and she was the one who recommended him."

Meg produced a constrained eye roll. "Honestly, I was surprised Charles had the gumption to fire the young man and make her unhappy given how gaga he was for her and what with them being barely past the honeymoon stage, but he had to protect his clients."

"Of course he did," Regan empathized. Her mind whirred. Was Jessie right about Corinne and Julien Rochette? It was all she could do to keep from blurting out something that would have challenged the immobility of Meg's eyebrows. She took a quick shallow breath, then another. She took a long sip of coffee.

The question she finally asked was delivered offhandedly. "I'll never understand what Corinne sees in Charles; do you get their relationship?"

"Of course I do; it's easy to understand, really."

Regan thought Meg's expression hinted at pride but she couldn't be certain.

"Most people don't realize it but Corinne runs the show. Charles treats her like a princess. If I didn't know better, I'd be tempted to think she's got something on him, but he's always been more in love with her than she is with him, so he tries harder."

She's got something on him — Regan had to force herself to stay in the moment. This wasn't the time to consider the possibilities of what Meg had just said. "How did they ever get involved, though? I would have run the other way if someone as difficult to be around as Charles asked me out."

"Oh, no you wouldn't have, Regan. Back then Charles was a love, and a catch. The term cougar hadn't been invented yet, but even *I* tried my best to be ahead of the times," Meg's laugh came out as a twitter. "Women threw themselves at him all the time, but he wasn't interested in anyone after his wife died, at least not until Corinne came along.

"His first wife died having Preston. I mean, really, who dies in childbirth nowadays? Charles was devastated, like it was his fault somehow. He spent all his time taking care of his son ... Preston was the spitting image of his mother when he was little ... Charles just adored that boy. You know, I don't think he ever even dated; he just worked hard, made money, lots of it, and spent his free time with his son. He's still attractive, but umph, he was a good-looking man back then." Meg squeezed her eyes closed for emphasis, the best she could do to make her point given her unmoving forehead.

"Corinne started working in the office right out of high school, gorgeous young thing she was, and Charles, well, Charles fell for her so hard he almost broke the floorboards. She wasn't interested in him at first, I think because of the big age difference, but eventually she warmed to him. And then she was a swell little mommy to Preston, which made Charles love her all the more."

"How old was Preston when Corinne and Charles got married?"

"Oh, he was little. He was his dad's best man. I went to the wedding and remember thinking how cute that was. He couldn't have been more than ten or eleven. Once they got married, Corinne got her real estate license, stopped working for the office, and started helping Charles out sometimes. They were the happiest little family you've ever seen, at least for a couple of years."

"For a couple of years?" Regan inclined her head slightly, trying to project just the right level of interest to encourage Meg to continue without seeming overly eager for details.

Meg inhaled deeply and exhaled slowly. "It was like the perfect storm hit about that time. The market took a hit; oh, it wasn't as bad as it has been recently, but Charles lost a lot of money. It got so bad that Corinne had to start really working, not just puttering, to help them hang onto some of their rental properties. Then Preston hit his teenage years — you know how teenagers can be — and it was like he became a different boy. Rumor had it he was into drugs a little bit — he may even have been picked up by the police once — and he was sas-sy," Meg divided the single word and made it into two, "to Corinne especially. She put up with his back-talk for a while, but even angels have their limits.

"Something finally happened with Preston, though. My personal guess? Corinne had enough and told him he'd get packed off to military school if he didn't shape up. Charles would have gone along with that, too, if she insisted. It might have broken his heart, but he'd do anything for her.

"Anyway, Charles must have been overwhelmed by his business downturn, his worry about his son, and I have to say, the way things fell apart between Corinne and Preston. I don't think he ever expected them to have one of those evil step-mother things, but for a while there, they sure did.

"Charles changed after that. They got past their financial troubles and Preston eased up, or Corinne reined him in enough he stopped fighting back, maybe that was it, but Charles never pulled out of his doldrums. It seemed like he was as down as he had been after his first wife died, but this time, instead of putting himself back together, he just gave up and never felt good about life again. He just seemed to stay bitter and started biting peoples' heads off, if you know what I mean.

"He even started treating Preston differently; poor kid went from being the apple of his dad's eye to a boy who, no matter how hard he tried, disappointed him.

"And then things just kind of mushroomed the way they do. Once somebody starts getting talked about in a particular way, well, people look at them differently than they used to. A person with a bad reputation can't do right any more than a person with a good reputation can do wrong.

"Charles gave people plenty of ammunition for their dislike of him, too. He started acting full of himself and mean. He was never nasty to me, or to Corinne, of course, but at one point a few years back our broker suggested, in the friendliest way of course, that," Meg suddenly looked past Regan, flashed a glowing smile, and then dropped her voice and hurriedly finished what she was saying, "he could benefit from an anger management course.

"Oh, super," Meg called across the office in a louder than normal voice. "You're here to relieve me."

"Ladies," Preston Alfrey acknowledged them both with a polite little nod. "Yep. Just my luck. I drew the short straw and got stuck with two-to-five floor time. What a waste at this time of year. Any action at all today, Meg?"

"None, Preston. Luckily Regan was in the neighborhood to do some shopping and kept me company for a while. She was telling me some thrilling stuff about the murdered man they found in her house. Turns out I knew him, isn't that exciting? Your mom knew him, too. Julien Rochette, that was his name and he was a friend of hers or her cousin, I can't remember which. And of course, your dad knew him, too."

Regan's mouth was open, but no words came out. There had been no way for her to stop Meg's chatter, and from Meg's perspective, she realized, no need for her to be circumspect once she got past the gossip about Preston's father. Regan was the only one, with her suspicions and assumptions, who was discomfited and felt caught red-handed by an Alfrey while talking about Julien Rochette.

She turned toward Preston slowly, trying to conjure a mask of innocent neutrality to cover her chagrin.

It wasn't necessary. Preston wasn't capable of noticing her expression. He had gone white and appeared even more unnerved by Meg's exposé than Regan had been.

"Well, good luck, Preston." Meg vacated the floor-time desk and began collecting her things. "Walk me out, will you, Regan?"

"Sure." Regan had to control her urge to jump to her feet and flee. As she followed Meg outside, she glanced over her shoulder at Preston Alfrey who had taken over the floor-time desk. He sat quite still and stared down at the desk. He still looked pale and shaken.

"Regan, you and Tom and your family have a Merry Christmas if I don't see you before then." Meg grabbed her around the neck and pulled her down into a hug that startled her back into the moment. She watched Meg ease into her car and wave a jaunty good-bye as she carefully edged out of the parking lot into Capitola Village traffic. Regan returned Meg's wave and then turned toward her car.

It was her turn to grow pale. Just as when she first pulled in, only two vehicles occupied the parking lot. But now Regan's rented Ford sat next to Preston's black Land Rover. She was staring at the answer to her most troubling question. How could Charles have attacked her when witnesses placed him at the Bradley holiday party? He could have had his son run her off the road.

She dove into her car, locked it from inside, and launched her car out of the parking lot and away from Preston Alfrey so quickly she caused a disgruntled driver to beep at her reckless maneuver.

Regan's ability to use a cell phone legally while driving had ended on a Bonny Doon mountainside. Her rented Ford defined basic and she hadn't even tried to set up her cell phone for hands-free use. Even if she had, right now there was no way she could have made a safe call while driving. The real problem with cell phones wasn't having only one hand on the steering wheel — the real problem was the distraction a remote conversation created. The more emotional the call, the greater the distraction, and in her present state of mind, she was bound to be a hazard on wheels, hands-free or not.

She pulled into the first vacant driveway she came to, retrieved her cell phone from her purse, and pressed Dave's office number.

"Dave Everett," the voice that greeted her was the professional one he used at work, but as soon as she said his name and he realized who he was talking to, he reverted to being her friend and ribbing nemesis. "Don't start by telling me you don't think I'm right about your termite guy, Jessie. Your house was tented. He did have a key, and he's bad-mouthed Julien Rochette to lots of people ..."

"Dave," she interrupted.

He continued unstoppably, "It's still preliminary, but we like him ..."

"Dave!" she practically shrieked. "It wasn't Jessie. It was Charles Alfrey."

"You don't like ole Chuck very much, do you? You keep bringing him up and blaming him for everything. First it was running you off the road, now murder. What's next? You plan on blaming him for California's budget mess?"

Regan usually found it hard to override Dave when he was on a roll, but she was rolling even faster than he was. "Let me tell you what I've uncovered before you start in."

"OK, shoot, but this better be more than your gut belly-aching again."

"Oh, is it ever. For starters, I've got confirmation that Charles knew Julien Rochette. Julien worked for him until Charles got rid of him, possibly for doing inappropriate things with keys, like making spare ones to use for break-ins. I've got someone besides Jessie who says Julien and Corinne Alfrey were close. I just watched Preston Alfrey, that's Charles' son, almost faint when that person said his father and stepmother knew Julien Rochette."

"Interesting."

"Interesting? *Interesting?* This puts Charles in the mix. I see all kinds of triangles here as well as motives and opportunities. Interesting." Regan repeated Dave's word but coated it with disdain.

"You still seeing visions of ole Chuck whacking you, too?"

"I was getting to that. There's another big black Land Rover in the family that needs looking at. It seems father and son like the same kind of vehicle."

"Both Alfrey men drive black Land Rovers?"

"That's right. I think Preston ran me off the road while his father set up an alibi."

"So you've got a whole bunch of coincidences here. I'll give you the Chuck-Julien-Corinne connection does create a sweet little triangle, but you lose me with the kid. Why would sonny try to run you off the road?" Dave was skeptical but not belittling.

"I don't know. Maybe Charles asked him to or he thought he was protecting his father." Regan wasn't satisfied with her answer but it was the best she could come up with on short notice.

"How would killing you protect his father? No one's been looking at Charles Alfrey for the murder of Julien Rochette."

"No one but me, Dave. Charles and Preston were there when I asked for information about who the listing agent was for our house back in 1994. They both heard me say the police were too busy to do an active investigation, but that I was going to figure everything out."

"Humph."

She could almost hear him thinking in the silence that followed.

"Tell you what I'm gonna do. I'm gonna personally go by Mr. Alfrey Junior's and ask him where he was the night you got smacked. I'll take a peek at his Land Rover, too. Then, I'll have a nice friendly visit with good ole Chuck. I'll ask him if he gave Rochette the key we found in his pocket or if he thinks the guy had one made all by himself.

"Don't thank me, Regan; just consider my hard work an early Christmas present." Dave made a fleeting attempt to end their conversation with his usual banter, but his efforts were overridden by his final utterance. "And Regan, until we get this all figured out, be careful, will you?"

Christmas Eve was spent waiting for her older son, Ben, to make it home to Santa Cruz. He left Los Angeles in the early afternoon and took the fast route up Interstate 5, a thorough-fare that lacked charm and diversions but could normally put him in Bonny Doon in a scant six hours. The road monotony he endured was the same as ever, but there had been snow over the Grapevine coming out of Los Angeles that tempor-arily stopped traffic until California Highway Patrol officers showed up, deemed the road safe, and began escorting drivers over the summit in twenty-cars-at-a-time groups.

Regan insisted on holding dinner for Ben. She caught her always-hungry younger son, Alex, microwaving a burrito at 6:30, and an hour later, caught Tom and Alex planning to share another one. When Ben finally arrived, their family supper was late enough that it wouldn't have been considered fashionable in any circle.

Christmas day was spent in transit, in airports, and with unforeseen and unforgettable phone calls. Alex, who came home from college five days before, had booked a Christmas Day flight because it was cheap and seats were available. His plan was to open gifts early Christmas morning in Bonny Doon and then hop on a plane for a five-hour flight to the east coast. With luck, he would arrive in time for a late Christmas dinner with his girlfriend Lindsey's family.

It was going to be a big deal day: Christmas combined with an official *meeting the family*. Regan's young and oh-so-madly-in-love son was nervous and too distracted to have a meaningful Christmas morning on the west coast, especially since he was well past the up-at-dawn-with-excitement days of little children and overslept. He had to rush gifts and breakfast to make his flight.

Tom, Regan, and Ben drove him to the airport in Regan's new car, a replacement for the one destroyed in her accident. She had wanted a Prius, a green one so she could say she drove a "green" green car, and the destruction of her six-year-old but perfectly serviceable Lexus gave her a guilt-free chance to fulfill her wish. When they went to the dealership the day before Christmas to pick it up, it even sported a big red bow.

By 4:00 they were back from dropping Alex at the airport and Tom and Regan had said goodbye to Ben. After his Christmas Eve driving debacle, he had decided to return to Los Angeles early to be sure he made his matinee perfor-mance in a play the next day. Ben said he didn't mind driving on Christmas too much since he'd discovered Margie's in San Luis Obispo was open, and if he took Highway 101, he could stop for one of the restaurant's famous giant burgers for dinner.

A few minutes after 4:30, their office phone rang. Regan picked up the call even though she had vowed no business would be conducted on Christmas Day.

"Merry Christmas," she answered, intending to tell who-ever was calling that she'd get back to them the next day.

"Regan, is this you?" She couldn't decide if the caller was slightly inebriated or just befuddled.

"I think so," she answered mirthfully and then added, "Merry Christmas," for a second time.

"Oh great, great. It's Bob. Bob Frisee. I'm so glad I got through to you."

Considering who was calling — befuddled, she decided.

"I need to get this off my chest, and in the spirit of the holiday I thought this was a good time to do it. Kind of clear the air before the new year begins, get a fresh start, reset the old friendship meter because I like you and I can't ... well ... I'm having a hard time with how I feel about you right now."

Regan did a quick search of her memory. Bob represented the buyers for one of her listings that sold just before Halloween. It seemed like a smooth enough transaction; nothing unusual came up and all involved seemed happy with the way things went. She hadn't run into him since that escrow closed.

"The thing is, I really have to complain about the way you treated me the day of the inspections, letting everyone into the house except me."

She frowned. She had no idea what he was talking about. She remembered being crowded into the tiny house with her clients, the buyers, and two inspectors with their ladders and assorted paraphernalia. Bob had scheduled the pest inspection and the physical inspection for the same day and time, but he had been a no-show. At the time she thought it very unprofessional that he hadn't been there with his clients, but the thought passed quickly amid the close-quarters confusion.

"I don't understand, Bob. You didn't come to the inspections."

"Oh yes I did," his statement was emphatic. "I saw all your cars and the inspectors' trucks parked along the street, so I know you were all there. I knocked on the door, then I rang the doorbell and knocked really hard, but no one would let me in. Finally, I went around back to see if I could get in that way. The back door was unlocked, but that vicious yappy little dog was in the laundry room where you put him to keep him out of the way. He darn near tore my leg off before I grabbed a broom and worried him into the bedroom with it. I was ready to give you a piece of my mind right then, but the inspections must have been finished, because when I went into the living room you had all gone.

"I bet you all went out for coffee or lunch or something to celebrate the inspections going well, too, and you didn't include me," he huffed. "Well, I've been as angry as can be that you never apologized for shunning me or even mentioned what happened."

"Bob," Regan tried to be as kind as she could, "the sellers didn't own a dog. I had another listing on that block, two doors down. The houses were the same color. Are you sure you were at the right house?"

"Did those sellers have a dog?" Bob practically whispered his question.

"Uh-huh. A little black and white Jack Russell Terrier."

"Oh-my-god." His words tumbled out as one. "Oh-my-god. I left them a nasty note on the back of my business card," his voice quavered, "they know who I am."

"Would you like the seller's phone number, Bob?" she offered. "You'll probably want to apologize to them and their dog ... given the spirit of the holidays and all."

"I guess you better give it to me. Oh, and Regan, I'm sorry for disturbing you today. Merry Christmas."

"And the same to you, Bob."

Regan was still laughing as she told Tom about Bob Frisee's dilemma when a phone rang for a second time; this time it was their home line. Tom assumed it was his sister from Florida and put the phone on speaker so Regan could join in, but the voice that greeted them was Dave's.

"I just got off the phone with one of the poor guys who drew duty today. He said he thought I'd want to know. I figured you would, too. Charles Alfrey came into the station house early this morning and confessed to the murder of Julien Rochette. Detective Harrison's pretty happy about a break in the case, but not about Alfrey's timing. He and a couple of other guys didn't get to have much of a Christmas. They've been interrogating him all day; he hasn't even lawyered up yet. Some Christmas present, huh?"

"Then it's over." Regan began quietly and rushed to a boisterous, "Tom, it's over. Julien Rochette can rest and I won't have to be afraid anymore."

Regan and Tom turned on the 5:30 news on KSBW and then switched to KION. They expected the Charles Alfrey confession to lead the local news, but the lead stories on both stations were heartwarming pre-produced pieces designed to be in keeping with the day. His story got no more than a cursory mention on either station and was positioned between current weather and the future weathercasts.

Regan had the *Santa Cruz Sentinel* out of their paper box earlier than most eager post-Christmas shoppers looking for December 26th bargains, and Tom greeted the morning much earlier than normal so he could read over her shoulder. But while there were a few more details in the newspaper than there had been on TV the night before, the story was still sketchy and unsatisfying.

The gist of the article was that Charles Alfrey, a prominent real estate agent with Bradley Real Estate — how the Bradley brothers who owned the company must have loved getting their name in the paper in that way, Tom noted — was being held in County Jail following an early Christmas morning confession to a murder that police believed had taken place in 1994. No charges had been filed as of press time. There were more details about the victim and the circumstances of his body being found than there were about the "alleged confession."

The address of their cottage was restated. Regan felt sorry for their neighbors. The mention of a murder and an address where a body was discovered was sure to bring out ghoulish sightseers driving by hoping to see — hoping to see just what, she didn't know — something, anything that might make them shudder.

Tom called Dave and asked if he was working later. When he said he was, Tom asked if they could stop by and get brought up to speed on the Alfrey situation. They scheduled a meeting for 3:30.

Dave was waiting for Tom and Regan when they walked into the police station lobby. He had their visitor badges prepared and shook hands with each of them, an oddly formal gesture for him. Regan thought he seemed unusually subdued.

Dave ushered them by the police break room and asked if they would like coffee to take with them for their sit down in his office. Morning dregs kept tepid by someone resetting the coffeemaker's ON button whenever it passed the auto-shutoff time were all that remained in the pot. Waffle paper sleeves stacked next to paper cups suggested optimism about the coffee's warmth that Regan didn't share, and the plastic container of artificial creamer with a metal spoon lodged in it failed to entice Tom. They had become spoiled coffee drinkers — their office was within an easy walk of Iveta Café and Kelly's Bakery, both excellent sources of fresh hot brew. Tom and Regan passed on Dave's offer.

Dave's office was essentially a cubicle with full walls and a door. It held his desk with his chair behind it facing the door, an inefficient way of using the space, but an arrangement he liked. Two folding chairs that normally rested against the wall were opened and facing his desk. He motioned for them to sit down as he squeezed behind his desk and took his seat. His door remained open, leaving them subject to the scrutiny of uniformed officers passing by.

Dave exuded professionalism. "Mr. Alfrey has confessed to murdering Julien Rochette during the last week of October, 1994," Dave began with official language and uncharacteristic detachment, "and has denied any involvement in your recent attack."

"What's wrong, Dave? There's a problem, isn't there?" Regan asked.

Dave's official manner dissolved instantly. "Oh man, one hell of a problem. Tom, can you close the door?"

Tom had to stand up momentarily and collapse his chair to do it, but he managed.

"That's better," Dave proclaimed once they had some privacy. He quickly lapsed into the Dave they knew. "This whole thing is messed up. The guy's got a silly motive for offing Rochette and he's got his murder facts all wrong. We'd probably kick him as a whack job looking to get out of the cold overnight except he knows about the cat litter and how the body was positioned, and he's a match for the one fingerprint on the plastic bag that didn't come from your home inspector."

"Could you fill us in from the beginning?" Tom asked.

"Sure." Without his procedural formality, Dave sounded despondent. "Regan, you remember I told you I was gonna run by, take a peek at Preston Alfrey's Land Rover, and ask him where he was on the night of your accident, right?"

She remembered.

"Alfrey junior said he'd been at the Bradley holiday party, but when I asked him if he was there between 6:30 and 8:00 he mumbled something about wanting to pick up some last-minute gag gift for one of the brokers and getting there late. His Rover looked clean and didn't have a brush guard on it, by the way. Was there one on it when you saw it in Capitola?"

"Uh, umm, maybe," Regan stuttered. She closed her eyes and pulled up a picture of Preston's Land Rover in the Capitola parking lot. "No, Dave, I don't think so."

"That's what I thought you'd say." He shook his head and seemed lost in a moment of pondering before he continued. "Anyway, good ole Chuck was at his son's when I made my visit so we got a chance for a nice little chit-chat as well. We were all friendly pals shootin' the breeze. We talked keys and pockets and about Rochette being Chuck's hire. I asked him if he ever heard any rumors about Rochette light-fingering any houses after he finished working on them. Nah, he said. He liked the kid, thought he was a good worker. It seems they were all buddy-buddy before Rochette disappeared. Alfrey even encouraged him to get a real estate license. And that's how our conversation ended; that's where we left it.

"When Alfrey turned himself in on Christmas morning, he told Detective Harrison our little tête-à-tête kicked his conscience into high gear, what with the season and all, and he decided to come clean after all these years. You know, I'm good at interrogation, making a point, and getting criminals to see the light, but not that good. I didn't see any light bulbs come on when I spoke to him.

"After he said he deserved a lump of coal in his Christmas sock, the first thing the duty officer asked him was why he killed the Vic. Well, he says he confronted Rochette at the house about making keys and using them later to rip off his clients, cat burglar style. That's completely counter to what he said the day before. It was kind of like he got the idea to say that because I asked him about it, you know what I mean?

"He says they had a big fight about it, and Rochette attacked him. He thought he was in danger of having the crap beat out of him by a younger guy, so he picked up a handy two-by-four and whacked the Vic with it."

"So, he says self-defense?" Tom asked.

"That's what he says."

Regan screwed up her face, "But if he was defending himself, why didn't he report what he had done? He wouldn't have gotten in trouble, would he, especially if Julien Rochette was stealing from his clients. Julien would look like a criminal and Charles would look like the good guy for confronting him, don't you think?"

Dave's smile was both artificial and mocking. "Oh good. You are paying attention, Regan. That's the way we cops read it, too. Alfrey came up with some lame reason about it costing him business if people thought he had made such a bad choice of hires and decided to just hide the body instead."

"Charles Alfrey is known for having a temper," Tom interjected. "Do the authorities think the murder was premeditated and not self-defense?"

"We think all sorts of stuff. It was suggested to Mr. Alfrey that he killed the Vic because he was jealous of the relationship the guy had with his wife. I listened to the taped interview. I've heard some good *that's news to me* responses, excellent reactions in fact, but nothing to compare with this guy's take. 'What do you mean?' he says. He's all Mr. Innocent and in the dark. When we suggested we had a witness who saw his wife in a compromising situation with the Vic, he stammered about how that was impossible.

"The thing is, maybe he's telling it like it is. We only have Jessie Bolton's version of what happened between Mrs. Alfrey and Rochette to suggest a jealousy motive and he's biased and guessing. Bolton's account would never hold up in court.

"But here's where things get really bizarre. We asked Alfrey again to tell us how he killed the Vic and he said again with a two-by-four administered to the head. He says he dumped the murder weapon into the triangle first, and there was a two-by-four at the bottom of the space with the Vic's blood and tissue on it, but he doesn't seem to know anything about the jewelry garrote. In other words, he doesn't know the real cause of death. Killers always know that kind of stuff."

"Couldn't he lie about how he killed Rochette?" Tom asked. "Self-defense sounds plausible if he hit the man over the head, but it wouldn't if Rochette was strangled."

"Detective Harrison's the one who's been talking to Alfrey. He's out of Los Angeles before coming to Santa Cruz — it's not like he's only run across murderers a couple of times — he's developed some pretty good ways of questioning his way around that. But what works for me and most of my fellow officers, is that Alfrey didn't leave any fingerprints on the medallion. He left a print on the bag — so what did he do, wear gloves while he choked the guy, and then took them off to bag the Vic and haul him up to the attic? We're going with Alfrey really didn't know how Rochette died."

"I don't understand," Regan's voice demonstrated her confusion.

"You don't understand?" Dave sputtered. "We don't even know what to charge him with. As it stands, he could be guilty of anything from just disturbing a policeman's Christmas to murder. Well, I guess with his fingerprint and the details he did know, even if he didn't do the deed, he has to be at least an accessory after the fact — but you get my point. We can get away with keeping him 48 hours and then we have to charge him or kick him loose. We may not even have that long if his family brings in a lawyer screaming habeas corpus, but in any case, we're about out of time here."

Regan volunteered, "Couldn't you charge him with orchestrating my accident?"

"Would you let it go, Regan?" Dave entreated. "Alfrey says he murdered Rochette. He says he didn't even know you'd been in a wreck. He hopes you're feeling OK, by the way. Why would he try to get someone to kill you to keep you from finding out about the murder, and then voluntarily come into the station, on Christmas Day yet, and confess? That makes even less sense than not knowing how he killed the guy."

Regan was silent as Tom drove them back to their office. "Regan? Are you with me?" he finally asked. "What's going on in your lovely head, sweetheart?"

"I keep trying to figure out why Charles would confess to a murder he didn't commit. I've been trying to think from his perspective; the only reason I can come up with is he's trying to protect someone."

"Alfrey's not known for his charitable spirit or empathy."

"He's certainly not known for it now, but Meg Dorsey introduced me to a different Mr. Alfrey. Her Charles of old was a nice man who was a great father and a head-over-heels in love husband."

"Kind of like me?" Tom grinned.

"Kind of. Yes. So let's say deep down Charles Alfrey is like you. Why would you confess to a murder you didn't commit?"

"I'd be willing to take the rap," Tom played with noir tough-guy language, "for the dame I loved."

Regan gave him an appreciative smile. "I bet you would. And I wonder if Charles would as well."

"You think Corinne Alfrey killed Julien Rochette?" Tom's eyebrows almost met his hairline.

"Let's say I'm mulling that idea over right now. Just for the sake of argument, let's say Jessie Bolton is right about Corinne and Julien, that they were *involved*."

"Fine. Let him be right. Why would Corinne have killed Julien if they were lovers?"

"Maybe Julien wasn't willing to share her and planned to tell Charles what was going on. She might have been afraid Julien could break up her marriage. According to Meg, Charles was a financial catch. If Corinne married him for his money, maybe she didn't want to risk losing her sugar daddy. They hadn't been married very long; she wouldn't have been able to get spousal support or anything from Charles if he divorced her."

"I already see some problems with your idea. You do agree that Alfrey at least helped hide the body, don't you?"

Regan nodded.

"If Corinne was the murderer, I think she would have needed help getting Julien into the triangle. I can't come up with a way she could have dragged him into the attic and across the beams all by herself. Besides, Charles' fingerprint was on the plastic bag, so he must have helped her."

"Right," Regan agreed.

"Now, you know how much I love you, sweetheart, but I'd draw the line at helping you hide your lover's body. Surely you don't believe Charles is a better man than I am?"

Regan stared straight ahead and said nothing, carefully hiding the merriment in her eyes.

"Hey!" He swiveled his head toward her, "You're having

to think for an awfully long time."

She turned toward him with a glowing smile and a little giggle. "Keep your eyes on the road, please. You know I think there's no better man in the world than you."

"Thank you. For a minute there I didn't think you appreciated me," he teased.

"If Corinne killed Julien to keep him quiet, Charles wouldn't have known he was hiding her lover's body," Regan suggested. "But maybe Julien wasn't her lover. Corinne and Julien could have had a history, but it might not have been romantic.

"Maybe what Jessie saw and thought was them being cozy was something else altogether. Couldn't he have misinterpreted what he saw because of his daughter's involvement with Julien — you know, he might have made Julien out to be a complete cad when really he was just a common crook? Suppose Corinne and Julien had a little business going before Corinne and Charles got married. I bet she was the one in charge of doing low level key-making details for Charles — she could have been the one giving Julien the keys he used for break-ins.

"Suppose she wanted to end their little enterprise after she married Charles and Julien didn't. Maybe he was forcing her to continue supplying him with keys. Or, Julien could have threatened to tell Charles what they had been up to, and she could have killed him to keep him quiet about *that* instead of about an affair."

"Same problem," Tom asserted. "How would she get Charles to help her hide Rochette's body? I'd rather you killed somebody to cover thievery than because you were fooling around with him, but I'd still be pretty upset that you were using me as an aid in committing felonies, and like you said," he flashed her one of his most charming grins, "I'm a terrific and understanding fellow and a much better man than Charles is."

Tom pulled into the office lot and parked. Regan undid her seat belt and leaned toward him, brushing her lips against his cheek. "And what if I whispered in your ear that it was all true and in the past, that since I'd fallen for you I had tried desperately to change my ways, but that my partner in crime had threatened me, even hurt me, to keep me in line. What would you do if I looked up into your eyes," she asked, acting out what she was saying, "batted my eyelashes and said, 'When I told him our stealing days were over, he hit me again. I was afraid for my life; I defended myself as best I could and accidentally killed him. Please don't turn me in, darling. Please, help me hide the body.'"

Tom stared at her in silence for a moment or two. "Damn, you're good. I'd probably help you ... uh, Corinne."

He recovered quickly. "No, wait." He held his hands over the steering wheel, "I've got problems again. First off, Charles wouldn't have bought a sudden violent struggle, nor would he have believed her poor defenseless damsel story when he saw the duct tape and the garrote. Those items imply premeditated, calculated murder. Cold murder. How would Corinne have explained those details?"

Regan shrugged, "I've no idea."

"If I were Charles Alfrey," Tom continued, "and any of what you're suggesting were true, I'd be getting pretty uncomfortable about now. Dave says Charles convincingly dismissed the suggestion that a witness saw Corinne and Julien Rochette in a compromising position, but Charles doesn't know who the witness is or the circumstances surrounding their supposition. If I were sitting in a holding cell with time on my hands, I couldn't get that suggestion out of my mind. I'd be wanting out and a chance for a long talk with my wife. Alfrey seems set on taking the blame for murder; I'd be having second thoughts about doing that if I thought I was being cuckolded or taken advantage of in any way."

"Tom, do you think it is possible Charles really did kill Julien in a jealous rage? It might not have happened at the house, but he might have known about the wall anomaly. Jessie could have told him about it, or Corinne could have, if Jessie pointed it out to her. Maybe he decided to hide the body there. Charles Alfrey is a fairly big man and Julien was described as slender. He could have managed by himself. If that's what happened, can you imagine what must have been going on in his mind when, years later, I started asking him questions, then the police did, and then Dave showed up with even more questions?"

"That makes more sense to me than the other ideas you've been considering. He may have assumed it was just a matter of time till he got caught," Tom said. "He would want to control the situation as much as possible. Alfrey may have been doing damage control by confessing so he could set up self-defense as his reason for killing Rochette.

"There might even be some outside chance that everything you thought about him masterminding your hit is right, that he did get some woman to call you and either hired someone else to attack you or got his son to do it — although I'm with

137

Dave, the Cooper kid seems more likely for that to me."

Tom fell silent again, rolling facts around in his mind. Finally, he said, "But killer or accomplice, why didn't Charles know how Julien Rochette really died?"

Regan managed, "That's a real mystery, isn't it?" before Tom's cell phone rang.

He slid it open. "Tom Kiley."

Regan watched closely as he listened to what must have been a question posed by his caller. Tom replied, "Yes, Dave. We're both here and we're both sitting down." He said nothing as he slowly turned to face Regan full on. Whatever Dave was saying was clearly impressing him. "I'll tell her," he said and closed his phone.

"What?" Regan was desperate for details.

"Dave says Preston Alfrey just turned up at the station house and says *he* killed Julien Rochette."

Part of Dave's job as Santa Cruz Police Ombudsman was media interaction. He was the spokesperson who got a microphone shoved in front of his face, and while the local TV audience watched, had to answer questions the media posed. Although he had never faced the camera in a suit and tie, he had spent some time getting his look just right. His goal was to convey that the police department could be friendly and approachable and was compatible with the free spirit of Santa Cruz. He had tried wearing a sports jacket with an open-at-the-neck shirt, a collared polo shirt, and a sweater over a shirt before hitting on his trademark Hawaiian shirt.

For the evening news two days after Christmas, Dave was resplendent in a Hawaiian shirt that managed to incorporate every color of the rainbow and a few only imagined in that meteorological phenomenon.

Sometimes he needed to be circumspect in answering media questions, citing the ongoing nature of an investigation for his lack of directness. Usually he seemed to enjoy his role. Tonight though, as Regan watched his performance, she noticed things like the beginning of an eye roll quickly altered into a mere non-judgmental look upward, or a smile she recognized as forced. He wasn't friendly or relaxed. He wasn't having fun tonight. He may have seemed composed to the evening news crew and audience, but Regan could tell Dave was spitting mad.

"That is correct," he stated coolly, "two people have confessed to the same murder."

"I understand the suspects are related?" the newswoman turned her statement into a question.

"Yes, Charles Alfrey and Preston Alfrey are father and son."

"And both have confessed to murdering Julien Rochette in late October of 1994?"

Dave repressed an eye roll. "That is correct."

"At the time of the alleged murder, how old would Preston Alfrey have been?"

Dave squelched another eye roll and stated serenely, "He would have been thirteen years of age."

"Will he be charged for murder as a juvenile or as an adult?"

"That decision hasn't been made yet." Regan noted Dave's jaw clench. "In fact, no charges have been filed against him at this time."

"Have charges been pressed against the father?"

"Not at this time."

"Why is that?"

Dave's pleasant smile was without a doubt forced, "The investigation is ongoing and any comment I could make at this time would be of a speculative nature."

"Would you care to speculate for our audience?"

"No, I would not."

The news reporter tried several other approaches to get more information out of Dave but wasn't successful. She finally thanked him for his time and ended the interview.

Dave's performance had raised a number of questions in Regan's mind. She punched his name on her speed dial. He picked up on the second ring. "Don't start with me, Regan. I know — the interview sucked."

"I'm not calling to critique your interview skills. I want to know what's going on with the Alfreys. I understand why you couldn't really say anything to the media, but can you tell me? I promise not to pass on anything you say to anyone." She hesitated for a second, "except to Tom, of course."

"We got lawyers involved now. As soon as Junior turned himself in, Alfrey senior lawyered up and told his son to do the same. You know what lawyers do: they look for guys like me to overstate so they can complain about muddying the jury pool and things like that. And you know how the news people are: they want a sound bite and they don't care if the information behind it is solid."

"Please assume you hear sympathetic noises from my end of the phone. I would make them, but I'm not sure how they should sound," she laughed. "You did seem irritated during the interview."

"Oh yeah. And you think I'm hot, you should hear what Detective Harrison's been saying — he's supposed to be running the show here, not a bunch of one-upping Alfreys. So, let's see — off the record, we got a real interesting story out of the younger Mr. Alfrey. He says way back when, his old man sent him by the house with instructions to flush the toilet

141

and run the tap water. Do you realtors do things like that if a house is sitting empty for a long time?"

"Guilty as charged. Empty houses sometimes show a bit of color in the water if nothing moves for a week or so ..." Her voice trailed off as she realized how what she was saying might sound. "Of course, we would never do something like that right before an inspection, at least most of us wouldn't." Dave's silence made her blush.

"Uh-huh. Well, the kid says that's what he was supposed to do. He says he was there doing his little job when in walks the Vic with some tools and supplies to do a little repair work. Junior says he didn't like the guy because he was dating Isabel Bolton. It seems young Mr. Alfrey, remember he's barely thirteen at the time, met Isabel when they did a summer school play together and he had this huge unrequited crush on her. He says that's all he had against the guy, but he hated him for it and told Rochette in no uncertain terms to leave Isabel alone.

"The son says Rochette just started laughing at him and calling him a wimpy little baby. He says he got so mad he picked up a two-by-four — I guess the same handy two-by-four his dad says *he* used — and took a swing at the guy. He says he didn't mean to kill him, just sock him in the stomach or crack a knee, but he got a lucky hit and bashed in the Vic's skull.

"Then he says he went high-tailing it home to daddy and told him what he'd done. Alfrey senior told him not to breathe a word about what happened, that he'd take care of things."

"Wow," Regan said. "So the police think Charles hid

Julien Rochette's body to protect his son? I guess he got worried when you started asking Preston questions and figured he'd better come forward and say he was the murderer."

Dave's frustration was clear even over the phone. "When Alfrey senior goes on trial, *if* daddy goes on trial, 'cause right now he's been released without charge, the most it can be for is as an accessory after the fact. He's gonna be a sobbing father with a lawyer going for some kind of jury nullification by arguing it was too late to help Rochette and he was just trying to protect his son.

"Then there's this complication with the way the law works: as an accessory after the fact, daddy is guilty of whatever junior is, but he can't be charged with more than junior can. An accidental killing in the heat of the moment should be manslaughter, but at thirteen ... so Preston's been sent home for now, too, while everybody cogitates."

"I understand why you're upset," Regan sympathized, "but Preston Alfrey will have to be charged with something more, won't he? He may have lashed out without thinking about the consequences, but then choking a man to death, even at thirteen, well that's hardly an accidental killing."

"You didn't let me finish and you're missing something big here, Regan, something huge. Junior has no more idea how Rochette was really killed than his old man does; no prints on the medallion either. Thinking in the Department is that he didn't do anything, that maybe he's just making up a story to try and protect his dad. That's the story his attorney's pitching."

"What do you think, Dave?"

"I think if we ever get either of these guys to trial, there's going to be a lot of finger pointing and blubbering." Dave's voice went into a falsetto, "'No, he's innocent. I'm the one who did it.' 'No. No. Pick me, I'm the guilty one.' No jury will have any idea who to believe beyond a reasonable doubt and they'll both walk. So yes, you could say I was irritated during the interview. I'm flaming furious."

🏠 🏠 🏠 🏠 🏠 🏠 🏠 🏠 🏠 🏠 🏠

It was hard for Regan to imagine a thirteen-year-old Preston as a killer, especially since he didn't have his murder facts straight — unless he was setting up his story with all the cleverness and cunning of a twenty-nine-year-old whose violent roots went back sixteen years.

If a workman making repairs to the house, possibly even Julien himself — now there would be the ultimate irony — left a piece of two-by-four laying around, it seemed possible they would have left some other random bits of construction material behind as well. Duct tape didn't seem to her like part of a construction kit, but when she ran her thoughts by Tom, he laughed and quoted G. Weilacher: "One only needs two tools in life: WD-40 to make things go and duct tape to make them stop." He told her that really was pretty good advice and that he kept both of those items in his car tool kit.

Maybe it was possible that Preston's story was correct to a point. Maybe he was a thirteen-year-old in the throes of beginning puberty who, still in the midst of a jealous adolescent rage, not only hit Julien Rochette, but discovered the tape and bound him with it, intent on finishing his warning about Isabel when his bashed victim regained consciousness.

Perhaps when that happened, though, instead of taunting a helpless and fearful Julien Rochette, Preston was the one who got the dressing down delivered by a still cocky-in-spite-of-his-circumstances Rochette. She could almost picture the thirteen-year-old raging and yelling for Julien to shut up and using the victim's necklace to choke off his taunts.

Her imagining stopped where it was. Using the necklace was cumbersome and the medallion didn't hold Preston's fingerprints.

What did work, if the mental picture she was drawing was accurate, was Preston taking another piece of duct tape and putting it over Julien's mouth to silence him. If the victim had been asphyxiated by tape over his mouth and nose, she could envision how Julien died. Preston might have accidently covered a struggling Julien's mouth and nose and then either not been able to peel the tape off quickly enough, or more cruelly, decided he liked watching Julien asphyxiate. But there weren't any remnants of tape on the corpse's face; Julien had been garroted, not suffocated with duct tape. It just didn't work.

Nothing worked, Regan sighed. Why couldn't she imagine a scenario that let the puzzle pieces coalesce into the face of Julien Rochette's murderer?

The authorities were probably right in releasing Preston. She didn't know the man well, but what she had seen of him suggested he was more of an order-follower than the master-mind of a murder and cover-up. If any cover-up was designed, he was more likely to have been used as a tool in its application than its instigator.

She didn't feel the same way about Charles Alfrey — he could calculate and he could be ruthless. But she had also seen that other side of him, the one he exhibited in the presence of his wife, the one Meg spoke of. That Charles might take the blame to protect a loved one, *would* take the blame. The problem was, if he said he killed Julien to cover for his son, why wouldn't he have described using a garrote to do the job? The only explanation she could think of was that he truly didn't know how Julien died.

She, like the authorities, kept getting stuck right there. The police had first tried to pressure more information out of the Alfreys, something that was unlikely to happen now that the men could only be interviewed under the watchful eyes of their attorneys with their whispered notes of caution. Then the authorities backed off to think about what approach to try next.

Regan decided on a different tack. She decided to get to know Julien Rochette better and see if the man in the triangle could tell her who killed him before Charles Alfrey put him there.

20

The first step in Regan's plan was to talk to the woman who knew Julien Rochette so well she had consented to marry him: Isabel Bolton. There was just one problem with that — she had no idea how to find Isabel other than by going through Jessie Bolton, and after the police let him know, she tipped them off to his hatred of the murder victim, he wasn't speaking to her.

The first time she called him, he hung up as soon as she identified herself. He did the same thing the second time she tried. And the third. She had Tom call him using a different phone number in case Jessie used caller ID and recognized hers. Jessie only spoke to Tom long enough to give him a message to relay to Regan: leave me alone. Regan suspected Jessie had phrased the message differently, but that Tom had softened it and cleaned it up for her ears.

She decided a face-to-face visit was her best hope of talking to Jessie. When she did a reverse directory search for his address by using his phone number, she discovered he lived near the historic town of San Juan Bautista, a community that grew up around the fifteenth Spanish mission to be built along California's El Camino Real.

Regan finished lunch at Jardines de San Juan, an extravagantly bowered outdoor cantina located in the town. She should have been cold sitting outside in January, but the weather this first week of the new year had been magnificent with inland temperatures in the mid-sixties. She ran across the street for a quick peek into Inka Line, a great little store with imported Peruvian goods, gorgeous earrings, and a delightful proprietor. Fortified by lunch and her mini shopping excursion, she told herself it was time to stop dawdling and get to the purpose of her visit.

Jessie's ranch was eight miles out of town toward Salinas. She was knocking on his front door less than fifteen minutes after leaving San Juan Bautista. He opened his door with a welcoming expression that vanished as soon as he recognized her. He started to close the door and she momentarily considered whether or not to block the door with her foot. She decided to plead her case instead.

"Jessie, please. We've known each other for a long time. I made the trip here just to see you for a few minutes. Hear me out and then if you want me to, I promise I'll leave you alone. Please."

"You wantin' to hear somethin' else to tell that piss-ant Detective Harrison? Suggestin' I was a murderer wasn't enough for you?"

"Jessie, I'm sorry. I never meant for you to become a suspect in a murder investigation. I'm sorry if the authorities troubled you. It wasn't my idea to blame you for Julien Rochette's death."

He opened the door a few inches wider. "Yeah, maybe you were just bein' dumb. What do you want?"

"For starters, I want you to know Charles and Preston Alfrey have both confessed to the killing."

"Yeah, I saw that on the news," his face was split by the first genuine smile she'd seen since the beginning of this unpleasant incident. "They seem to have taken me off the hook, all right. Either of them say why they did it? Or which one of 'em did it? I owe somebody some steaks, remember?"

"I know why they both said they did it."

He let out a huge sigh. "I never was very good at holdin' a grudge against a pretty woman who was gonna tell me some back-fence talk." He emitted another even longer sigh. "Come on in," he said, opening the door wide.

Jessie's décor was simple, masculine and rustic in feel, and sparse. He favored sturdy plaid furniture with heavy uncarved frames. His coffee table was well-worn pine that hinted to visitors it was OK to put their feet up on it. He had rifles and guns displayed high on the walls where most people would have hung pictures. The one incongruous decoration in the room was a large ornately framed photo of a bride and groom which hung above the mantel of his heavy stacked-stone fireplace.

Regan had seen photos of Isabel before. Jessie never let an inspection or meeting end without producing a recent picture of his daughter, so she immediately recognized the bride. The size and placement of the picture meant it demanded the attention of anyone who entered the room, but Regan stared at it because of the bride's beauty.

"Oh Jessie," she gushed without any need of artificial

flattery, "I forgot how beautiful your daughter is."

Jessie's smile was luminous. "My little girl was the most beautiful bride you ever laid eyes on, and I'm not just sayin' that like a proud papa."

She moved closer to the photograph and looked at it more carefully. Had the photo been an ancestral one, where the newlyweds held rigidly still for the sake of the needed long exposure, nothing about the bride's eyes would have caught her attention. But to Regan, who earned her living reading nonverbal cues from her clients, something about Isabel's eyes didn't seem right. She remembered smiling so much when she married Tom that her cheeks ached the next day. Brides were supposed to be happy, but though Isabel was smiling in the photo, her eyes weren't. They seemed somehow cheerless.

She was probably reading more into the bride's expression than was really there — all the events, tension, and ensuing exhaustion that came with a grand wedding could have caught up with the girl just as the photo was taken — but Regan thought she saw something that didn't belong in the eyes of a bride on her wedding day. Isabel's eyes were filled with buried pain.

"You admirin' her dress?" Jessie asked.

"Umm, yes, her dress and her hair," Regan felt only a bit dishonest with her answer. "It's fun to try and guess the year of a marriage from the style of the gown and the bride's hairstyle. I'd guess your daughter got married sometime between 1998 and 2001, and in the summer."

"You're a pretty good guesser. Isabel and John got married in 2000. My little girl had a traditional June wedding at Mission San Juan Bautista and then there was a big reception at the groom's spread in Aptos."

"You told me they stayed in the area, didn't you? Do they still live nearby?"

Regan sensed Jessie's body tightening. "What did you want to talk to me about?"

She tried to sidetrack him. "2000. I bet you have grandchildren by now. How many grandchildren do you have? Do you get to see them often?" she asked brightly. "Oh, I was going to tell you about the Alfreys ..."

"You were going to ask about Isabel, weren't you? It's not enough the police asked her if she thought her dad killed her boyfriend? Now *you're* lookin' at botherin' her with this Rochette murder thing, aren't you?" His perception was dead on right, and his resultant growing anger was aimed directly at her.

"That is what I wanted to talk to you about, Jessie. I was hoping you'd tell me how I can contact Isabel," she confessed.

"Out! Get out! You're not my friend. You leave my daughter alone, you hear?" He shooed her toward the door, and although Regan was taller than Jessie, his anger was fierce enough to be intimidating. She did as she was told, moving hurriedly out the front door.

For a fleeting second, she recalled Jessie's guns and envisioned the outraged father reaching for one of them, ready to dispatch her and hang her from a fencepost in warning to other snoops. When the door banged closed explosively behind her, she froze for just a heartbeat, waiting for a sharp pain to pierce some part of her body.

151

🏠 🏠 🏠 🏠 🏠 🏠 🏠 🏠 🏠 🏠 🏠

Jessie had thrown her out before she got all the information she sought, but she felt confident that she had learned enough to find Isabel. Regan made an assumption: Isabel and her husband had taken out a marriage license either in San Benito County where they had been married, or in Santa Cruz County where the groom lived. Since she was already near Hollister, San Benito County's government seat, she decided to start there at the combined office of the County Recorder, Clerk, and Assessor.

San Benito County was larger than Santa Cruz County in area but about a fifth the size in population. Government still had a small-town feel; it wasn't uncommon for county employees to greet their patrons on a first name basis.

"I know the bride's maiden name and the groom's first name and that they got married in June of 2000, but I can't remember their last name," Regan said to the clerk, ready to lay out a make-believe story if she needed to, but the clerk stopped her with a question.

"What was the bride's name?" the plump young woman dressed in a slightly too tight polyester dress asked. "Maybe I know them."

"The bride's maiden name was Isabel Bolton."

"Oh sure, Jessie's daughter."

"That's right. Do you know her married name?"

"Umm, I should, but I can't think of it. I still think of her as Isabel Bolton, probably always will. Just a sec," the cheery young worker typed a few keystrokes into her computer. "I looked up Bolton in 2000, but I didn't get a hit. Are you sure about the year?"

"Yes, I am."

"Well then, I'd guess they got their license in Santa Cruz County. Lots of people go there, especially if one of them works there."

Regan thanked the woman for her help and began her drive back to Santa Cruz and its much more formally run County Government Building.

A quick search of the information board told her the County Recorder's office was only one flight up so she took the stairs. Regan found an available clerk, a sinewy woman with frizzed ear-length salt-and-pepper gray hair and the pinched, disappointed look of a thirty-year smoker who had kicked the habit on doctor's orders but had resented life every day since. She began the story she had prepared on the drive from Hollister.

"Hi, I'm a little embarrassed here and I hope you can help me out. My friend got married in 2000, June of 2000, but you know how it is, she kept her maiden name," she giggled for effect. "Well, the thing is, her husband John is coming to town on business and she asked if he could stay with us for a day or two."

The gatekeeper across the counter looked up at Regan over the top of her glasses and silently maintained her discontented expression.

"Well, of course I said that would be fine." Regan paused to give the clerk time for an "Uh-huh" but none was forthcoming. "Now I realize I may have to introduce him to someone while he's here and, oh this is the embarrassing part," she leaned in toward the unresponsive clerk and stage-whispered, "I can't remember his last name. Could you look up their marriage license and tell me what it is?"

"That will be fourteen dollars, payable in cash, by personal check, or by money order," the bored civil servant replied.

"No problem." Regan looked through her purse and retrieved her checkbook.

The disinterested bureaucrat continued parroting the counter notice that faced Regan. "I need the full name of both parties named on the license, the date of the marriage, or at least the year of the marriage, and the address where the marriage certificate copy is to be mailed."

Regan's voice went up an octave, "But that's the point — I don't know the groom's last name. And I don't need a copy of the marriage certificate, just the name."

"That's fine, I can look it up with the information you have. But it will still be fourteen dollars made payable to Santa Cruz County Recorder Vitals Department."

A few keystrokes and a check for fourteen dollars later, Regan had the name she needed and was on her way to the nearest phone book, hoping John and Isabel Minetti had a listed phone number.

"Hello." Isabel answered the phone in a soft clear voice.

"Is this Isabel Bolton Minetti?" Regan included Bolton in Isabel's name to make sure she had the right woman; no need to let an unexpected name and marriage date coincidence cause her to pour out her heart to someone with no idea what she was talking about.

"Yes." There was a hint of suspicion in her gentle voice, like she expected Regan to try to sell her something with her next sentence ... which in a way, was exactly what she hoped to do.

"Isabel, is it OK for me to call you Isabel? I've seen pictures of you so often I feel like we've met. My name is Regan McHenry. I'm a real estate agent and your father was, is, so proud of you ..."

A warm giggle interrupted her. "Say no more. I hope my father didn't bore you with every detail of my life."

"No, no," Regan smiled as she talked. "But I do know you love horses and are an accomplished rider, you were a very good student, spent a little time as a professional model, and made a beautiful bride."

"Is your memory that good or did my dad overwhelm you with photos and chatter?" Isabel's easy-going giggly laugh came out again.

"It's a little of both, Isabel." Regan paused and took a deep breath. "I have more reason to know and remember things about you than most people your dad worked with. I'd like to meet you in person and talk about why that is; but I have to be honest with you, your dad has been trying to prevent me from contacting you. He's afraid that what I want to talk to you about ... the person I want to talk to you about ... is a painful memory for you. He may be right, but it's important, Isabel."

Isabel remained quiet for so long that Regan began to wonder if she was still on the line. "Isabel? Isabel, are you still there?"

"It's about Julien, isn't it?" Isabel's voice had lost all trace of merriment and vitality; it was scarcely more than a whisper.

"Yes, it is."

"I read about him in the newspaper ... and then for a while the police thought my father ... was it your house?"

"Yes."

"I need to talk to you, too, regardless of what my father thinks. Could you come here, to my place, tomorrow, while my husband is at work? I don't want to talk about Julien in front of him; it would be too painful for both of us if he heard me talk about Julien."

"Whenever you want will be fine. I appreciate you seeing me; please be assured I'll respect your privacy. Thank you, Isabel."

Regan intended to introduce herself when Isabel opened her front door, but she stood there open-mouthed instead. Jessie's photos, good as they were, understated Isabel's striking beauty. She had a delicate frame and a small heart shaped face that made her seem fairy-like, a fragile being that might require a magic spell to keep her earthbound. She was a petite woman, shorter than Regan anticipated, and she looked up at her through a dense fringe of lashes with steady, deep blue, almost violet eyes.

"Did he suffer?" It wasn't what she expected Isabel's greeting would be; it caught her by surprise.

Regan tried to read her, to determine the answer she wanted. A pat "No" would have been the easiest answer to deliver, but Isabel hadn't known the truth about Julien for so long … besides, she couldn't lie to those eyes. "I think he did, Isabel." She found herself almost tearful as she spoke.

The woman dropped her head and took a quavery breath in response and nodded a couple of times. Isabel invited Regan in with a solemn "Please come in" and silently led her to the kitchen. She directed Regan to a chair at the kitchen table and slipped into the seat opposite her.

Isabel's eyes remained downcast. "I don't want to know how he died. I don't want to know the details," Isabel said, battling for control, fighting to come away from the brink of weeping.

"I don't think I could tell you the details. There are certain things the police hold back." Dave hadn't admonished her, but she was smart enough to realize he had probably told her more about how Julien Rochette died than he should have.

"I don't know how to feel about what happened to him." Isabel pressed her lips together hard as her eyes filled with tears again. "I loved him so much. At first, I was certain he hadn't abandoned me like my father insisted, and I was terrified something had happened to him. But over time ... I abandoned *him*." Her magnificent eyes glistened as she met Regan's gaze, "There's a part of me that feels almost relieved he's dead. It means he still loves me. Do you understand?" Isabel shook her head. "I'm an awful person. I didn't deserve him."

As she spoke, Isabel's hands assumed an almost prayerful pose on the kitchen table; Regan wordlessly covered them with her own.

"And then there's John. He's such a decent man, such a good man. He's always been wonderful to me. I had reservations about marrying him ... I told him how I still felt about Julien. But he said he could wait for me to love him ... and I did come to love him in a way ..." she shook her head again. "He deserves better than me."

"I think if you asked him, he'd disagree. You're hurting right now. It will pass. Old wounds have been reopened, but now they can heal. Let yourself mourn for Julien; lay him to rest. See what happens after that. You may look at your husband with new eyes soon. You can do that, can't you?"

Isabel produced the weakest of smiles, and nodded. "I'll try."

Both women sat in silence until finally Isabel said, "You wanted to ask me about Julien. What do you want to know about him?" Her hands formed into fists and her voice gained strength as she spoke.

Regan followed her lead and began her explanation in a business-like tone. "Two men have confessed to killing Julien and the police don't know which of them to believe. It's even possible neither of them killed him. I've heard some pretty contradictory things about Julien, about who he was, about his character, some of it from your father. I want to know who he was, really. I think knowing him might make it easier to figure out who killed him. I thought of you. I'm sure no one knew him better than you did."

"Julien was a work in progress. Probably everyone who said anything about him was right. My father said he was wild and unreliable. That was probably true of him for a while, but he was changing, growing up maybe, looking forward and taking responsibility for his future, for our future. He had stolen things from some houses he worked on for Charles Alfrey, but he'd never been caught. He stopped doing that. He said he was one of the lucky few who had learned from his mistakes without having to pay for them. He felt like it was a blessing, like he'd been given a second chance and that he better use it to make something of himself."

"Your father said Julien dissuaded you from going away to college."

Isabel's response was quick and amused, "My father insists to this day that's what happened. He's mistaken. Julien encouraged me to do whatever I wanted. I was the one who didn't want to leave. I never wanted to become a serious actress. That was always my father's dream for me, not mine.

159

"Julien was getting his real estate license. He promised he'd work hard and be a big success and make as much money as Charles Alfrey. After we were married, he was going to put me through school, veterinary school, that's what *I* wanted to do. That was our dream. We had it all worked out but we were realistic; we knew money would be tight starting out. He was going to work here for a while to get some experience while I went to Foothill College in Los Altos. It's a junior college so it would have kept my expenses down, but they have a good veterinary program there. After two years we were going to move near Davis. I'm a good student. Getting into the vet program at the University of California at Davis is hard, but if I got accepted at Carnegie Mellon, I was confident I could get in there, too.

"We had such wonderful plans before Julien ..." she bit her lip and looked at Regan with eyes devastating for both their beauty and for the sorrow they held, "... before Julien was killed.

"You said two people confessed to Julien's murder. From the news, I know both Charles and Preston Alfrey were in police custody for a while. They both said they killed Julien? Did either of them say why? It's hard enough to think Charles Alfrey might have done it, but Preston, well, that's just impossible."

"Preston said he killed Julien out of jealousy over his relationship with you."

"Preston wasn't jealous of Julien. He adored him."

"That's not what he said. Preston said he had a crush on you since the summer play you did together and he didn't like Julien dating you. He said he ran into Julien at a vacant house and when he warned him to leave you alone, Julien goaded him and called him a baby, and he ..." Regan stopped, realizing she was close to telling Isabel details she didn't need to hear, details that would only create another painful image she would have to work through. "He said he killed him in a kind of jealous adolescent rage."

Regan expected the details, sketchy as she had kept them, might cause Isabel to grimace, but there was no sign of hurt on the woman's face. Isabel smiled indulgently, recalling fond memories.

"No, that's not possible," Isabel said. "We did *'Bye, 'Bye Birdie* that summer, Preston and I. I was Kim in the play and Preston was my little brother, Randolph. We did feel almost like brother and sister by the end of the summer. If he loved me, it was like a sister." She shook her head in an emphatic No, "He did not have a crush on me.

"Julien used to come by and pick me up most days after rehearsal. Preston had to be at rehearsal every day but Randolph wasn't a big role. He spent a lot of time just hanging out and being bored. Sometimes Julien would take him to the back of the theater and entertain him. I remember one day Julien had a yo-yo with him and he did tricks for Preston. Preston wanted to learn how to do *around the world* and Julien was working with him on that when the string broke. The yo-yo flew through the theatre and hit Miss James, the drama teacher, in the behind," Isabel giggled at the memory. "She wasn't hurt or anything like that, but she banished both of them for the rest of the day's rehearsal."

"Isn't it possible that Preston developed some sort of feelings for you that he hid — pubescent boys can do that sort

161

of thing. Could he have grown jealous of Julien?"

Isabel's eyes glistened. "No," she said simply. She paused for a moment savoring her remembrances. "No, Preston was going to be our best man."

Regan tilted her head questioningly but said nothing as she waited for Isabel to continue.

"I remember it was after dress rehearsal. Almost everyone had left, but I was up on-stage double checking my position during one song — the blocking for that song always gave me trouble — when Julien came up on stage, got down on one knee and pretended to propose. He was just play acting, or what do you call it — floating a trial balloon — he didn't really propose for a few more months. The next thing we knew, Preston came running up the center aisle, jumped onto the stage, and flew at us. He threw his arms around both of us as best as he could and pleaded, 'Please let me be your best man, Julien. I was my dad's best man. I know how to do it.' He was so cute, Julien promised him he had the gig." Isabel's laughter tinkled merrily; it was as lovely as she was. "So you see, it's not possible he killed Julien."

"The authorities released Preston. They seem to agree with you."

"Then why did Preston confess?"

"The police seem to think he was trying to cover for his father."

"For Charles Alfrey?" The slightest frown flitted across Isabel's brow.

Regan pulled her lower lip into her mouth. "Isabel, I'm sorry." She hesitated, trying to frame her next words with as much care as possible. "It may be that Julien didn't stop breaking into houses. There was a key in his pants pocket, a key to the house where he was found, our house, now. Charles says he discovered Julien was making keys and using them to gain entry, and when he confronted him about it, they got into a fight. Charles said in defending himself, he accidently …"

"No. No. That never happened." Isabel's statement was so firm and certain she could have convinced any jury. "Charles never found out about Julien's past. Julien talked about telling him, but the break-ins had ended more than two years before he met me. I discouraged him from confessing. When he decided to go for his real estate license, we realized a record like that could prevent him from becoming licensed. He felt guilty for not telling Charles, but I convinced him that confessing what he had done in the past would have been a bad idea. He agreed. Charles Alfrey never knew. That's why Julien felt he had been given a second chance. If Charles Alfrey killed Julien, it didn't happen like that, at least not for that reason."

"Can you think of any other reason Charles might have for killing Julien?" Regan asked her next question cautiously; she was guessing — floating her own trial balloon with Isabel. "Could he have been upset because of Julien's relationship with Corinne?" Regan gave Isabel time to consider but stared into her eyes looking for any hint of evasiveness or deceit.

Isabel looked down momentarily. Then her lashes slowly rose again revealing the young woman's dazzling near-violet eyes. She met Regan's gaze full on. "It's possible," she said in a clear, measured voice. "His relationship with Corinne Alfrey was the only thing Julien ever lied about to me."

"What? How?" Regan was so taken aback, she stammered.

"Julien knew Corinne. She got him his job with Charles Alfrey when she was working for Bradley Real Estate. He told me they were cousins, distant cousins, but related, and that was how he knew her. We were out one night. We'd gone to a movie, I can't remember which one, it doesn't matter anyway, but I can certainly remember Corinne's reaction when she saw us. We were walking on Pacific Avenue right by the Cinema 9, holding hands, going to Julien's car. We were talking; you know how people can be talking and not see anything that's going on around them?"

"People in love? Yes, I know how that is," Regan offered an understanding smile.

Isabel nodded pensively. "We came around the corner heading to the parking garage between Walnut and Church, and there was Corinne. I've seen her picture in real estate magazines since then, colored pictures. She's a pretty woman and always smiling, but as many times as I've seen her photos, they can never make me forget the look on her face that night.

"Her eyes were hardly visible; they were just slits of rage. She snarled, snarled like the cougar that jumped out at my horse one day when I was riding. She spit out her words so they hissed, 'What are you doing with him?' It was me she seemed to be angry with. Julien kind of turned sideways, just kind of took a step toward her and moved his shoulder like an offensive guard. He tried laughing and said something like, 'Hey couz, you meeting your hubby for some dinner?'

"Corinne didn't say anything for a bit and then she kind of came up with a snide little laugh. 'Exactly,' she said and then she kind of pushed out each word separately, 'I'm meeting my *husband*.' She almost made 'husband' sound like a curse word. And then she just pressed her way through us, between us, and walked down the street. But the look she gave me as she passed was unforgettable. I felt if Julien hadn't been there to protect me, she could have ripped out my heart.

"Of course I asked Julien what was going on. He said Corinne and Charles had had a big fight at work that day and she probably wasn't over it, that he shouldn't have teased her about meeting Charles for dinner because it obviously made her angry. That wasn't what Corinne was angry about. We women can tell when another woman hates us because of a man, can't we?"

"Yes we can," Regan replied.

"Julien was more than Corinne's cousin." Isabel issued a sour chuckle, "I said that to him; I said they must be kissing cousins at least. He grabbed my arm so hard it hurt and shouted at me that there wasn't anything between him and Corinne, that there never had been, and that I needed to believe him and trust him."

"Did you?"

"I half-believed him. I knew he was lying to me about there never having been anything between them, but I wanted to believe there wasn't anything going on then. I did decide to trust him about that. He asked me to marry him a few days later. He wouldn't have done that if he still had feelings for her, would he?"

Isabel's question was rhetorical. She was serene with the certainty of Julien's love which the knowledge of his murder had given her. Regan didn't want to hint at youthful naiveté or love leading to blindness. Isabel didn't need to hear anything that might cause her more anguish than she'd already carried for the last sixteen years.

"You knew him better than anyone else," seemed like the right thing to say. "What about Charles? Do you think he knew about Corinne and Julien's past?"

"Like I said, it's possible. That's another reason I trusted Julien. If he and Corinne were involved before she got married, well that was before me as well. I had no right to be upset with Julien for what he did before he met me. Charles Alfrey hired Julien and treated him well, paid him well, too, for the work he did. If Julien and Corinne had been a couple in the past, he probably felt the same way I did.

"You know how you can still feel a twinge; I guess you'd call it jealousy, but baby jealousy, if your love looks at an old flame in a certain way? That's all I felt, probably all her husband felt, if he knew. After a while, even that little jealousy sensation goes away. If it wasn't over between Corinne and Julien, surely Charles Alfrey would never have hired him. He wouldn't have wanted him around."

22

Regan only stayed on Highway 1 for a few miles after she left Isabel's house. The beach called her. She took the Rio del Mar exit and followed the road until it deposited her in the parking lot near the Cement Ship. It was usually a challenge to find a parking space there, but it was a weekday and early January. Few people shared her desire for a walk on the beach so she had her choice of parking spaces.

A week of pounding El Niño rain was expected to begin the next day, but if she hadn't heard last night's weather report, she would never have guessed what was coming by looking skyward. At mid-day the sky was crisply blue and devoid of clouds, even the one or two decorator clouds that usually hovered over Monterey Bay.

She hit the hatch door button on her dashboard, got out, and walked to the back of her new Prius. She took out her windbreaker and replaced it with her purse and shoes.

The beach that stretched from New Brighton through Rio del Mar and to Seascape was her favorite feet-on-the-sand beach in Santa Cruz County. Tom had proposed to her as they strolled there and they came back often for long walks.

167

Usually they headed south toward Seascape to walk past the ship house, a curious structure built on a long narrow lot at the ocean's edge. The house was high and narrow, built with a pointed end like the prow of a ship. The original owner may have intended only to guarantee a beachfront view from every room, but subsequent owners had nautically enhanced the structure with porthole windows, a high-hanging dingy, and a deck where a Marilyn Monroe statue perpetually fought to control her skirt, not from subway air vent blasts, but from sudden ocean gusts.

Regan wasn't walking for pleasure today, though. She needed to think about what Isabel told her. She headed north toward the shorter beach and walked past the Cement Ship. Regan did her best thinking while walking. If she got lost in thought and forgot to pay attention to her surroundings, she would run out of beach and be forced to turn around and come back to the moment and solid surroundings — and nothing could be more solid, symbolically or in reality, than the partly submerged World War I era ship made of rein-forced concrete.

In Isabel's mind everything was resolved: Julien wasn't using pilfered keys to break into houses, Julien and Corinne may have been a couple at one time but that was long over, Charles wasn't jealous of Julien, Preston adored Julien and wasn't jealous of his relationship with Isabel. All neat, all tidy. But in Regan's mind, very little was that clear.

Charles may not have known that Corinne and Julien had a history when he hired him. If he did find out, he may have felt more than baby jealousy, as Isabel called it.

Jessie might have been right. His warnings to his daughter

may have come more from what he observed between Corinne and Julien than from any comparison he made to his own rowdy youthful self. And if Charles had found out Corinne and Julien were still involved after he and Corinne married, goodbye baby jealousy — hello green-eyed monster.

Charles would have been enraged by a continuing affair. His broker told him he needed help with anger management; he might well have been capable of murder. If only Charles had known how Julien died, she thought, everything would fit together so well. But it seemed he didn't know. That missing knowledge created problems.

She considered murder from different directions. Charles hid Julien's body and confessed to murdering him, but he didn't know how Julien died. That meant he helped with the cover-up, but not the murder. Yet he was willing to say he was a killer and take sole blame for Julien Rochette's murder. Was it possible Charles confessed in exchange for the real killer's silence about some hidden secret in his past? It seemed unlikely.

Would Charles sacrifice himself to protect someone he loved from facing a murder charge? Charles loved his son; did Charles confess to protect him? After her conversation with Isabel, who insisted Preston wasn't jealous of Julien and wouldn't have killed him under any circumstances, Regan didn't believe Charles needed to protect his son from a murder charge any more than the police did.

If he wasn't covering up for Preston, was he covering up for someone else? If so, who was Charles protecting, and why? Regan walked faster and pulled her jacket tighter around her as if that would make her think more clearly. The only person she could come up with was Corinne. Could Charles be covering for her?

Twinges of jealousy. Great clobbering masses of jealousy — she knew all about them. Lots of houses got sold because of divorce. She'd had clients who, after leaving their mate for another, still were furious when the person they deserted started to pull their life together and move on. She often saw that anger increase when the abandoned spouse began a new relationship.

Deserters carried guilt with them when they walked out; that was probably why they often were so good at making up reasons why they left — "my wife doesn't understand me," "my husband is so distant, I grew lonely" — she'd heard many variations on those themes. But one thing remained the same regardless of why the spouse left: when the abandoned partner moved on after a crushed marriage, the marriage-ender felt abandoned.

If Corinne and Julien had been involved, it was Corinne who left the relationship. She married Charles Alfrey, a man defined by Meg Dorsey as good-looking and rich. If anyone had a right to be jealous, it should have been Julien Rochette. But he had moved on. From what Isabel said, it sounded like he had gotten his life together and found love with her.

The story about Julien and keys and break-ins was in wide circulation. Isabel said, while the story was true, it had taken place in Julien's past and that no one knew about his unlawful history. But she knew. Julien told the woman he loved about his past. Regan guessed that he might well have told another woman he was involved with, too. Someone spread the key story. Corinne seemed like a natural pick for the tattletale.

Regan was alone on the beach; she talked to herself as she walked, pretending to be Corinne. "Getting his real estate license ... found a new woman ... moving on, is he? I could kill him." Saying the words out loud rather than merely thinking them made imagining Corinne saying them easier, but her mind still resisted the idea. She knew Corinne — they weren't close friends but they were friendly. She liked her. Everyone liked her. Nothing she had ever seen in Corinne's behavior suggested she was the sort of person who would be murderously vindictive. Nothing that is, until she heard Isabel describe her run-in with Corinne. Isabel's account presented a side of Corinne that Regan didn't recognize.

Stories of abandoned lovers who murdered their exes made headlines. Spreading cruel stories about exes happened all the time. But murdering your ex because he had moved on and then somehow convincing your husband to help you hide the body? That was a story she had never seen in the news. No, she must be getting way off base.

Wasn't it just last week that she had breathlessly called Dave, certain that Preston Alfrey had been the one who attacked her on Empire Grade just because he drove a black Land Rover and had gotten pale when he came upon Meg and her talking about Julien Rochette at the Bradley office? Now she was thinking of Corinne as a possible murderer.

"I'm in danger of becoming as crazy as Linda Cooper — the only difference between us is a noun substitution — where Linda sees aliens, I see Alfreys.

"Why is it so easy to believe the worst about a person? In another minute I'll be thinking Corinne was the one who ran me off Empire Grade." Regan stopped walking, startled by her own words.

She had never gotten past believing Charles was somehow involved in her crash. Even when he had the solid alibi of being seen at the Bradley office party at the time of her attack, she believed he was guilty. Her mind raced. Was Dave right? Was she letting her dislike of Charles blind her? Dave said something about Corinne getting to the party late because she had been in Bonny Doon with clients. She may have been, probably was. Would the police have verified what she said? Corinne wasn't a suspect for any crime; maybe they hadn't. *I should check when Corinne finished showing property on the night I was forced off the road.* A plan took shape in her mind.

Back up. Corinne drives a cute little car, a Miata, not a menacing big black SUV. How could she ...

Regan's mind raced again. Corinne could have parked her car at the Santa Cruz office, very few people would have been around to see it on the night of the office party, and even if they had, they wouldn't think it out of the ordinary for it to be there. Then she could have taken Charles' Land Rover, the one he left at the Bradley Santa Cruz office when he hitched a ride to the party with his broker. She probably had access to a key for it. He might not even have known she borrowed it.

There was a problem with her theory, though. Charles' Land Rover didn't have a brush guard and the vehicle that forced her off the road did. It was a troubling detail but she wasn't going to let it stop her imaginings for now.

Corinne could have called her from a nearby bar so there would be a background din that sounded like party noises as she pretended to be an out-of-area real estate agent. She wouldn't have had any difficulty sounding like a realtor; Corinne had been one even longer than she had.

Regan imagined Corinne using a bar like the Jury Room on Ocean Avenue, an old Santa Cruz mainstay located right across from the County Courthouse. For years the bar had a sign out front inviting visiting beach-goers and Santa Cruz residents alike to "Stop in and Have One for the Road," an amazing invitation considering that a few blocks away Ocean Avenue blended into the notoriously twisty and dangerous Highway 17 that climbed up and over the mountains to San Jose. The sign was gone, but the bar was still popular and loud; it always sounded like there was a party going on inside. It was also close to where Charles left his Land Rover overnight.

Regan produced a mental map. Corinne could have called her and still had plenty of time to drive up Graham Hill Road to Felton, continue up Felton Empire to Empire Grade Road, turn left toward Santa Cruz, and be in position to pursue her as she drove into town for her meeting with the fabricated agent and her clients.

Did Corinne know where she and Tom lived? If she didn't, she could have found out easily enough. Regan researched ownership records on title company websites looking for addresses. Corinne would have the same kind of access that she did.

Regan stopped short a good quarter-mile from the end of the beach and began jogging back toward the Cement Ship. She needed to make a few calls.

🏠🏠🏠🏠🏠🏠🏠🏠🏠🏠🏠

On the day of her accident, there were only six houses for sale in Bonny Doon and she and Tom had two of the listings. She reached Patty Kindig, one of the other four listing agents right away, and left messages for the other three. Regan had created a good story about an agent trying to steal her clients and asked for their help to catch the agent in a lie. All three agents responded to her message by noon the next day. Their promptness wasn't a surprise. She knew from firsthand experience that her story was sure to hit a nerve with them.

"So Frank," she said to the last agent returning her call, "now she says she showed your listing to my clients on December 4th, that she met them there late in the day, and that she should write the offer and be the procuring cause for the sale if they buy the house. I have no idea if she's telling the truth or not. She's a Los Gatos agent so I don't know anything about her, you know, like if she has a reputation for trying to steal commissions. Maybe she's telling the truth and my clients are playing games, but they say she never showed them your listing. Someone's lying; either she is or they are. But it occurred to me you'd be able to check your lockbox records and see if she did show the house that day. I said some pretty harsh things to her. If my clients are the story-tellers, I owe her an apology. If she's the one telling lies, I want to complain to her broker."

"Hang on, I can check online," Frank Murdock said. "December 4th, right?"

"Uh-huh."

"She's a rat bastard. There were no showings that day — no showings that whole week. Go get her."

"Thanks, Frank. That's exactly what I intend to do."

She'd had the same results from the other calls. If Corinne Alfrey was in Bonny Doon on December 4th, she wasn't there to show property.

23

Dave was the perfect host. He escorted her into his tiny police station office where he had a chair unfolded and waiting for her. He motioned for her to sit, and then sat at his desk, tilted his chair back, entwined his fingers, folded his hands over his mid-section, and listened silently as she outlined her reasons for suspecting Corinne Alfrey of murder.

Since her grounds were pure conjecture, Regan also presented him with her plan to entrap the murderess. He didn't interrupt her once as she spoke, and he kept his eyes on her, never once letting them drift to the stack of papers on his desk, papers that she suspected needed his attention.

He flipped his chair to full upright as she finished speaking, put his elbows on his desk, and supported his face with balled fingers. "You know what your problem is, Regan?" he asked softly.

A smart-alecky reply occurred to her but since he had been so accommodating, she decided not to use it.

"You're always so darn sure of everything — right up to the minute you completely change your mind. Then you're off in another direction because this time you're *really* sure. I get so dizzy trying to keep up with your whirling dervishness, someday I'm going to fall on my face and smash my glass eye."

"You don't have a glass eye. Your prosthesis is made of medical grade plastic acrylic. You can fall on your face all you want and it won't break. You told me so yourself."

Dave produced a bitter smirk. "That's another thing you do — you take me literally when it suits you, but when you want to go around me, you say, 'When you told me not to do that, I had no idea you meant it literally.' I can't win."

"I'm glad you realize that," she offered a tormentingly demure smile.

Dave heaved a huge sigh. "If you're right about the Alfrey woman, what you want to do could be dangerous. You'll need protecting in case she comes after you; that's gonna take valuable police time and resources, two things in short supply right now.

"You've laid out all your brilliant insights," so much sarcasm dripped from his words it seemed likely to collect in splashy rivulets that puddled on the floor, "now let those of us who know what we're doing handle this — stay out of our way."

He switched from irritated exasperation to pleading concern. "I worry about you. Stay out of the way for your own good."

Regan leaned toward him with raw enthusiasm, "Then you do agree that Corinne didn't have an alibi for the night I was attacked? You think it's strange she'd lie about where she was that night, too, don't you? In fact, you *do* think that it's possible Charles Alfrey was trying to protect her — that she's

177

the one who killed Julien and forced me off the road?"

"Whoa. Whoa there. I didn't say I agreed with your latest harebrained ideas. All I said was *if* you were right …" Dave left his statement dangling as Regan leaned back in her chair. Her smile grew to one of pleased satisfaction.

"I'm not going to do anything dangerous. I'm just going to present an offer on one of Corinne's listings."

"And drop the bomb on her you think she's a murderer who tried to kill you, too." Dave waggled his hands on either side of his head. "If she is, she's gonna go nuts."

"I'm not going to say anything about suspecting she attacked me. I may not even intimate that I think she's a killer. I'm just going to hint that I know more than I should. But I'm going to play kind of dumb, let her think I haven't put everything together yet, but that I'm close. I'll be in an office surrounded by potential witnesses. What is she going to do?"

"It's what she might do after you leave that office that worries me."

"I'll be fine. I'll have you and Tom watching out for me, not to mention all that costly police protection you'll arrange."

Dave tried a different tack. "What about your new buddy, Isabel? She's your source for a lot of the info that got you so worked up. None of her scoops could be considered evidence of anything. She has as many 'feelings,'" he made quotation marks with his fingers as he said the word, "as you do. Based on what you told me she said, cops wouldn't even bother to interview her.

"Even so, with all this muscular protection you think

you're gonna get, suppose your Dr. Jekyll and Mrs. Alfrey decides it'd be easier to get rid of Isabel, the person who put the bug in your ear about her in the first place, than it is to get rid of you. She might figure if you couldn't get any corroboration for your notions, that'd leave you looking like some kind of crazy lady who makes things up."

Dave screwed his bent index finger into his cheek, batted his eyes, and prattled in a bad southern accent, "Oh why, oh why, would my friend Regan say such dreadful things about me? Do you think she hit her head in her recent accident and rattled her brain?"

"That's why I have to shake up Corinne. I've got to make her think she needs to worry about what I already know or am about to uncover. I need to push her to do something rash." Regan pointed her finger at him, working hard to keep her face serious, "You have a good point though. I'll have to be careful not to mention names, especially not Isabel's."

"Right about now I wish I could have you put in protective custody or held for creating a public nuisance." His words were delivered with a sense of underlying disappointment; at some level he truly would like to do what he suggested and lamented the fact that he couldn't.

"Dave, in the past I've done some chancy things, either because I didn't know any better or because I was deliberately keeping you in the dark. I promised to keep you in the loop going forward. And I am."

His voice was stern, "I think you said you weren't going to play detective anymore."

She waved her hand. "I may have *said* I wasn't, but I never promised. There's a big difference." Her final attempt

179

at levity fell flat with both of them.

"I'm not looking forward to doing what I proposed — if you can think of a better way to test out my theory that doesn't involve me making Corinne think she better get rid of me, I'd like to hear it — but it seems to me we're all stuck here, doesn't it?"

Regan felt melodramatic but made her speech anyway. "A young man was murdered and his killer has gotten away with it for quite some time. I might be wrong about Corinne. Charles, or even Preston, could have killed Julien and attacked me, but I'm convinced we're looking for a killer whose last name is Alfrey."

Dave nodded slightly — involuntarily — in agreement.

"Now it looks like she, or he, may continue to get away with murder because that family is better at hiding the truth than a derivatives trader. Someone has to do something about them. The authorities aren't about to file charges against an Alfrey any time soon, are they?"

Dave shook his head, "Doesn't look like anything is in the works. Preston doesn't seem real for the Rochette murder and Charles Alfrey, well, we know he's involved, but he's a well-connected man in the community. The D.A. doesn't want to ruffle prominent feathers unnecessarily, especially when he doesn't know what charge he can make stick. The D.A. tries to take Chuck down without sufficient evidence, and his fanny will be nothing more than chum for the lawyer-sharks the Alfreys hired. Nope. D.A.'s gonna sit on this one for now and think about it long and hard.

"Oh yeah, FYI, all three Alfreys are licensed pilots to boot. Any or all of them are as free as birds to fly away on a

long vacation if the D.A. starts making them feel too uncomfortable." Dave raised his hand to simulate a plane taking off
and flying into the air, "Shhuushh."

"Dave, if I play this right, maybe we can clear one or two
of the Alfreys, or make a strong enough case against one or
two of them that the D.A. will have to take some action. I
need to try."

"Does Tom know what you're up to? Is he OK with what
you want to do?"

"We talked it over. He's concerned about my safety like
you are, but he agrees with me that something has to be
done."

Dave rolled his eyes, his prosthetic eye perfectly mimick-
ing his sighted eye. "Oh, to have been a fly on the wall during
that little talk."

🏠🏠🏠🏠🏠🏠🏠🏠🏠🏠🏠

Regan enjoyed feeling like a stealthy predator as she set
up an appointment with Corinne. She needed to be face-to-
face with her quarry when she sprang — she couldn't risk
talking to her prey and accidently letting anything slip prema-
turely — so in the back-and-forth needed to set up the
appointment, Regan avoided participating in person. Instead,
she relied on texting, email, and phone messages to arrange a
5:00 meeting the next evening, ostensibly to present an offer
on one of Corinne's less salable listings.

Corinne left a message that 5:00 was fine, but that her
clients wouldn't be able to attend. Regan emailed that didn't
matter, congratulating herself all the while that her hasty

research had paid off; she had specifically looked for a listing with absentee owners for her bogus offer so there would be no chance of having company as she confronted Corinne.

Regan expected the Bradley office would be almost empty when she pulled in at 4:55, given the hour and the rain. A strong rainstorm, the first of a series of storms that were predicted to dump enough rain to overflow Loch Lomond reservoir and break Santa Cruz' three-year drought, had begun in earnest.

As she pulled into a space close to the entry door, the sky opened up in a sudden drenching downpour, the kind that makes it seem like a good idea to stay put instead of running for the nearest cover. She waited for a minute, hoping the responsible cloud would pass. When it didn't, she opened her door and made an umbrella-less dash for the awning above the entry door.

She let herself in and reflexively began shaking rain from her hair and fluffing it with her fingers.

"In here, Regan," Corinne called, motioning to her from inside a glass-enclosed conference room near the entry. "Are your clients coming?"

"They said they were, but they live in Ben Lomond," Regan pointed upward in reference to the storm and shrugged. "Let's give them ten minutes."

"The office receptionist has gone, but if we use this room, we should be able to see any arrivals."

Regan pulled the conference door closed behind her for privacy. She put her briefcase on the meeting room table and took out the folder with her offer, but she didn't open it and give a copy to Corinne.

"You don't want me previewing your offer, Regan? It must be awful," Corinne laughed.

Regan let Corinne's comment slide. "I'm glad you agreed to hear the offer tonight. Are you sure you're up to this?" she asked solicitously. "You must be exhausted. From what I've seen on the news, the last couple of weeks haven't been great for your family."

Corinne inhaled deeply, closed her eyes, tilted her head upward and shook it. "Oh my, oh my. You could say that. Detective Harrison, such an annoying little man, has been calling Charles and Preston into the police station at the most inconvenient times; I think he does it just for the harassment value. He even bothered me until he realized I didn't have anything to add to their statements."

She looked at Regan as if seeing her for the first time, "That's right. The man that both my husband and my stepson say they killed was found in your house, wasn't he?"

Regan nodded wordlessly.

"Small world."

Corinne seemed to drift into a world of her own, possibly considering that irony. Regan took her silence as an opportunity to begin directing the conversation — to begin her search for a guilty conscience. "You knew him, didn't you?"

It was hard to read Corinne's reaction to the question. Her face remained cloaked in a completely neutral expression, but her eyes seemed to betray consideration of answers being weighed rapidly.

"Um-hum." One corner of Corinne's mouth twitched, barely hinting at movement. "He worked for Charles for a while."

Another silence followed. Regan decided not to speak first this time.

"We were sort of related, too. Distant cousins."

"My condolences for your loss ... for the loss of your cousin, I mean. The past few months must have been difficult for your extended family, too. After the body was found, the police said it fell to his mother to ..." Regan didn't finish the sentence. "How is she holding up?"

"I wouldn't know. We don't keep in touch. He really was a distant relation."

"Oh," Regan puckered her brow but replied evenly, "I thought someone told me you two were close."

Corinne's response was quick this time. "Whoever told you that was mistaken," she snapped. It was a momentary lapse. She immediately fashioned a placid face and controlled her voice. "Who told you that?"

"It's hard to remember; I've spoken to so many people."

When Regan was satisfied Corinne had nothing more to say, she began her ruse. "The police identified the murder victim ... your distant relation ... but since he was killed so long ago, they called him a ... what is the term? Ah yes. They called him a cold case and said they had more pressing matters to work on.

"Well, you know it's strange, I'd never say I was one to believe in ghosts or anything like that, but I can't seem to stand spending much time in our little cottage. I was really looking forward to fixing it up, too, but it just seems like there's ..." she drew her shoulders up and in and produced a bit of a shiver, "a presence. So even if it's not a priority for

184

the police, *I've* got to figure this thing out. Maybe when I do, he'll leave, or at least, rest."

Regan gurgled, "I sound so kind of out there, don't I?"

Corinne responded with a bemused smile and a slight shrug.

"Anyway, like I said, I've been talking to lots of people and collecting little bits and pieces of information about the murdered man that the police don't care to pursue. You know: who he knew, what he was like," she bracketed "who the women in his life were," with pauses. "I'm looking for skeletons in his closet ... oh," she winced, "that was a poor choice of words.

"I'm close to figuring it out, Corinne." Regan paused dramatically and stared at her, testing. "In fact, I was going to share what I've uncovered with my friend on the police force the day after Christmas ... but then, first Charles and then Preston confessed. That really threw me. I didn't know what to think at first." Regan found it easy to make her last statement with genuine consternation.

"It's just as well you didn't tell anyone what you suppose you know, Regan. The truth isn't always what you think it is, and no one is quite who you think they are — except for Charles, that is — he's always the white knight galloping off to protect the ones he loves ... and fair maidens."

Fair maidens? A fleeting frown crossed Regan's brow. Was Corinne referring to herself?

"It's complicated, Regan, and getting more so all the time, that's all I can say now that we've been advised by our attorneys not to discuss anything. But I can tell you neither Preston nor Charles is a murderer." Her words seemed honest and sincere, and filled with as much integrity as her reputation.

"I think you're right, Corinne. I can't see Preston as a killer, especially since he was so young when the crime was committed. I assume he confessed just to take the focus off of his father. But I don't understand why Charles would confess to a murder he didn't commit ... unless, of course, he was trying to protect someone else."

Regan smiled enigmatically, trying to express sympathy while implying more knowledge than her words indicated. "I have one more person I want to talk to, just to confirm my theory; after that I will be ready to go to the police."

Corinne's eyes evaded Regan's. "Have you talked to Isabel Bolton, yet?" she asked.

Corinne's sudden introduction of Isabel's name gave her a start. She intended to be vague about her investigation, naming no names. She tried to sound offhanded, "Isabel Bolton? Is she the daughter Jessie Bolton was always talking about — the model? What does she have to do with any of this?"

"Yes, Isabel is Jessie's daughter. I don't think of her as a model, though. I think of her as an actress. I've seen her perform. She was always quite convincing as a wide-eyed innocent in large part because of the way she looked, but I understand she's quite a *good* actress, capable of other roles, too. I believe she knew my cousin quite well."

Corinne glanced over Regan's shoulder at the lobby clock, signaling an end to their dialogue. "It's quarter after five. I think it's time to give up on your clients. Let's go over their offer."

In the cat and mouse game Regan had been trying to play, it seemed the mouse had just escaped into the safety of her hole, and had even suggested other prey for Regan to chase.

Regan's cell phone rang at that moment. She retrieved it from her briefcase, flipped it open, and looked at the caller ID, "Speak of the devil." She pressed the answer button, put the phone to her ear and said, "Hi Gordon," to Tom, who was calling at the time they had prearranged.

"How's it going?" he asked. "You okay?"

"Yes, I made it without any difficulty." She pretended to listen to the man on the line. "I do understand. Don't worry, I'll tell her that. Stay warm and dry," she signed off and flipped the phone closed. "They gave up on getting here. There's a tree down on Highway 9 so they turned around and went back home. They want me to tell you their offer may not be everything your clients are hoping for, but it's the best they are willing to do."

Regan ran through her bogus offer quickly. It appeared to be from Gordon and Georgina Bradshaw, the names of a couple she had worked with briefly. She made them all cash buyers so she wouldn't have to involve a mortgage lender, and had her "clients" offer an insultingly low amount of money. She wished she could advise Corinne to tell her sellers that she apologized for the offer and didn't expect them to waste time putting together a counter, but had her offer been genuine, her fiduciary responsibility to her clients would have precluded a statement like that. If she said such a thing, she would blow her cover.

Corinne said what she couldn't: "Regan, this is a terrible offer. Is it even real? Are these people serious about buying or just throwing out offers, hoping to hit a really desperate seller? I know, I know," she put her hands in front of her chest, "they're your clients, wonderful people and all that, making a great offer given the market conditions, and you have to present all written offers, but really, don't wait up for a response.

"This offer doesn't warrant me rushing to communicate it, and I do want to get home. I'll call my clients after we've all had dinner. Let's get out of here."

Corinne snapped off the conference room light as they left and peered into the section of agent cubicles. The overhead lights were all off. The low illumination of the night security system in the reception area was all the light that remained on in the office. "It looks like everyone's left. I'll lock up and walk you out."

Only Corinne's Miata and Regan's new Prius remained in the parking lot.

"Is that car yours?" Corinne asked, as she finished locking the office door. "Where's your old Lexus?"

"I had an accident in November. That car gave its life for me."

"It got totaled? That sounds like a serious accident. You're OK, though?"

"I'm fine. The rescue team said I could have been killed, probably *should* have been killed, but I got lucky."

There was a break in the rain so neither of them had to make a dash to their car. Corinne walked around Regan's Prius, picking her way through the puddles that glistened in the parking lot lights. "Dressy pumps with three-inch stilettos — what was I thinking?" She scrunched up her face as she missed a hop and landed part way in a puddle. "Are you going to get vanity plates like you had on your old car?"

"I'm not planning to. I think I'll try anonymity for a while."

"But Regan, every fourth car in Santa Cruz is a Prius. How will I know for sure it's you if I don't see your 'Regans' license plate?" Corinne offered a crooked little grin.

Regan was glad the parking lot's minimal illumination prevented Corinne from looking at her too closely. If she had, she'd be aware of the extraordinary expression that flashed across her face. She'd been easy to recognize in her old car as she turned onto Empire Grade Road the night of her attack — and Corinne knew how to spot her.

Corinne beeped her car door unlocked, opened the door, and tossed in her purse and the folder with Regan's offer. "You drive carefully now, you hear? We wouldn't want anything to happen to you. The road's wet, probably slippery, and you don't know how your new car handles all that well yet. You wouldn't want to have another accident. You might not be so lucky a second time." She smiled pleasantly as she got into her car.

The silver BMW was parked just past the entrance to the Abbey Coffee Shop and pulled out as soon as she passed. It caught up with her quickly, before she reached the left turn onto High Street. It flashed its lights one time. Regan peered in her rear-view mirror, but it was too dark to see the driver.

When she turned off Empire Grade for home, the BMW stayed close behind her. But unlike when Seth Cooper had followed her, she took no evasive action. She drove straight home and into her half of the garage.

Tom pulled his BMW into the garage next to her. "How did it go?"

"No problems. Corinne now thinks I'm a little out there for feeling the ghost of Julien Rochette is hanging out at our house, and I'm set up as a danger to her if she's guilty and as a jerk if she's not. If it turns out I'm wrong about her, I'll have to bake her some of our open-house chocolate chip cookies and deliver them with a sincere apology.

"I didn't get any revelations out of her, just some confirmations, a curious insinuation, and one comment that was a bit disturbing — but then, it's not like I expected her to confess to killing Julien."

"Let's sort it out over a glass of wine," Tom suggested.

"That's the best proposition I've had all day."

"Really? And just how many other propositions are we talking about here? More than one? Fewer than five? Should I be worried or jealous?" Tom ended his queries with a laugh that was easy and jovial. Then his smile almost disappeared, "I'm glad that part's over and you're home."

Regan took a pot of pork tagine with dried cherries and apricots out of the refrigerator and put it on the stove. Tom opened a bottle of zinfandel and poured each of them a glass of wine. They sat at the breakfast bar in the kitchen enjoying the blended aroma of cumin, cinnamon, ginger, and turmeric that soon began escaping from the simmering dish.

"For starters, I forgot how much I like Corinne," Regan said. "I feel a special kind of empathy for her. It makes sense, I guess, we seem a lot alike. I don't just mean that we're close in age, have raised sons, and have been realtors for ages; in many ways, I think we look at the world in the same way."

Tom took a sip of his wine to savor for a few seconds and waited for Regan to add a "but" to her statement. When one wasn't forthcoming, he said, "I've never heard anyone in the business say anything negative about her, or about you," he smiled. "You said Corinne confirmed some things you knew?"

"Uh-huh. She acknowledged Julien Rochette worked for Charles. She corroborated what I'd heard before, that they were related, so she knew him. She was offhand and casual about that, but I cracked her unruffled veneer when I said I'd been told they were close."

191

"I thought you weren't going to name information sources?"

"I didn't. That's why she got agitated; she wanted to know who told me that. Tom, Corinne made a curious statement about Charles always being reliable — that he could always be counted on to rush in to protect those he loved and fair maidens."

"Fair maidens?"

"I'm glad that phrase gave you pause, too. That's what she said. At first I thought it was a revelation, like she might be referring to herself as the fair maiden that Charles was ready to protect, but then she asked if I had talked to Isabel Bolton."

Tom frowned, "She brought that name up, not you?"

Regan nodded.

"Misdirection?"

"Maybe. She went into a kind of riff about what a good actress Isabel was and how well she could play the innocent little damsel. I have to admit, it was unsettling. I've only met Isabel the one time, but she was very believable. I'm usually pretty spot-on when it comes to sizing people up right away and can trust my instincts, but my record has hardly been perfect recently. You might remember that close call I had last summer because of a misread," she blew air out of puckered lips.

Tom nodded, "That *was* a big deal — both the close call and the misread."

"I'm feeling a little less certain about my capability after that. I've had plenty of opportunities to size Corinne up; I've known her for years."

"So you believe her rather than Isabel?"

"Not exactly," she was hesitant and frowning. "I'm still reluctantly going with a probable misdirect. The problem is … Isabel paints Corinne in such a different light than everyone else does … but I don't see a connection between Charles and Isabel, and yet there has to be something between the murderer and Charles because he helped hide Julien's body. If Isabel was the murderer, why would Charles protect her?"

Regan got up to stir the tagine and put in a handful of large, round couscous. Tom began drumming his fingers softly on the kitchen counter. "There might be more to Preston's confession than anyone thinks," he said.

"What do you mean?"

"I'm just thinking out loud, OK, but suppose Preston really did get into it with Rochette, not because he was jealous of him, but because he saw something upsetting happen between him and Isabel."

"What would he have seen?"

"I don't know. Let's say Preston saw Rochette being abusive to Isabel, or at least thought that was what was happening." He shrugged. "Inexperienced little kid sees some kind of intense foreplay or hears some lovers bickering and makes more out of it than he should — just a thought."

"You think Preston might really have killed Julien and that Charles was protecting him like he claims? But where does protecting the fair maiden part fit in?" Regan asked, as she returned to her seat and took a sip of wine.

"Well again, just for the sake of argument, suppose Rochette was killed elsewhere, garroted somewhere else and brought to the house for disposal. If you want to, follow what

Corinne implied and take a look at Isabel being Rochette's killer."

Regan's imagination immediately kicked into high gear. She made jealousy the motive for murder, but it was Isabel who was in a jealous rage when she discovered Julien was still involved with Corinne — maybe Jessie Bolton had a better understanding of the victim than anyone else — and then ...

Her imaginings were stopped short by Tom's logic as abruptly and with the same dissonance as a DJ scratching a record.

"No, forget what I said. I can already pick that idea apart. If Isabel killed him, why would she ask for Charles' help with the body? At the time of the murder, she was young and living with her father who hated Julien. She would have turned to her father for help disposing of the body and Jessie would probably have been only too happy to bury Julien somewhere on his back forty."

"Not necessarily," Regan breathed. "Suppose Preston saw Isabel kill Julien or happened on her with Julien's body. Preston told the police he had a huge crush on Isabel — she's the one who said that wasn't true. She was over eighteen, an adult. If she killed Julien, maybe she used Preston's feelings for her to manipulate him into making up the story about an accidental killing. She could have convinced Preston that if he was caught, he wouldn't get in much trouble since he was a minor. Maybe she told Preston to tell his father that he'd murdered Julien. Maybe Charles believed his son *had* killed Julien, just like Preston said he had when he confessed to the police."

Regan nodded, "That could be what happened, couldn't it? Charles, thinking he needed to protect his son, helped hide Julien's body."

Tom squinted his blue eyes, a sign he was deep in thought. "If Isabel killed Julien, she certainly didn't do it in our cottage — she wouldn't have had access. If she committed murder and then was able to convince Preston to say he was the killer and he got his father to help them dispose of the body, why would they bother to hide Julien where they did?"

Regan didn't have an answer for Tom's question. She shrugged. "Making Isabel a murderer is getting too complicated, isn't it?

"I'm back to thinking about Corinne as the guilty party. When I'm not face to face with her, it's easier to go back to thinking chilling thoughts about her and to believing what Isabel says about her is true."

"What else happened during your set-up with Corinne?"

"I told her the police were not actively investigating Julien's death but *I* was, and implied like crazy that I was one interview with some unnamed person away from solving the murder. I hinted I was extremely close to telling the police what I knew. Corinne didn't react outwardly at all — but that doesn't mean she wasn't squirming on the inside," Regan quickly added.

"Do you have a case-breaking interview in mind or were you just saying that for Corinne's benefit?"

"It was just for show, although the more I think about it, I would like to talk to Julien's mother. Dave said she told the authorities the medallion that was used to choke him was a twenty-first birthday present from a girlfriend. I'd like to

195

know if she remembers who that old flame was. It couldn't have been Isabel; she would have been too young, only fifteen or so when Julien turned twenty-one. I want to know if it was Corinne. Even if it was, I'm not sure what that tells me, but I'd still like to know. Talking to Mrs. Rochette is on my *TO DO* list.

"I haven't told you what happened as Corinne and I were leaving the Bradley office; wait till you hear what she said. Corinne asked me if I was going to get vanity license plates for my new car. When I told her I thought not, she asked how she'd recognize me without them, and then she told me to be careful driving, that she wouldn't want me to have another accident.

"Everything she said could be taken at face value and mean nothing ... or it could be taken as demonstrating she knew how to recognize me, like the driver who attacked me did, and as a warning."

Tom leaned back in his seat. "I don't like the sound of that at all. Let's be extra careful with you for a while."

Regan's phone rang just as they were finishing dinner. Caller ID indicated it was Corinne on the other end. "Put her on speaker," Tom instructed.

She nodded. "Hi, Corinne. I'm putting you on speaker phone so I can keep working on dinner. Let me know if I sound too tinny."

"No, you're fine," Corinne sounded sunny. "This won't come as any surprise, I'm sure, but my clients have turned down the Bradshaw's offer. They aren't even responding to it. They instructed me not to say thank you for it; actually, they instructed me to say something a lady like me shouldn't, so I won't repeat what they said."

"Sorry if I made your evening difficult. I won't hold it against you if you made me out to be the bad guy and yourself the innocent forced-to-do-my-job agent to your clients."

Corinne laughed, "Good, 'cause I did. But just to show you there are no hard feelings on my part, I'd like to show a listing of yours tomorrow — but only if you'll agree to meet me and my clients there to answer questions about the property."

"Oh?" Regan raised her eyebrows and looked at Tom. "Which one, and when?"

"It's going to need to be late. I'm working with a couple who can only look after work, so 7:00 tomorrow night. It's your listing on Irwin in Boulder Creek. I know it's vacant. Does it have power on?"

"It does. I'll get there a little early to turn on the lights and crank up the heat."

"Thanks, Regan. See you tomorrow, then."

"What do you think?" she asked Tom. "Irwin is private and vacant. Lonely. And it's going to be dark and rainy at 7:00 tomorrow night; it's unlikely any witnesses will be out and about. It seems like a great place for an ambush, doesn't it? She could say she found my body when she got there ... but do you think she'd risk being that obvious?"

"I don't know, sweetheart. If I were her and intent on harming you, I'd probably lay low for a while, give you time to let down your guard."

"Unless she bought everything I said," Regan held up her

197

hand with her index finger almost touching her thumb, "and believes I'm this close to turning her in. If she thinks that, she probably feels she has to take a chance and act fast."

"She might. I don't want you taking any chances," Tom knitted his brow. "Dave better get the police to spring for some overtime."

25

"So this is how it's going down, Regan," Dave stated with authority as he finished placing a tiny transmitter into one of her favorite pins, a large folksy multi-metal piece with a two-story shingle house fronted by a picket fence and a leafy tree. He pinned it to her jacket lapel. "An officer in an unmarked car is going to follow you down Felton Empire Road, not so far back he couldn't help you if somebody wanted to play bumper cars, but he's gonna leave a little space between you and himself in case they want to try. You're the sacrificial goat, remember?

"If nothing happens on your drive, you're gonna meet your pal at the property right on schedule. She's gonna think you have no idea what she's up to and that you're alone. Course, the guys in the surveillance van parked across the street will be able to hear every word either of you says and so will I. I'll be close by, inside the closet in the office, locked in ..."

Regan erupted with nervous giggles, "It's going to be just like when Linda hid under the stairs."

"What are you talking about?" Dave was serious,

completely in cop mode.

"Haven't I ever told you what happened to Linda Lynley, a broker I know?" Regan asked wide-eyed. "She was holding an open house on a remote country property — no cell service. It was a couple of months after 9/11, you remember how the whole country felt back then, and this car full of 'swarthy men,' that's what she called them, pulled up — no women, just men. She decided they were up to no good, probably planning a terrorist attack in the heart of rural Aptos. She panicked and hid in a closet under the stairwell.

"They came into the house and she could hear everything they said from her hiding spot. Turns out they were a foursome who had just finished a round of golf. They looked around for the longest time until finally one of them said, 'this house is perfect, just what my wife and I have been looking for.' He even added something about not having an agent yet." Regan waved a hand dismissively, "Never mind about that, that's kind of insider stuff ... it meant there was a chance for her to double-end the sale ... make a double commission," she chuckled.

"Well, she figured there was no politically correct way to bounce out of the closet and explain she had hidden because she thought they looked like terrorists," Regan snorted, "so she had to stay in the closet. The men didn't leave for the better part of an hour; probably they assumed the agent was somewhere on the property and would be back any minute," she could barely catch her breath she was laughing so hard, "and she just sat in the closet until they left. She never heard from them again."

"You want to calm down, Regan? You sure you can pull

this off; I'd say right now you're borderline hysterical."

She stifled a giggle, "I'm fine. Really. What you said just struck me as funny. You ... locked in the closet," another chuckle escaped.

She sucked in her cheeks and tried to be serious. "Really. I'm totally together," she said making her voice deeper than it normally was. She held her hand at the top of her head with her palm facing her and slowly drew it down in front of her in a straight line until it was below her waist. "Calm. Centered."

Dave watched her for a couple of seconds, shaking his head, "It's always such a great joy working with amateurs."

When Regan got caught at a red light at the bottom of Felton Empire Road, waiting to make a left turn toward Boulder Creek, she couldn't resist waving in her mirror to the driver who pulled in behind her. She was sure he was the officer in an unmarked vehicle that Dave said would follow her to Highway 9.

Highway 9 was a busy road at any time of the day, but through Felton, Ben Lomond, Brookdale, and Boulder Creek, just before 6:30 at night, it was rush hour, and clogged with people coming home from work. Once she hit that stretch, Regan knew there would be no accidents — too many witnesses and too hard to make a getaway.

She turned onto Irwin Street before coming into down-town Boulder Creek and crossed the San Lorenzo River on a little neighborhood bridge. With all the rain, it was a stressful crossing. The runoff-swollen river seemed like it might grab the bridge at any moment and whisk it downstream.

On the far side of the bridge the road paralleled the river, sometimes immediately next to it and sometimes far enough away for a house to be built between the road and the river. The house where she was to meet Corinne — in the hope that Corinne would ... what Regan wondered ... try to kill her — was situated like that.

She pulled down the long curving Irwin house driveway at 6:50 and parked. She seemed to be alone; there were no signs of Dave or of police officers nearby. Regan could hear the sound of the rushing river as soon as she opened her car door. When she opened the gate of the high privacy fence that separated the house from the driveway, the sound intensified and overwhelmed her ability to hear anything else.

She stumbled through the darkness toward the house, fervently wishing there was a motion sensor light that would come on and help her find the stepping stones through the marshy garden to the porch. She vowed to have one installed as a housewarming gift for the new owners.

Her thoughts were filled with mayhem: *If I wanted to get rid of someone tonight, I'd conk them over the head right here, in this pitch-black bog, and dump them in the river.* Regan turned her head from side to side, nervously searching through the dark night for any signs of a bat-wielding attacker sneaking up on her.

She clicked on her meager keychain light. It didn't help her avoid a misstep into the muck, but once she reached the porch, it gave her enough illumination to find the lockbox, retrieve the house key, and unlock the front door. She reached inside and clicked on the first switch she felt. The porch light came on.

In the sudden brightness, Regan could see her left shoe

was in no condition to walk inside. She slipped it off, decided to take off its mate as well, and left both shoes on the porch.

Once inside, she turned on every light within reach and reveled in the now bright living room, kitchen, and hallway to the office where she hoped Dave must already be hiding. She felt emboldened by the light and ready for anything that might happen.

But nothing did.

She waited barefoot in the brightly lit house for a good ten minutes before she noticed one of the marketing flyers was out of the Lucite display holder on the kitchen counter and slid partway under it. The flyer was photo-side down and had handwriting on the back:

I'm so sorry to get you out in this weather, Regan. My clients seem to be no-shows just like your Bradshaws were. No hard feelings, I hope. This makes us even, don't you think?

I hope you have that breakthrough you're close to soon so we can all get on with our lives.

Corinne

P.S. When you talk to her, give my regards to Isabel Bolton

"Dave," Regan spoke to the pin on her jacket lapel, "Dave, you can come out now. Corinne's not coming."

There were sounds of a sliding door being moved and Dave appeared. She handed him Corinne's note. He read it quickly and then spoke into a handheld device, "Operation shut down. Return to base. Repeat, operation shut down.

Game's over, guys.

"I guess you're not as smooth as you thought, Regan," he smirked. "From this note, I'd guess your gal pal was onto you the whole time," his grin split his face from ear to ear. "I hate spending the time and money we did for this wild goose chase, but if it turns out to be a good teachable moment for you, it may be worth the heat I'm gonna take from Detective Harrison for spending some of his yearly budget on this little gambit. Come on," he coaxed, "tell me what you learned."

"I learned Corinne is not going to crack as easily as I thought."

"Wrong answer." His response was filled with irritation. "Besides making it clear she didn't like you wasting her time last night and isn't above getting even, she's wishing you well and telling you she's not worried about you uncovering anything juicy by talking to people in Julien's past. Does that sound like something a murderer would be saying? You can't spook someone with nothing to hide, Regan. She didn't do anything wrong. That's why this whole little exercise came to nothing.

"What I was hoping you'd say you learned is that you don't know what you're doing and have decided to leave things like investigating murder to the police," he muttered.

"But you told me the police are underfunded right now and can't afford to actively work on solving Julien Rochette's murder." Regan felt an almost overwhelming urge to stamp her foot as she came back at Dave, but controlled the childish impulse.

"Yeah. And you've just burned through some of their scarce resources with these shenanigans. Besides, after the twin Alfrey confessions, things have been moved up a notch. Satisfied?"

She gave a half shrug and pulled her mouth into a pout. "What about catching the person who pushed me off Empire Grade?"

"That we're working on very seriously."

"But I still think they're related ..."

"And *we don't*, Regan." It wasn't the first time Dave had been exasperated with her, but it was as close as he had ever come to flat-out shouting at her. "Let's close up and get out of here," he growled.

26

The consolation of sleep eluded Regan. At first it was because she was still tense from her expected confrontation with Corinne, but after her nervous energy dissipated she remained sleepless because of Dave's words. She knew she was getting special treatment and more information from him because of their friendship than would normally have been forthcoming from the police.

She didn't want to abuse that friendship and never wanted to put him in an awkward spot because of it, so she vacillated between feeling like a spoiled child and Cassandra, the cursed prophetess of Greek mythology.

Dave was right, of course. She was a real estate agent, not a detective — not even a private investigator, another category of being that the police sometimes considered nuisances. She was behaving like a spoiled child.

But a murder had taken place in their new cottage, and someone had made an attempt on her life. How could she possibly sit by quietly and let the police plod along at their frustratingly slow pace, obstinately refusing to see the connection that was so apparent to her. She felt like Cassandra ranting — Cassandra rightly ranting, knowing, but not being believed. *I want to leave everything to the police, Dave, I really do, but what happens if they never believe me?*

At 5:30 she gave up; there was no point in trying to sleep any longer. After such a wearisome and frustrating night, she skipped her morning tea with its gentle introduction to the day in favor of a harsh jolt of coffee. The caffeine rush changed her outlook.

It wouldn't be taking advantage of Dave's friendship if I offered my condolences to Julien Rochette's mother, she rationalized as she flipped through the phone book in her home office. There were no listings under Rochette.

A Google search produced several news stories about Julien Rochette and one other local hit for a T. Rochette. Regan brought up the story about T. Rochette which included a profile. T stood for Terese ... talented glass artist ... doing innovative work ... just celebrated her fiftieth birthday. Julien would have been forty if he had lived; the woman wasn't old enough to be his mother.

A check of Santa Cruz County property owners using title company records came next. The artist owned a house. No other Rochettes did. It was possible Mrs. Rochette lived outside of Santa Cruz County. Regan repeated the same search for the surrounding counties and got no more property-owning Rochettes.

The police would have Mrs. Rochette's contact information. *Why not call Dave and ask for it? Because my intentions aren't necessarily innocent,* she answered her own question.

Her fingers typed and clicked furiously as a new idea occurred to her: Santa Cruz Sentinel, obituaries, November,

December. *Don't forget the year,* she reminded herself. The discovery of Julien Rochette's body made the newspapers; a small notice appeared when his identity was uncovered, but she saw no mention of a funeral for him on the first Google search page.

There had been an autopsy which would have slowed the release of his body for burial. She reordered the search results to put hits in chronological sequence and skipped to page two in a methodical search for information about Julien Rochette's funeral.

After a couple of false starts, she found what she was looking for. The announcement listed facts about Julien's life and then continued with what interested Regan:

Survivors: Mother Aimee Rochette of Aptos; numerous cousins, aunts and uncles in New Orleans, Louisiana. Services: Memorial Service following 11:00 a.m. Worship Sunday, December 13 at Coast Church, 1400 State Park Drive, Aptos.

She had two ways to go in her pursuit of Mrs. Rochette. She could repeat her computer search for Rochettes in New Orleans and then pick up a phone and start calling strangers to ask if they were related to Aimee Rochette of the Santa Cruz area. It was possible she would find a related Rochette that way. But at the moment, Regan, who would never have called herself a religious person, at least not in a traditional sense, felt the need to pray.

The church was a plain affair, likely built in the late sixties by an unassuming congregation with an eye on function and maximizing square footage. It was located on a frontage road near Highway 1 but set at the back of the parcel and buffered from the freeway by the parking lot and mature trees that had been carefully preserved during construction. The effect was that the church felt utilitarian, yet friendly. Regan hoped its congregants would resemble their spiritual home.

There were two cars parked in the lot, no more or less than she would have expected to find at a mid-sized church at 9:00 a.m. on a weekday. She parked next to an aged mustard colored Volvo covered with peeling bumper stickers that touted various environmental and social causes and asked observers to "visualize whirled peas."

Regan pulled the sanctuary door open just enough to gain entry and immediately pulled it closed behind her. It was brighter inside than she expected; there were many more windows than were apparent from the church front, and unlike the churches of her youth with their dark stained-glass scenes, these windows were filled with frosted glass, effective for keeping out distractions but letting in light.

There was a plain wooden cross at the front of the sanctuary. It hung over a carpeted two-stepped raised platform that was littered with speakers, leaning guitars, and a keyboard. Judging from the number of instruments ready to be taken up, it seemed likely Sunday services could rock the attendees' souls or at least be boisterous celebrations.

The platform featured an unadorned boxy altar at center-front. A stout woman, who Regan judged to be past retirement age, was picking flowers up off the altar where she had strewn them and was arranging them in a hefty vase. Though Regan had entered quietly, the woman noticed her immediately. She continued working but called out to Regan, "Hello, there. I don't believe we've met, yet. I'm Edie, Edie Palmeroy."

Regan clacked down the uncarpeted central aisle toward Edie Palmeroy, feeling noisy and disruptive and wishing she hadn't worn high heels. She held out her hand when she reached the platform. "Edie, you must have a good memory for faces. I remember houses and voices, but I'm not good with faces. You're right, we haven't met. Regan McHenry."

"Are you looking for a new church home or have you already decided to join our congregation?"

Regan hoped she had guessed right that Aimee Rochette was a member of the Coast Church. "Neither, I confess. I was hoping to find out how to contact one of your members."

"Oh? And who might that be?"

"Aimee Rochette."

Edie Pomeroy, so warm and accepting only a moment before, screwed her face into a cold look of disapproval. "Hasn't she been through enough without you people wanting to bother her? She hasn't changed her mind about doing an interview."

"No. No, I'm not looking to interview her; I would like to talk to her, though." Clearly Edie knew Aimee Rochette and felt protective of her privacy. Regan selected her words carefully, "We have a unique connection."

Edie raised one eyebrow and squinted her other eye. "What kind of connection might that be?"

"Kind of a ghoulish one, I'm afraid. Her son Julien was

murdered in my house."

Edie Palmeroy clearly hadn't expected that answer. "Oh my!" she gasped. Her hand involuntarily flew to cover her heart but she was holding a tulip and only succeeded in smacking her chest with the flower. "Oh, Dear Lord."

"I wanted to offer her my condolences, let her know how sorry I was about ... everything ... maybe give her a hug, and ... and maybe get one back in return." Regan thought she might be laying it on a little too thick, but Edie's reaction was the one she hoped to get.

"Oh yes, I know she would want to talk to *you*. She'll be back day-after-tomorrow. I know her schedule because I'm feeding her cat."

"She's away?"

"She's in New Orleans visiting her people. She has friends here, of course, but after what happened, the knowing for sure, I mean, well she needed to get away and be with family over the holidays. You understand, I'm sure."

Regan nodded. "Of course."

"You give me your phone number. I'm sure she'll call you as soon as she's back and settled."

Regan had hoped to get rather than give contact information but decided she better not push. If she were a reporter, she might have made up a similar story to get Edie's sympathy, and while Edie seemed favorably inclined to her right now, she might have second thoughts if she felt Regan was being reporter-like aggressive.

"Thank you, Edie. That sounds perfect. Please tell her not to rush; tell her to call me when she's ready." Regan took a card and a pen out of her purse. She crossed out her business number and wrote in her home phone number. "She can call me at home."

Regan's cell phone rang as she was leaving the church. She opened her car door and slipped into the driver's seat as she answered, "This is Regan."

"Hi, Regan, Linda Coo ..." the caller's voice faded momentarily, "voice from your past ... sorry we ... showed up."

"I didn't catch what you said. Could you repeat it?"

"I ... on my way ... Highway 17," the caller's phone scratched. "Do you remember me ... I'm sorry I left you hanging ... December. We all got ... little drunk and those nice people I met at the party ... not so nice. You remember? I stood you up at the West Cliff ... you have listed."

Regan was jolted to attention. Even with the call fading in and out, she knew the voice. "Linda, it's a terrible connection, I'm missing most of what you're saying."

"Damn 17." After another momentary lapse the caller asked, "Any better? I'll talk fast," she said and laughed. "I flaked last December, I should say my clients did, oh well, let's not get into that. I want to make it up to you. Can we see the West Cliff house tonight at 7:30? I have some reliable clients ... perfect for ... to show them the lights around the bay."

"My clients are home," Regan offered. "Have you contacted them for an appointment?"

"I've tried, but," she was gone again. "So could you come to be sure we can ... in?"

"Sure, Linda. I'll meet you there at 7:30." She sounded

overanxious and too accommodating but Linda didn't seem to pick up on her eagerness.

"Super. I'm looking forward to a great showing, maybe even a sale," she gushed before she hung up.

Regan hurtled through the self-locking door separating the police reception lobby from the secured personnel area before it could close behind the female officer coming in the opposite direction. In her haste, she hadn't stopped for a visitor's badge — she hadn't even paused to ask if Dave was in or if she could see him.

"Hey! You can't ..." the flabbergasted officer did an abrupt about-face and rushed after her.

Regan knew the way to Dave's cubby-hole office and reached it before the exasperated policewoman caught up with her. It was good Dave was in because, as the officer gave chase, she undid the strap over her handgun and was ready to draw her weapon.

"Dave," Regan was breathless, "the woman who tried to kill me called again!"

Dave looked up, saw the look on the policewoman's face and where her hand was vis-à-vis her weapon, and responded to what he recognized as a situation more pressing than what Regan was telling him.

"It's OK, Christy, I know her. She's not a problem. Maybe

a little crazy, but not in a dangerous way," he laughed and motioned the pursuing officer away. "You trying to get shot bursting in here like that?"

"She called again. She wants to meet me at the West Cliff house tonight," Regan was too wound up to notice what had just happened. Her voice went up an octave as she hurled her exciting news at Dave.

He pointed to the seat across from his desk. "You want to sit down, take a deep breath, and tell me what you're in such a tizzy about this time."

"I recognized her voice — I think she intended me to — it was the same woman who called the night I was forced off the road."

"One more try, OK? Wind it down a bit," he cranked his hand to illustrate what he meant. "Start from the start and tell me what you're trying to say."

Regan leaned back in her chair and took the deep breath Dave had recommended.

"I got a call from a woman who identified herself as Linda. She said something about our not having connected in December. Her phone kept cutting in and out — but she said she wanted to meet me at the house on West Cliff Drive tonight. It was the same woman both times, Dave. Last time there was background noise to keep me from hearing too clearly; this time she said she was on Highway 17 and used that as an excuse for disguising her voice, but I recognized it anyway."

"Linda? As in Seth Cooper's momma? Tinfoil Linda Cooper?"

He had a huge smile on his face.

"That was the name she gave, but that's not who it was calling."

"Oh, really? And just who was it calling?"

"Corinne Alfrey," Regan practically shouted the name. "That's whose voice I recognized."

"Why me?" he shook his head. "You know there are expensive contraptions that let cops filter background noises and do voice matching. I'm not sure how they work, but I know they do. We haven't got one here in Santa Cruz; only the big guys like the FBI and Homeland Security have them. I always thought it would be cool to have one, though, if we had the budget for it, but now it turns out we won't need one. We can just have you give a listen. That's great, Regan, given how tight money is."

He was teasing. That meant he wasn't taking what she told him seriously. "I am good with voices, Dave. It was the same woman both times." Regan's tone had a steely edge to it.

"Like I said, glad to hear it. And you're absolutely sure it was the same woman both times?"

"How many times do I have to say I am?"

He raised his hands off his desk, leaned back in his seat, and folded his arms with his hands behind his head. "You want to tell me again what she said her name was the first time she called you," he grinned. "Oh, and just for the record, what did she say her name was this time she called you?"

"Linda." Regan acquiesced. "She didn't say the last name clearly either time."

"But it sorta' sounded like Cooper, didn't it? Ya know betting for money is illegal in California, especially betting in a police station, so we either have to take it outside or make it

216

just a lunch wager, but I'm ready to bet you the mysterious Linda is really Linda Cooper in all her Crazy Momma glory. Whadda-ya say? You still think she's Corinne Alfrey?"

"I do. I'll take that wager if you promise to be a gracious loser. When I win, I'm going to want lunch at The Crow's Nest."

At 7:00 that night Dave was in position, parked at Majors Creek Road where it opened onto Empire Grade and Regan was ready, as he had so expressively phrased it, to rock and roll.

Tom walked her out to the garage and her car. She kissed him goodbye, noting the worry clouding his blue eyes.

"I could lie down on the back seat. No one could tell I was there," he appealed.

"If anything happened and you were there, what could you do to help?" She didn't give him time to come up with a reply. "Besides, Dave is going to follow me down and the police will be waiting ..."

"I'd feel better," he replied softly.

"I'll be fine." She gave him a second goodbye kiss and smiled up at him as she got into her car and backed out of the garage.

Regan was paused at the stop sign at Empire Grade Road, ready to turn toward Santa Cruz, when she saw the dark truck with a brush guard parked across the street. It was blatantly there, under the power pole light and impossible to miss, taunting, daring her to continue her journey. She came close

217

to panicking and had to fight the impulse to turn around and rush home into Tom's arms.

Headlights appeared from a car approaching from behind her. She had to make a decision quickly: flee or turn now, before the car came too close and its innocent driver got caught up in the perilous game about to be played.

Regan checked left on Empire Grade a final time, looking for headlights going in the Santa Cruz direction, and seeing none, moved onto the road. She rounded the first gentle turn which came up almost immediately and checked her rear-view mirror as the road straightened again. The truck was behind her.

Dave's position was only three hundred yards down the road but it seemed like it took hours to reach him. She slowed her car and quickly flashed her lights to high beam and back to normal before she passed him, part of a prearranged signal. The truck behind her flashed its lights, too, as if to parody her.

At a straightaway, the truck drew close enough she could make out ominous brush guard-created horizontal lines across its headlights. She swerved slightly, trying to see behind the truck, looking for Dave. She caught glimpses of other headlights, but they seemed to be disinterestedly far behind. *That is you, Dave, isn't it?*

Reagan peered into her mirrors with compulsive frequency. The truck was always there, sometimes coming close enough that she emitted an involuntary moan, but it never made a more threatening move.

Even on those rare occasions when Regan drove conservatively, Western Drive, her prearranged turning point, was only ten minutes down the road, but getting there followed by the looming black truck seemed to take twice that long. Every minute and every mile stretched into the boggy slowness of nightmare running while being chased by a monster.

When she finally reached Western Drive, she slowed and signaled a right turn. The truck behind her slowed and responded with a similar signal. *What are you doing using your turn signal?* Regan flipped off her blinker before she made the turn. The truck did the same.

Bay Avenue, the next right turn after Western, would have been a more direct route to West Cliff Drive, but it was a busy street. Any driver following her down Western Drive and then onto the empty roads between its termination and West Cliff Drive was likely following her deliberately. Her route invited violence. The truck moved closer, seemingly positioning itself to accept the invitation — but then backed off and remained reticent.

The stop light where Western Drive crossed Highway 1 turned green as she approached. She crossed without pausing as did the looming truck and a couple of other trailing vehicles.

In front of her were the empty roads by the warehouses and research buildings of the industrial park that was squeezed between residential areas of Santa Cruz. The stretch was deserted at night, the perfect place for an ambush. Regan was drenched with sweat and exhausted from tension. *She's going to shoot me this time.* Regan cringed in her seat, waiting for a bullet to smash through her window and then through her body.

She didn't use her left turn blinker to signal a turn onto

Delaware Street and she didn't signal a right turn onto Swanton Road. The truck didn't signal either, but stayed close behind her.

She didn't obey the stop sign at Swanton and West Cliff; there was no danger of a collision if she didn't. All that was to her right was the entrance to Natural Bridges State Park, and at this time of night the entrance was gated, blocking the road. West Cliff drivers, seeing the dead end, would be forced to turn onto Swanton before they reached her.

Instead of stopping, she gunned her engine, sped left onto West Cliff Drive, and sprinted through the first of the tight curves as the road followed the sea cliffs edging the ocean. The dark truck parroted her moves as if it was attached to her back bumper by a short chain.

In front of her a police car suddenly flicked on its bubblegum lights and pulled out from the curb, blocking the roadway. She veered sharply to her right and stopped as she had been instructed to do when the police car made its move. The black truck swerved and came to a stop just inches before hitting the police car, paused momentarily, and then attempted a back-up maneuver. Dave pulled in almost against its rear bumper, sealing the vehicle in a tight formation.

A police officer emerged from his cruiser before the truck stopped moving completely and rushed toward it with his weapon drawn. The officer ripped the driver door open and began shouting sharp commands to the driver inside.

Tom pulled his BMW to the curb well back of Dave's car. He'd been unwilling to wait at home, the long-suffering spouse sitting by the phone hoping for the best, and had been behind Dave during Regan's interminable drive.

Regan stayed in her car and breathed deeply and rapidly, feeling like her lungs would never be able to hold as much air as she needed. The truck driver's hair fell across her face as she twisted wildly and tried to escape the police officer's grasp. Regan couldn't understand the woman's hysterical words through her closed window, but when she opened her car door in response to Tom's rap on her window, she heard a desperate command shrilling from the woman.

"Run! Get to the water! I can't protect you anymore. Tell my son they've taken me. Run!"

🏠🏠🏠🏠🏠🏠🏠🏠🏠🏠🏠

Tom and Regan were already seated at a table at the Crow's Nest, one with a good view of the boats coming and going into the yacht harbor, when Dave strode in audaciously and sat down on Regan's side of the table. His face was split by the broadest and most satisfied Cheshire cat smile she had ever seen.

"What's good here, and expensive, since you're paying?" he asked, directing his question at Regan.

"I asked you to promise you'd be a gracious loser. It never occurred to me to ask if you'd be a gracious winner," she scowled.

"I bet it didn't. But see, I am being gracious. I'm getting my victor's lunch at the restaurant you wanted." His smile threatened to swallow his whole face. "Has she made any more noises about her pal Corinne or is she accepting the error of her ways?" he asked Tom.

"You want to field that question, sweetheart?"

221

"No, you two can talk among yourselves. I'm just going to sip my tea and watch the boats go by."

"Still sulking, sounds like," Dave chuckled. "You shouldn't take it so hard, Regan. You were right about some things. You got the description of the truck that ran you off the road right: it was black and it did have a brush guard ... sorry, cow catcher. Looks like you were right about a big thing, too — it was the same woman who called you both times. Oh, and don't forget, you got what she said her name was right, even if it was hard to hear her when she said it."

Dave changed directions abruptly. "OK, enough needling. This has been a messy case, hard on a lot of people, and something that's not likely to end with us all feeling swell because justice has finally been served. At least you can feel safe again, Regan. It's really looking like Crazy Momma was behind the attack on you."

"I know I said the voice was the same on both calls, and I'm sticking to that, but I still can't believe Linda Cooper could have put together such an elaborate plot. And what was she screaming when you caught up with her."

"She had some cockamamie story about following you until you could get to the ocean. She claimed someone in her alien abductees support group — yeah, I know, only in Santa Cruz," Dave laughed, "told her you needed her help and that she had to follow you to protect you."

"Who in her group came up with Regan's name?" Tom cocked his head and frowned as he asked.

"The department shrink has been asking tinfoil lady that question; she doesn't know. He seems to think she came up with your name on her own, that she remembered it from the eviction proceeding, but filed it in the wrong place in her brain and then swirled it around until it popped out in a new context. Rather than being someone she was afraid of, Regan here became someone who could magically help her. Some kind of transference he called it, I think."

"Did she admit to attacking me?" Regan asked.

"No, she's pretty out of it. She hasn't said much of anything. They've got her under a 72 hour hold in the psych ward at Dominican Hospital right now. From what I hear, she's pretty much shut down and curled up in a ball. They think she's gonna be court-ordered to stay a lot longer."

"That poor woman."

"The thing is, she was waiting for you near your house night before last. That points to her being able to do the same the night you got whacked. Just how her son fits into all this, what with him following you home and all, we don't exactly know, yet ..."

Regan stopped him with a hand on his arm. "Dave, it might not have been Seth who followed me from the courthouse. The truck was Seth's, we know that, but if I had to swear he was the driver, well ... I couldn't. I didn't get a good look at who was diving. All I really could tell was that the driver had longish light-colored hair. I assumed the driver was male; I could be wrong about that. Seth isn't a big man; his mother is probably about as tall as he is. They'd look about the same size in the driver's seat. I didn't see Linda Cooper in court. It's possible she was sitting in the truck watching me when I left the courthouse, and that she's the one who followed me home."

Dave pressed his lips together until they disappeared and

223

then pulled his mouth into a straight line, "That would explain a lot. You think that's what happened?"

Their conversation was interrupted by a buxom young server dressed in a tight black spandex skirt and a short white tank top that missed the top of the skirt by a good three inches. Both rode up as she moved. Tom and Dave grew unusually indecisive, Regan noted with amusement, and both seemed to need lots of information about what the best things on the menu were. The server had to lean over repeatedly to point out her favorite suggestions.

When she left to place their order, tugging her skirt as she went, both men's eyes followed her appreciatively until Regan asked, "Dave, what about Julien Rochette's murder? Any progress there?"

"I thought we all might be able to back off a bit on that subject now that we know his murder isn't related to your accident." Dave faced Tom as he spoke, but his sideways glance to watch Regan's reaction left no doubt his statement was directed at her.

Dave's response threw Regan's thoughts into turmoil. She wasn't ready to accept that the attack on her and Julien Rochette's murder were unrelated. Yet, hadn't she just admitted Linda Cooper could have been stalking her? She had to be reasonable, didn't she? She had to accept facts. She knew what Dave would say if she cited her gut feelings again. "I mean about the Alfreys' confessions," she said. "What's going to happen to them now?"

Dave shook his head. "Everything about them keeps getting downgraded. The thinking right now is since Preston admitted to taking a swing at the Vic but didn't kill him, the most he might be charged with is assault. Then there's always the problem that he was only thirteen at the time.

"I already told you how messy it gets with Alfrey senior. No one believes they can make a murder charge, even a manslaughter charge, stick. The only thing everyone agrees on is that Alfrey disposed of the body," he shook his head with frustration.

"His attorney is deep in negotiations with the D.A. The more time that passes, the more likely it is there won't be any serious charges filed. By the time his lawyer finishes pushing, Alfrey will probably get to cop to some charge that gets him a stinging slap on the wrist and some community service time, no more."

"But what about justice for Julien Rochette? He was murdered."

"I warned you justice was unlikely here. It's frustrating as hell to be in law enforcement sometimes. Everyone thinks our system is about justice and truth, but really a lot of the time it's about who's got the best lawyer or who's better at obscuring the truth." He looked down at the table. "Sorry. I don't have better news for you."

By the time their lunch arrived, even the server's constant self-conscious skirt tugging couldn't lighten their collective mood. What had begun as Dave's celebratory victory lunch was eaten in subdued, even maudlin silence.

28

More than two weeks had gone by since Regan gave her phone number to Edie Palmeroy and asked her to have Aimee Rochette call her. Regan had almost forgotten about Mrs. Rochette — suppressed thinking about her was probably a better way to describe it — when she listened to her answering machine and heard Aimee Rochette's voice for the first time.

"I do apologize for my reticence in calling you," the woman began. Her voice was melodious and gentle, refined, Regan thought. She spoke with a southern cadence, a quality that was more a matter of pacing than of anything that could be called a drawl. Regan was certain she would guess where her caller grew up if she ever heard her pronounce *New Orleans*. "I would like to speak with you when it is convenient. My phone number is 555-7388 if you would be so kind as to call me."

Regan replayed the message and copied down the phone number. She picked up her handset and keyed in the number, but then, instead of pressing 'talk' to dial the number, she returned the handset to its cradle.

The day Regan had gone to the Coast Church in search of Mrs. Rochette, she badly wanted to speak to Julien's mother. Now she wasn't sure if it was a good idea. The saying "let sleeping dogs lie" flitted through her mind. It might be better to delete Aimee Rochette's message and crumple her phone number than to return her call.

The past two weeks since she and Tom had lunch with Dave at the Crow's Nest had been a struggle for Regan. As hard as she tried, she couldn't reconcile objective facts with her feelings.

She was certain that the woman who called her the night Linda Cooper followed her was the same woman who called her the night she was attacked. If that was so, it followed that Linda Cooper was her attacker, and that Linda's motive for her attack was something bound up in the wretched woman's troubled mind. Regan considered the objective facts: Linda was apprehended in Seth's truck — the truck that followed her home from court and closely matched her description of the vehicle driven by her assailant. Linda knew where to wait for her. The same woman's voice was on the phone both times. Everything seemed to point to Linda as her attacker, and if she was, then Regan's assault had nothing to do with Julien's murder. And yet, she couldn't accept that conclusion; she still felt her attack was related to her poking around and asking questions about the long ago killing.

Again, objective facts: current police budgetary constraints, the coldness of the case, and the confession by two men who didn't know how the victim died meant that, for the time being, Julien Rochette's murder would remain unsolved. That was unacceptable.

Regan sighed. She had great sympathy for Julien's mother and she didn't want to meet her without being able to offer help. She had asked Mrs. Rochette to call her, but now she was afraid that talking to the woman and revisiting Julien's death might make both of them feel worse than they already did.

Regan was overcome with shame for her misgivings. Her discomfort was trivial compared to what Mrs. Rochette must be feeling. If Mrs. Rochette was willing to talk, she had no choice but to return her call. She picked up her handset again and pressed 'redial.'

Aimee Rochette's answering machine came on after the fourth ring. "You have reached the Rochette residence," it explained before a similar voice began talking over it, "I'm here, I'm home, please bear with me while I turn off the recorder." An earsplitting beep signaled the end of the outgoing message. "Oh, I am sorry; I'm never fast enough answering my phone. This is Aimee. With whom am I speaking?" Her voice held no wariness, only genuine interest in knowing her caller.

"Regan McHenry, Mrs. Rochette."

"Mrs. McHenry." She said nothing for several seconds after her acknowledgement. "Please don't think ill of me when I tell you I am somewhat ambivalent about speaking with you."

A small ironic smile formed on Regan's mouth. "I understand; I hesitated returning your call."

"Well then, as long as we are of a like mind, perhaps we should speak. Telephones are such impersonal instruments, though. Would you be willing to come to my home tomorrow afternoon so we might meet one another and speak directly?"

Aimee Rochette lived on one of the streets that twisted through Seacliff in a seemingly random way. The community got its start as a beach getaway after the S.S. Palo Alto, originally built as an oil tanker and affectionately called The Cement Ship by locals, was no longer needed following World War I and was moored at Seacliff State Beach. It was used in turn as a casino and night spot, the center of an amusement pier, and as it continued to deteriorate and break apart, as a fishing pier, and finally a closed monument. Initially people built in Seacliff catch-as-catch-can, not worrying about much other than having simple amenities and a place to sleep when they came to the beach.

The house Mrs. Rochette rented, like so many of its neighbors, was serviceable but short on charm. It had been cheaply built using mostly cinderblock for walls. The roof had a low pitch, angled enough that the builder couldn't get away with using tar and gravel, but not steep enough to demand more than a modest number of shingles. The original owner had probably wanted to avoid spending vacations mowing lawns or watering gardens and had finished the property with no-fuss landscaping. Over time, as the take-care-of-themselves plants had become sparse and leggy, lava rock had been deposited around the survivors for weed control; bits of exposed plastic ground cover visible in spots under the rough orange rocks attested to that. And from the look of the front yard, it was clear Mrs. Rochette wasn't a gardener.

The front door, a faded yellow and slightly paint-challenged affair, opened in response to Regan's knock and was held ajar by a small woman, who in every way possible sharply contrasted with her unkempt house. Her hair was white with just one streak remaining to suggest that it had once been almost black. It was pulled back severely from her widow's peak into a timeless French twist devoid of even a single escaped hair. She wore a pale lavender sweater set — cashmere Regan guessed — topped by a string of evenly sized pearls. Her earrings were pearls as well, perfect matches to her necklace. Mrs. Rochette's outfit was completed by a neatly pleated grey wool skirt and a pair of low-heeled perfectly polished pale grey pumps.

"Mrs. McHenry? Do come in," she invited.

Aimee Rochette had created a foyer in the otherwise open floor plan with furniture placement and a small oriental rug. She had positioned a tall cabinet with its back to the area so it obscured her living room. A substantial painting on its finished back hung above a graceful Queen Anne console which displayed a flower-filled vase and a porcelain figurine of three dancing maidens. She escorted Regan around the cabinet room divider and into the living area.

Mrs. Rochette's home was cluttered with objects and pieces of furniture, treasures acquired over generations. In her own living environment, Regan required light and open spaces, but as a visitor rather than someone who had to live in the midst of such abundance, she appreciated its appeal for the same reasons she loved visiting Savannah, Georgia antique shops when she and Tom vacationed there.

"I have still-warm beignets. How do you feel about coffee with chicory in the blend? Would you rather have tea? I have both China black and herbal; which do you prefer?" She rushed forward in a blur of anxious questions, almost talking over herself. "I'm not giving you a chance to answer, am I? Please sit down. I'm a touch nervous as you may have noticed. I'll only be a minute." With that, she left Regan alone in the living room.

Regan had noticed Mrs. Rochette's nervousness. She shared a bit of it herself. She sat down as instructed.

Mrs. Rochette made no attempt to disguise the house's coldly functional structure; it vanished on its own, cast out by the intricacies, highly polished patinas, and richness of her decor. To those who only saw her house from the outside, Aimee Rochette seemed to live in shabby 1960s surroundings — to anyone invited into her home, it was obvious she lived in a genteel time and in a world of her own making.

Mrs. Rochette returned with a tray holding two each of daintily embroidered napkins, coffee cups, spoons, and small dishes; a silver creamer and sugar bowl that matched the coffee pot; and a plate filled with powdered sugar covered beignets which, as promised, were still warm.

She poured coffee for Regan and added a great deal of milk. "Sugar?" she asked.

"I don't know. May I taste it before deciding?" Regan's answer had been a straightforward one — she hadn't had chicory coffee before and didn't know if it would need sugar — but Mrs. Rochette took her words as wry humor which caused her to laugh lightly and put her at ease.

"Oh, Mrs. McHenry. This is a difficult situation, isn't it?

231

We do share a bond, not one either of us would have chosen to share, I'm certain. Both of us are afraid to say Julien's name out loud or acknowledge that he was murdered, aren't we? There, I've done it; I've said it. Now we may be able to speak more easily. Edie said you had questions you would like me to answer. That's why you contacted me, isn't it, Mrs. McHenry?"

"Yes. But I thought you might have some questions you'd want to ask me first."

"What would I want to know from you? The circumstances of your finding my son's body? I'm not interested in that."

"Have the police been keeping you informed about their investigation? I may know some things they haven't told you."

"I doubt you know anything that matters." Mrs. Rochette smiled forlornly. "I'm certain the police don't understand much about my son's murder at all."

"Mrs. Rochette, I want you to know how sorry I am for your loss. I have sons myself. I can't imagine anything more horrible than losing one of them, especially by murder."

"There are worse things," she said evenly. "Now please, ask me your questions."

Regan nodded. "I'm trying to understand who Julien was. I've heard many things about him. I'm sorry, not all of them have been positive, I thought you ..."

Mrs. Rochette stopped her. "You have children so you know you love them whatever they do, but sometimes they dishearten you. May I tell you a story which I think will explain more than I can in any other way?"

232

"Of course. Yes."

"My family traces its beginning back to the 1700's in the Vieux Carré, the French quarter of New Orleans. Old families like mine share a similar history and all seem to be distantly related to one another in some manner through long ago marriages. That was the case with my father and his best friend.

"As young men, both were sent to Korea in 1950 to fight in that conflict. Both men left young wives and baby daughters at home when they went off to war. My father's friend came home safely after the war; my father had a different fate. He died in Korea as a hero whose bravery and sacrifice saved the lives of several men, including that of his best friend.

"My father's friend and his wife took my mother and me into their home and looked after us like we were close family. When my mother died an untimely death, they truly became my parents and their daughter became my sister as surely as if we shared blood.

"My sister and I married fine New Orleans men the same summer and my husband, Christian, and I were blessed with our son Julien two years later. But my poor sister had tragedy after tragedy in her life. She had three miscarriages and then bore a stillborn son. She finally rejoiced in the birth of a healthy baby girl, but it seemed God allowed her only one person to love at a time: her husband was taken in an automobile accident before their daughter reached her first birthday.

"My husband's employment brought us to Santa Cruz. I fell in love with the area and stayed on with my son even after my husband passed six years later. Raising a child alone was difficult. My sister and I struggled with single parenthood in our separate localities and talked on the phone about our challenges every week.

"Julien was not always an easy child. There were times he made poor choices with friendships and came close to trouble, but compared to my sister's child, he was an angel. Rinny was a wild thing. My sister had family around her, but even with that support, her daughter grew more and more dangerously out of control. When she was about to start her last year of high school, my sister took a drastic step and moved here with her daughter. She thought ... we thought, a fresh start might help Rinny and that we could be stronger together and help one another finish childrearing.

"Our idea seemed to work well; Rinny graduated and began walking a straighter road. There was an added blessing as we saw it: Julien and Rinny became very fond of one another — we thought they fell in love. We anticipated they would wed when they were older." Mrs. Rochette closed her eyes and tilted her head back as she took a deep breath. "You can imagine how surprised we both were when she accepted an offer of marriage from another man. An older man. A widower with a son."

Regan's eyes opened wide and her lips parted. "Rinny?" she asked.

"A pet name for Corinne." The corners of Aimee Rochette's mouth hinted at an ironic smile. "After Rinny's wedding, my sister, who had never developed an affinity for this area as I had, felt that now that her daughter was settled, she could return to New Orleans. We old friends and

234

scheming mothers were disappointed things didn't work out between our children, of course, but I expected Julien would be devastated and confused by Rinny's decision. He was not.

"Rinny was close-mouthed with her mother and a distant child, but Julien always shared his feelings and dreams with me, even those that might cause me pain. He told me he and Rinny had a plan, a grand scheme which would let them start their young lives in style. He told me nothing had changed between Rinny and him, but that her husband was a rich man with more money than he needed. Rinny would stay married to him for a short time and then divorce him. She seemed to think she would be entitled to many of his assets. In the meantime, she and Julien would quietly continue an affair …" her voice trailed off.

"Mrs. McHenry, I was raised in the Catholic faith. What they were doing was a mortal sin." Tears welled in Mrs. Rochette's eyes. "I pleaded with my son that their plan was evil and that he needed to give it up and give Rinny up." Her voice choked. She drew herself into a rigidly upright pose and pulled her elbows inward, trying, it seemed, to control her emotions by tightly controlling her body.

"I couldn't condone what my son and Rinny were doing." Her eyes pleaded for understanding, "but I couldn't disown them either." Her mouth quivered, "And I couldn't tell my sister; I couldn't break her heart. I also couldn't continue in my Catholic faith. How could I make the same confession every week and take communion, knowing that my silence was giving tacit approval to what our children were doing?" Mrs. Rochette turned her face away from Regan before she continued.

235

"According to Julien, Rinny was a good mother to Preston Alfrey. I understood firsthand how much that can mean to a child and that biology didn't matter when it came to parental kindness. Julien worked for Rinny's husband sometimes, even helped out occasionally with his son. And all the while they continued … and I said nothing more.

"It was on one of those occasions when he was helping out, driving Preston Alfrey to summer school for a play the boy was in, that my son met a girl and things began to change for the better. Julien said he was smitten with her the moment he saw her. He described her beauty and said it came from inside her as much as from her lovely features.

"The last message from him was such good news that I kept it, replaying it over and over. I tried to reach Julien to make certain he would bring his fiancée to Thanksgiving dinner. Then, when I discovered he was … missing," she stopped. "I saved the recording; I wanted to keep his voice with me. May I play it for you?"

"Yes," Regan answered hesitantly, "if you want to."

Mrs. Rochette went to the front side of the cabinet she used as the room divider and removed a red and gold lacquered box from the top shelf. She returned to her seat and placed the box on the table next to the beignets. She twisted the brass clasp to align the latch and opened the container. Her movements were slow and precise as if they were part of a religious ritual performed in the presence of sacred relics.

The box looked empty from Regan's perspective, but when Mrs. Rochette reached inside, she produced a small tape, the kind used in answering machines before they went digital, and a small cassette player. She loaded the tape and pressed play. Regan leaned forward, anxious to catch every word.

Julien's voice, stronger and richer than Regan anticipated it would be, filled the small living room. "Mère, I've made up my mind. I know you will be pleased. Isabel has consented to be my wife. I've told Rinny we are ended. She's married to a good man. I told her to work at being happy with him; if she does, I think she will be. I told her I didn't think it would be good for us to see one another anymore. I plan to give her back the medallion and find another job."

"The medallion … that was used to …"

"C.J.R.," Mrs. Rochette nodded. "I told the police it was a gift from a girlfriend and that it was Julien's initials; his full name was Christian Julien Rochette. Both of those statements were true, but the initials also stood for Corinne Josephine Richard, Rinny's name. He put it on a long silken cord and wore it always, so it would be near his heart."

Mrs. Rochette carefully removed the tape from the player and returned both of them to their sarcophagus. "I didn't know for sure — although in my heart I did, but I hoped I was mistaken — until his body was discovered in your house and the police told me about the medallion. I didn't know what to do. I have accepted my son's death. I believe Julien's soul has been saved because he repented before his death, but repentance doesn't necessarily let one avoid punishment. Perhaps he needed to be punished in this world for his sins.

"Rinny is my daughter almost as much as Julien was my son. If I tell the police about her, it won't bring Julien back and it will destroy my sister.

"And Rinny has also repented; I'm sure she has. She has

237

kept her marriage vows and helped her husband raise his son. She has been a good wife and mother for the past sixteen years."

Her words were delivered as a statement, but Regan could tell that Aimee Rochette was begging for confirmation, pleading for Regan to agree with her, and by doing so, make what she said true.

"Mrs. Rochette, you were in New Orleans at Christmas; you don't know what happened here, do you? Corinne's husband confessed to murdering Julien."

Mrs. Rochette blinked as relieved tears filled her eyes, "Then Rinny didn't …"

Regan took Mrs. Rochette's hand and held it firmly. "Preston Alfrey came forward the next day and said he was the murderer, not his father."

"The child?" she breathed.

"Neither of them knew about the medallion."

For a minute Aimee Rochette was completely still, then she felt the woman's hand begin to tremble as she held it. "She used her husband," her breath came in shallow pants, "and she used the *child*." And Regan understood what could be worse than losing a son to murder.

29

Every time she was caught by a stoplight, Regan reached over to her passenger seat and took the tiny cassette out of the lacquer box. She rolled it between her fingers, listening for a slight rattle that would indicate the tape had loosened with age. She heard nothing. The tape was as clear and sound as the quality of Julien's voice. With each green light she returned the tape to its resting place in the box and tried to concentrate on driving, suspending her plotting until the next stoplight.

It was at one particularly long light that she settled on blackmail. She needed a few supplies to implement her plan; by the time she turned off Mission Street at Bay and headed for home, she had made her purchases. She was ready.

Tom's car wasn't in the garage when she opened the door. She was pleased he wasn't home yet — she only wanted one person to hear what she had to say. Regan sat the lacquer box on her desk while she looked up Corinne's cell phone number. She dialed confidently. She was prepared for Corinne live and, uncharacteristically for her, for her answering machine as well. Corinne's outgoing message was

239

all warmth when it greeted her. Regan wasn't cordial; her voice was as hard and pointed as her message.

"This is Regan McHenry. It's surprising the mementos mothers keep from their dead sons and how foolish old sentimental women can be about sharing them. I have something one of them just gave me because she trusts me to do the right thing with it, but I think," she slowed her speech and delivered each word purposefully, "you'll be as anxious to own it as the police are to have it."

🏠🏠🏠🏠🏠🏠🏠🏠🏠🏠🏠

Regan walked into the Crepe Place on Soquel Avenue five minutes late. She was compulsively punctual; her slight tardiness was part of her plan. Those who waited were made to feel subservient. She had agreed to meet Corinne at the restaurant at 1:30, after most lunch goers had finished eating. The day was warm enough that she had instructed Corinne they should meet outside in the garden portion of the restaurant where the tables were spaced farther apart and they could have a private conversation.

She wore her favorite dark red jacket over a black pencil skirt. Her outfit was accessorized with simple black pumps, a squarish black leather purse, and a gauzy black scarf wrapped in a loose circle around her neck. According to a seminar she had taken early in her real estate career, what she wore constituted a power outfit. That was also part of her plan.

She intended to control every detail of her meeting with Corinne. This wasn't a friendly lunch get-together like she often had with other realtor friends, but if anyone noticed

240

them or recognized either woman, that was what it would seem to be.

Corinne was already seated at the round table near the back of the garden. Her adversary had positioned herself to watch her arrive, *no dead man's hand for her, no opportunity to slip up behind her*, she noted as she sat down next to Corinne.

She greeted Corinne with a larcenous smile, opened her purse, and took out a typed piece of paper and the cassette. Once she was satisfied Corinne had seen the cassette, she returned it to her purse. "I transcribed what's on the tape. It's remarkably clear even after sixteen years, so clear I thought it shouldn't be played here."

Regan took up her menu and pretended to study it as Corinne read the transcript. She looked up and announced, "Oh good, Corinne, here comes the server."

Corinne folded the page Regan had given her in half and slipped it onto her lap and under her napkin as the server asked, "Have you two ladies decided what you would like today?" Both women indicated they had and quickly placed their orders.

"How did you get this?" Corinne sounded baleful.

"I told you. It was given to me. I'm supposed to deliver it to …"

"You know what I mean," Corinne hissed. "Why did she give it to *you*?"

"After what you did, she thinks you should be punished, Corinne, but she couldn't bring herself to give Julien's tape to the police; she still thinks of you as a daughter. I told her I'd do the dirty work and she trusted that I would. I am a trustworthy and reliable person, after all — much like you are — so she gave me her only copy." Regan's statement and her smile were full of callous irony.

"You know, Corinne," Regan sniggered, "I think we are alike in many ways. Think about it. We're both well regarded and respected in our community, intelligent, competent — resourceful, too. What most people fail to realize about us is that neither one of us would pass on seizing an opportunity, especially one that was dropped in our lap, as it were.

"Our pasts are even similar; I didn't realize that until after I talked to Isabel Bolton. You were abandoned by the man you loved, a man you trusted to love you always. My ex-husband left me for another woman. I understand how that made you feel.

"We both are married to men who love us, men we control, who would do anything for us — men we don't necessarily feel the same devotion to — sometimes don't even like that much."

"But you and Tom ..." Corinne began.

Regan interrupted her, "Seem happy enough together just like you and Charles do. That's another thing we have in common, Corinne: we're both good actresses, aren't we? There is one big difference between us, though. You made Julien pay for what he did to you; I was never able to get even with my ex.

"How did it feel?" Regan leaned toward Corinne and licked her lower lip, "Good?"

Corinne's expression contained the barest hint of a smile and there was a brief flutter at one corner of her mouth. "Revenge is intoxicating. You should try it sometime. It feels great."

Regan gasped, startled by her own exhilaration.

"What do you want, Regan?" Corinne asked. Her voice was flat and harsh.

"I want to know what happened. I think I'll enjoy hearing the details as much as you'll enjoy reliving them." Regan smiled pleasantly. "Then I'll probably want something tangible … in exchange for the tape."

"I understand." Corinne took a long sip of water and then smiled slowly, "Sisters in crime. Details then. Julien and I probably shared a racial memory, if there is such a thing, of living well. There must have been servants and wealth in our background, given where our families came from, but by the time we came along, it was all in the past. We wanted a comfortable life," Corinne arranged her face in a cavalier smirk, "it was our birthright.

"Julien wasn't averse to taking small shortcuts to get what we wanted, but I was the one who, like you said, decided to seize an opportunity when it presented itself. I got a job at Bradley Real Estate as a receptionist after I graduated from high school and met Charles Alfrey there. I thought he was creepy at first, kind of a dirty old man. I flirted with him anyway," she said scornfully. "It made me feel powerful, seeing how badly he wanted me and how I could manipulate him. Then I found out he was rich. I came up with the idea that, since California is a community property state, I could marry him, divorce him after a few years, and be a well-to-do woman when I married Julien. I thought we could jumpstart our lifestyle that way.

"Julien was horrified when I told him my idea. He said he

loved me and wasn't about to give me up and sit by while Charles Alfrey ..." she broke into genuine laughter. "Well, I explained to him that wasn't what I had in mind. I told him we could be lovers the whole time I was married to Charles."

Regan thought Corinne looked triumphant as she spoke. Her eyes twinkled, and she seemed as amused by her plan now as she likely had been when she explained it to Julien.

"He wasn't as open to the idea as you might think, but I was always able to coax him into seeing things my way." The pleasure drained from Corinne's face and her eyes grew cruel as she continued, "at least I was until Isabel Bolton came along. The irony is he would never have met her if it hadn't been for my stepson.

"Julien called me, probably right before he left this message for his mother, and told me he was going to marry her. *Marry her.* Here I was with Charles for us, for our future, and he said he was going to marry Isabel Bolton." Corinne shook her head, slowly at first, but then more rapidly. "Bastard.

"I'm not sure what I intended to do to him; I wanted to get his attention, somehow make him see he couldn't discard me like that. We used to meet in empty houses that Charles had listed. I'd give Julien a key to the house and then I'd go by and take the lockbox key inside so no other agents could open the door and surprise us. I'd set up a nice little spot for us while I waited for him. I'm practical, too, Regan. Sometimes if the owners left a bed behind, I'd wait for him there instead."

"Is that what you did at our house? You met there?" Regan asked.

244

"More than once. We liked your house. It was very private and it had a bed and nice shades on the bedroom windows," Corinne offered emotionlessly.

The server arrived with their crepes and beverages. He asked if either of them would like freshly ground pepper and refilled their water glasses. To Regan, anxious for Corinne to continue, his normal routine seemed interminable. By the time he finished fussing and got to his cheery, "Please let me know if there's anything else I can get for you," Regan was ready to burst.

As soon as he was out of earshot, Corinne continued. "Like I said, I'm not sure what I intended to do exactly. I brought duct tape and a handkerchief to stuff in his mouth to make him be quiet and listen to me. None of what I may have considered doing mattered anyway; the minute I saw him, all I wanted to do was make love to him. I persuaded him he at least owed me one last time.

"And that's what we were doing when in came Preston Alfrey, big as life. Charles must have given him a key and sent him by to do a little water running." She dropped her head and heaved a dramatic sigh. "The kid went nuts. He started screaming something about Isabel and his father and ran out of the room. Julien barely had time to get off me when Preston came back. He'd found a big old board somewhere in the house and he swung it and caught Julien in the head. Julien went down and just lay still. He was bleeding like crazy and Preston was as white as a sheet. He started screaming, 'I killed him. I killed him. I didn't mean it. I'm sorry, Julien.'

"Can you imagine what was going on in my mind? I

couldn't have Preston tell his father what I'd been doing with Julien; he'd leave me. All the time I spent being married to him would have been for nothing. I'd be out on the street. And I couldn't count on Julien to take care of me anymore because," she twisted her face into an ugly semblance and derided, "'he was in love with sweet little Isabel.'

"Then the perfect solution hit me: I'd let Preston believe he *had* killed Julien. I told him to go home, that I'd take care of the body, but if he ever told anyone about what he had seen or what had happened, I'd tell everyone he was a murderer and turn him in to the police." Corinne grinned, "I thought I'd figured out a clever way to get him to keep his mouth shut about Julien and me.

"I barely got Preston out the door before Julien started moaning. I bound him up with duct tape. I needed to keep him still so I could talk to him, make him understand how much he was hurting me. We'd been through so much; I was sure deep down he still loved me."

Corinne looked at some distant image that only she could see and then turned to Regan, "He kept floating in and out of consciousness, but during one of his lucid moments he said we were finished. How could he walk away? How could he abandon me?" For little more than a heartbeat, Regan could see genuine pain in Corinne's eyes.

"Is that enough detail for you? It better be. I don't want to talk about it anymore. If you want any more ghoulish details, use your imagination, Regan. I'm sure you can make up the rest," she said angrily. "Tell me what else you want."

"I will, but I want to know about Charles first."

"Ah, Charles," Corinne breathed, "my knight in shining

246

armor." Her words were sarcastic and disparaging, but she blinked rapidly as she said them and quickly rubbed her hand across her cheek. "I misjudged Preston. He ran home all right, but rather than keeping quiet, he unloaded to his dad that he had killed Julien. I guess he blubbered something about jealousy and Isabel, at least that's what Charles thought he heard, and told Charles I was with the body."

"And Charles came to help?" In her mind Regan was doing what Corinne suggested; she was filling in the details of what probably happened then.

Now that she had moved past Julien's death, Corinne seemed willing to continue. "That's right. I pulled the bloody sheet where Julien fell around him like a shroud and was trying to figure out what to do next when Charles started pounding on the door and yelling for me to let him in. My heart practically stopped — I was so scared that Preston had told him about Julien and me. I told Charles I had come by to collect the agent showing cards and discovered Preston with Julien's body and that I couldn't stand to look at it and had covered him with a sheet. Charles threw his arms around me and said I was wonderful for trying to protect Preston.

"We didn't know what to do with Julien. And then Charles said he thought there was an opening, a place where we could hide him, that he had seen in a report about the house. He climbed up in the attic for a minute. When he came back down he said he had a plan."

Corinne began giggling. "He told me to be brave — and said that we both had to go buy all the cat litter we could find, but that we needed to get it from several stores so no one would wonder what we were doing. I left Julien ... with

247

Charles. When I came back, Charles had big garbage bags with him and his car was full of bags of cat litter." Her giggles escalated into aberrant laughter. "He had bent Julien up and pulled a bag over him. Somehow Charles managed to get him up into the attic and to the place where he put him. I don't know how he managed, but Charles was muscular and probably high on adrenalin: it must have made him strong.

"It took us almost until dawn to finish with Julien. My job was to hand up the piece of wood Preston used to hit Julien and then bag after bag of cat litter. I never believed we'd get away with it, but we did. At least for sixteen years. That's it, Regan. That's the whole story, all the details. Now, what do you want? Money? I can get you money, but I'll need a few days."

"Yes. Let's start with money. I bet you've set some aside, haven't you?"

"I've been putting cash away in my own name and investing it well." There was real pride in her voice as she told Regan about her secret hoarding. "How much is it going to cost me to get that tape? And how do I know you haven't made copies?"

"I'm promising you I haven't. But you won't know that for a while, will you? If I come back for a second installment when I've disposed of what you gave me, then you'll know I was lying." Regan forced out a cruel laugh.

"But I wouldn't worry about the tape too much. What I'd worry about, if I were you, is what happens when Mrs. Rochette wonders why the police haven't contacted her. When that happens, and she does go to the police and says she gave me a tape of her dead son saying some incriminating things about you, you're paying for me to say, 'what tape?' What you're really going to be buying is my silence."

The server appeared with their bill. Corinne reached for her purse but Regan stopped her with a raised hand. "No. I'll get it. You can pay me back later." She gave the server a credit card and when he ran it through his hand-held charger, signed the tab.

"Thank you, ma'am. That's *very* generous." The server dipped his head in a little bow before he left.

"I need a number for the tape, Regan. And because we've both spent so much time understanding the importance of written contracts, why don't you put it in writing? Put your number at the top of the transcript." Corinne uncovered the folded transcript, took it from her lap, and handed it to Regan with a pen she had taken from her purse.

A number. Regan couldn't allow herself to ask what a life was worth or consider how many lives Corinne had shattered. No number could make up for what Corinne had done. She only had to decide what her silence would be worth to Corinne. She forced down the anger she felt. This part wasn't about retribution. She needed a small enough number that Corinne would readily agree to pay it. Regan wrote "$100,000" on the paper and handed it back to Corinne.

Corinne smiled triumphantly. She refolded the page so the text and Regan's number were hidden. "Regan, since you seem to appreciate the potential illicit value of tape recordings, I assume you are recording today's luncheon conversation. So, for those of you who may get a chance to hear this, Regan McHenry has just attempted to blackmail me for $100,000. Am I right in assuming blackmail is a felony?

"Since I knew she was recording what I said, I invented the juicy story you just heard. It was a pretty good one, don't you think, with all that sex and gore? I wasn't there so I don't know how Julien Rochette died. In fact, all I know is that my stepson, Preston, says he accidently killed Julien in a fit of jealousy. Oh, and I also know my husband. I know he would try to protect his son. He told me how he hid the body, how he buried Julien Rochette in cat litter. That's all I know.

"Why don't you ask Regan what she thinks happened? I'm of the opinion that she has a better imagination than I do. Too bad you couldn't see her face; she seemed full of prurient interest while she listened to the part about how my lover and I used her house for our trysts."

Regan's face flushed and her mouth dropped open.

Corinne wrote a hasty line on the blank back of the transcript and turned the paper so Regan could read it, but didn't hand it to her. The note said: "Agreed. I'll need 48 hours to get the money together." She quickly pulled the paper back and pushed it into her open purse. "I'll hang onto this. Evidence," she grinned.

"Good seeing you, Regan," Corinne said as she stood to leave. "Let's get together again soon, especially since we are so much alike." She turned and sauntered out of the Crepe Place with her head held high.

No, Corinne. I was mistaken. We aren't anything alike.

30

"Don't take it so hard, Regan, just because she outsmarted you. Hey, you're an amateur — like I keep trying to tell you."

"She didn't outsmart me. I have her confessing on tape."

"Yeah. Right before she takes it all back. Have you listened carefully to what you recorded? I have. She doesn't really confess to anything except adultery," Dave chuckled, "and even that confession might just be for your dirty little mind. There's nothing about the real cause of death, nothing about the medallion, which her fingerprints aren't on either, you know. Shoot, she doesn't even give up anything on her husband and son that they haven't already said."

"But when you play it with Mrs. Rochette's tape ..."

Dave's expression was frozen in a scoffing grin; he shook his head. "No way. She knew what you were up to from the time you called her to set up lunch. She was ticked at you and planned out what she was going to say to mess with you. At least that's what any jury listening to that tape would say after Corinne Alfrey's lawyer explains it to them.

"After hearing Mrs. Rochette's tape and yours, jurors won't like her, but they won't convict her of anything. Nah, you'll get on the witness stand, cite your real estate license instead of law enforcement experience, the jury will fall off their seats laughing, and they'll believe Corinne Alfrey was playing with you right from the get-go. I might even have to testify about how she's done it to you before. Remember Irwin Street?"

"What about the note she showed me, agreeing to pay $100,000 for the tape and my silence?"

"What note would that be?"

"What do you mean? I told you about the note." Regan sounded irate.

"And may I have a copy of that note? Now don't get me wrong, Regan, I believe there was a note, but I'm pretending to be her lawyer questioning you on the witness stand. Doesn't look good for the prosecution, does it?"

"But the prosecutor will have my sworn testimony."

"Whoop-de-do." Dave circled an index finger in the air. "The defense will have your gal pal's sworn testimony saying you're making stuff up. Just because something's true doesn't always mean a jury will believe it; nothing here looks like it's beyond a reasonable doubt.

"Then there's the whole question of whether or not your recording is even going to be admissible."

"Why wouldn't it be admissible? The wire you were going to make at Irwin Street would have been admissible. Why wouldn't mine be?"

"Big difference. That recording would have been made according to proper procedures and kept in the evidentiary chain. Who knows when, or where, or how you got your tape. Maybe it was an old recording you spliced together to make it sound like a confession. Don't take it personal, Regan, I'm just playing her lawyer again."

"But I have a receipt. I can prove I bought the spy recorder the day before Corinne and I had lunch, and I tipped the server at the Crepe Place one hundred percent so he'd remember us having lunch. I couldn't have recorded it earlier and tampered with it."

Dave laughed out loud. "I have to give you credit. That tip idea was pretty clever, good for the server's wallet, too. It's not going to help with the recording, though. Grand Jury wouldn't even indict her would be my bet. If they do, her lawyer'll chew you up in tiny little pieces and spit you out all over the courtroom floor."

"Maybe," she admitted. "But I don't think we'll have to rely on any recording. She's hooked, Dave. She doesn't know whether or not I'm a blackmailer, at least not for sure. If she knew, she wouldn't have played it both ways; she wouldn't have written that message for my eyes only."

Dave made a face Regan recognized: first he sucked one cheek in, then he released it and pooched his lips forward in an exaggerated pout. He was pondering. "Tell you what let's do," he said finally. "Let's invite Alfrey senior in for an evening of entertainment ... play both tapes for him. Let's see what he has to say after he has a listen."

"And what happens if he doesn't have anything to say after he hears the tapes, Dave? Remember he'll have his very highly paid, very savvy lawyer with him while he's listening. You're right. There's nothing on either tape that incriminates him any more than he's already done himself, and his attorney will remind him of that."

"I'm not looking at getting Alfrey. Even I'm beginning to feel kind of sorry for the guy, what with him being in the clutches of a nasty piece of work like his wife. What I'm looking for is getting him to roll on the missus. I'd roll on my wife if I found out she did to me what your buddy Corinne Alfrey did to her hubby. Ask Tom what he thinks; I bet he'd agree," Dave beamed. "He'd give you up. In fact," he joshed, "I'd like to know what he thinks about how convincing you sounded when you were saying you control him, oh yeah, and that you don't even like him very much. I'm gonna have to tell him about that."

"That's my point, Dave. You and Sandy, Tom and me, our marriages aren't like the Alfreys. She really does control him; I've seen her do it. He won't, what did you call it, roll on her? She'll have an explanation ready for him, and even if it's one that anyone could poke holes in, he won't. He'll believe her because he'll want to. And he'll keep quiet and continue to protect her."

"I'm not buying it, Regan. You're going all goofy here, like you think you can do some ten-minute psychological profile on the guy just because you have some undergraduate degree in psychology or something. I say he rolls. I'm gonna give the tapes to Detective Harrison, the officer running the investigation, and see if he agrees with me."

"It was behavioral science. My degree was in behavioral science. But you're right, that doesn't qualify me to know that Corinne is a murderer or that she can get her husband to cover for her. It's the years I've spent watching people; that's my training. Understanding people is part of my job, Dave, and I'm good at it. Give Corinne her 48 hours. When she comes up with my blackmail money, you won't have to play anything for her husband. When she pays me to be quiet, it's tantamount to confessing."

He only took a second to think about it. "You have no idea how it pains me to agree with you. Deal. But consider it a favor, OK? You know you're going to owe me big-time here. When I explain about your taping misadventure to Detective Harrison and ask him to assign one of our scarce officers to babysit you for the next 48 hours, I'm gonna take some heat *again* for being too cozy with a do-it-yourself detective like you."

Regan nodded, "I know."

"Hey, Regan, there's another possibility you missed. What happens if you are as wrong about Corinne Alfrey this time as you were about her trying to run you off the road? Suppose she turns up at the police station screaming bloody murder that you tried to blackmail her?" He laughed explosively, "If somebody's got to come arrest you, I'll volunteer."

Tom listened intently, his elbows on the arms of his office chair and his fingers spread wide and touching their opposites. He frowned occasionally and leaned back farther and farther in his chair. He tapped his index fingers together intermittently as Regan told him what she had done and what Corinne had said on the tape.

"I'm convinced she murdered Julien Rochette because he ended their affair and was planning to get married. Dave says there's another possibility — I think he brought it up in pure jest — that Corinne is innocent and will try to have me arrested for attempted blackmail. That seems to be the outcome he'd find most entertaining; he said he'd volunteer to be my arresting officer."

"I think it's unlikely he'll have that opportunity," Tom smiled, "poor Dave." He rocked forward in this seat, compressing his fingers and hands into a position resembling prayerfulness and touched his index fingers to his chin. "I can think of another possibility, one I don't like very much. Corinne may decide you are indeed a blackmailer."

"That's what I'm hoping she'll do. When she tries to pay me off, she's caught."

"Blackmailers have a bad reputation; they tend to be a greedy lot, never satisfied with one payment. You said yourself she was concerned you'd give her a tape but keep a backup. Assuming she did kill Julien Rochette, and what's more troubling, has gotten away with it for all these years, she may think she can get rid of her blackmailer, you sweetheart, and get away with killing you, as well.

"For the next forty-eight hours at least, you're tied to a stake waiting to see if a cougar is going to come get you. It feels like we just did this. Didn't you put yourself out in a field, staked and alone a couple of weeks ago, and didn't you think Corinne was going to come devour you then?"

"Yes, I did; it feels like I'm about to start bleating when I speak, I've been playing the goat so often, but remember, nothing happened to me. It'll be the same this time. She'll think she can pay me, test me out for a while, and get rid of me later if she needs to and after she's had time to come up with a nice plan for my disposal. What she doesn't realize is the game's up the minute she shows up with cash in hand."

"Until she's in custody, keep your head down, OK?"

"I will. But Dave was going to have a meeting with Detective Harrison, the officer in charge of the Julien Rochette murder, right after I left his office. He was going to give the detective the tapes and talk him into waiting forty-eight hours before doing anything with them and ask for some police protection for me for the next couple of days. Knowing Dave, I'm sure there's already a cop assigned to waste good taxpayer money keeping an eye on me."

"I'm glad to hear it. As an added precaution, though, I'll keep close to you, too, if you don't mind."

Regan responded coquettishly, "Not a bit. I always like it when you're close to me."

His eyes crinkled. "Good. OK, Tom 24/7 begins right now. Oh," his next words came out like a deflating balloon, "or not. I've got a listing appointment in half an hour. 24/7 Tom is going to have to wait for a couple of hours to begin following you around — until then, you'll have to stay close to me. Come with me; we can present ourselves as the dynamic team of Kiley and McHenry."

"Right there, the way you phrased it," she teased, "I would have said McHenry and Kiley. I'm going to pass. We're both competitive people. If we start competing with one another for the client's attention, it could get messy.

"I've got a bunch of paperwork to do and some calls to make. I'll stay here in our nice safe office and work while you go be the dynamic solo act of Kiley himself. When the last agent leaves the office, I'll drop and cover, or at least lock the doors and set the overnight alarm, and wait for you to come back sporting a new listing."

"I should be back by 7:30. We can catch dinner in town." He picked up his laptop and a folder with listing documents, and holding one item in each hand, put his arms around her awkwardly and kissed her with the kind of passion he usually reserved for home. "Maybe we can make it a romantic dinner."

Regan waved goodnight through the glass door to Kathy Valdez, the last person leaving for the night. She twisted a lever to close the mini-blinds sandwiched within the door's dual panes, and was setting the back door alarm when she heard the reception desk phone ring at the other end of the office. It was late for a call to the office — after 5:30 most clients called their agents using their individual lines — but there were always a few people who had misplaced their agent's card or were new to the process and called the office number. Regan finished activating the alarm and sprinted for the phone.

"Kiley and Associates, this is Regan," she answered.

"Regan McHenry?"

"Yes."

"Mrs. McHenry," the masculine voice on the line sounded serious and professional, "this is Detective John Harrison. I'm the lead investigator in the murder of Julien Rochette."

"Detective. Dave mentioned he was going to be speaking with you."

There was hesitation on the other end. "Oh yes," she could almost see him shaking the cobwebs out of this mind. "It's been a long day," he sighed. "Yes, he did speak with me.

"Mrs. McHenry, you were present when the body of Julien Rochette was discovered, I believe? I need you to come by your house on 11th Avenue to point out where certain things were the day the body was found. I'm going by the house right now — it may be after hours for you but not for me — would it be possible for you to meet me there now? I shouldn't take more than fifteen minutes of your time and I'm anxious to move the investigation forward."

She glanced at the wall clock over the reception desk. It was just after 6:00. She should be able to make it to the house, and if Detective Harrison was good to his word about taking no more than fifteen minutes of her time, get back to the office in time to meet Tom for dinner.

"Yes, I can do that. I should be there within twenty to twenty-five minutes."

"Excellent."

Regan decided to leave a note for Tom. She was confident she'd be back before he was, but just in case and given the talk they'd had before he left, she didn't want him worrying. The tiniest twinge of misgiving slipped into her mind as she wrote. She'd heard of Detective Harrison. Dave said he was heading the investigation into Julien's murder, just as the man who identified himself as Detective Harrison did … she couldn't quite figure out what was giving her pause, but something was.

You're being paranoid; you're being silly, she chided herself. *It's OK; embrace trite clichés*, she argued back in a one-woman debate. *How could it hurt? Better safe than sorry.* Regan went to her office and picked up her cell phone. She pressed speed dial for Dave's number.

"You've reached Dave Everett. Please leave a message, or if this is an emergency, call 9-1-1." He was probably home or on his way home, his day concluded. He might be in the midst of dinner with Sandy and ignoring his cell phone. This was hardly an emergency; all she wanted was confirmation of Detective Harrison's authenticity. She hung up without leaving a message.

She dropped her cell into her purse and slung her purse over her shoulder, ready to leave the office by the back door, when she remembered she hadn't yet set the front door alarm. She returned to the front of the office and punched in the door code and heard a beep indicating the system was fully operational.

The pesky wary woman in her head had one more bit of advice for her: *Caution can be a virtue, Regan.* She reached into the top drawer of the reception desk and took out a phonebook. Dave might have left the building, but the police station was manned around the clock. She dialed the main listing for the Center Street Police Headquarters.

"Police Department," a crisp male voice offered.

"Hello. This isn't an emergency or anything like that," she apologized, half embarrassed to be making the call. "May I speak to Detective Harrison of the homicide division?"

"He's in the field, ma'am. May I take a message?"

"No, thank you, officer; there's no need."

Regan hung up and chastised the cautious voice in her head, her suspicions put to rest. *He's in the field and no doubt on his way to our house. You can be such a silly worrywart.*

Regan pulled into the driveway next to the unmarked car already parked there. Attaining the rank of Detective was a big deal in the police hierarchy; obviously one of the perks that came with the rank was driving something other than a police cruiser.

She was surprised to see a light on in the house and the front door slightly ajar. She had expected Detective Harrison to be sitting in a cold, dark car waiting for her to get there and let him in, but apparently, he had his own key. She wanted the police to actively investigate Julien Rochette's murder, but their house was a private residence now, not an active crime scene. The police shouldn't be opening doors — they should need knock-on-the-door permission to enter. She made a mental note to get the house locks changed as soon as possible.

Regan pushed the front door open wide enough to let herself in and then closed it firmly behind her. It was dark where she stood; the light was coming from another room. "Detective Harrison?" she called loudly.

"In the back bedroom," the voice she recognized from the

phone responded.

Detective Harrison had his back to her when she entered the bedroom. "Detective Harrison," she said again, this time in a conversational voice. He turned toward her slowly. She recognized the danger before he fully faced her.

From behind her a jovial Corinne Alfrey said, "Regan, may I present my stepson, Detective Harrison."

Regan spun around. Corinne was smiling and aiming a gun with a disproportionately long barrel in her direction. She'd seen enough movie hit men with silencers on their weapons to recognize what the barrel lengthening add-on was.

Preston Alfrey grabbed her arms from behind and pinned them back uncomfortably. He practically lifted her off her feet and deposited her in an upright wooden chair.

"Do sit down," Corinne invited hospitably as he forced her to sit. She maintained the gun's position while Preston noisily ripped duct tape from a roll and wrapped it around her wrists, binding them to the back of the chair.

"Comfy?" Corinne asked sweetly.

All of Regan's attention had been focused on Corinne and the gun. When she finally looked at Preston she saw a marked contrast in their appreciation of her situation. Preston's face looked pinched and pale, not at all like his stepmother's gleefully assured and smiling countenance. He didn't say a word to her.

"Preston, why? What are you doing here with her?" Regan was more mystified by his presence than frightened by what was happening. Had she misread him? She thought of him as another of Corinne's victims, but he was behaving like an accomplice.

Preston said nothing. He looked away, unwilling to make eye contact.

"You know what to do, Pres. Go get a drink somewhere to stiffen your spine. Talk to a couple of people. Hand out a business card or two. Be obnoxious so they remember you — establish a good alibi — and, what time is it now?"

Preston checked his watch, "6:25."

"Call Seth Cooper at 6:45. Don't forget to give him the street address — make sure he knows where it is — and don't forget to tell him Regan's here and that she's laughing about getting his mother committed.

"That's all you have to do. You can go home after that, just like last time. Just like last time, I'll take care of everything. Preston? You understand, don't you? I don't like this any better than you do, but we have to protect Charles. Julien made me marry your father. It's true I didn't love him at first, but I grew to love him." Corinne pleaded, "He has protected you for sixteen years. If she gives your father that tape of Julien bragging about what he made me do, it will destroy him. You love your father, don't you, Preston?"

Preston gulped air and swallowed visibly.

"Preston, that's not what the tape is," Regan wailed. "She made you believe you killed Julien, but it's not true. She killed him after you left. Ask the police how Julien died. It wasn't because you hit him in the head — he was ..."

Her words were cut off by Corinne's smack across her mouth, but it was Corinne who recoiled as if Regan had somehow escaped her bonds and struck her. Corinne cradled her hand; she had hit Regan so hard, she hurt it.

Regan's focus blurred, and for a moment she saw the cliché stars described in cheesy novels. She could taste blood. That sensation forced her back to the real world. She missed some of Corinne's words but heard enough to understand how Corinne was playing Preston this time, "… she'll say Charles knew what Julien made me do all along and that your father hated him and murdered him because of that. She'll set your father up for first degree murder," Corinne exhorted. "She'll destroy all of us. She *has* to be stopped."

Preston glanced directly at Regan for the briefest of moments and whispered, "I'm sorry." Then he dashed out of the room before she could speak again.

Regan could hear the front door slam and the car in the driveway start up. Then everything around her grew silent and she was alone with Corinne Alfrey.

Corinne was immediately composed, wholly unaffected by the preceding drama. "Well, Regan, it would appear we have some time to kill."

Regan ran her tongue inside her lower lip and discovered the source of the bloody taste in her mouth. She swallowed hard and lowered her expectations about instant rescue. If the cop that the real Detective Harrison had assigned to her was going to hustle in and free her immediately, he would have done so by now. What could he be waiting for, she wondered? Then she had a hopeful thought: her tardy protector was probably waiting for backup. Preston Alfrey could be in a police cruiser right now, protesting his innocence while being driven to the county jail.

"My guess is Seth Cooper will be here within five to ten minutes of Preston calling him, so that gives us almost half an hour."

"I don't understand. What does Seth Cooper have to do with any of this?" Regan asked.

"He's going to kill you in a rage because you got his mother committed, he's such a devoted son, you see. And then when he realizes what he's done, he's going to be so remorseful, he'll turn the gun on himself. Preston doesn't know how deeply Seth's guilty conscience will affect him, of course, only that he can be a hothead," she chuckled.

You can make your move any time now. Regan badly wanted to shout to her as-yet-unseen guardian, but she had to settle for the thought instead.

Corinne began unscrewing the silencer. "There's no need for this any longer. If you managed to get out of Preston's hands and looked like you were going to get away, I would have shot you; but now, since Seth's going to do it, a silencer looks too studied for a young man with a temper."

"The police will know it's your gun, not Seth Cooper's, once they check the registration. They'll never believe it was a murder-suicide; they'll catch you because of the gun."

"They'll think he bought it illegally; they're not going to be looking at me about it. My fingerprints won't be on it. See, Regan," she held up her free hand to show off her old-fashioned white cotton gloves. "I'm wearing gloves. Unlike my husband, I always wear gloves when I have messy things to do.

"There's no record of me owning this gun anyway. Louisiana is a nice gun-friendly state, not at all like California where you have to go through all these machinations just to buy a handgun. Last time I went home to New Orleans for a

265

visit, I just walked into a gun store, reminisced about growing up there, and plunked my money down on the counter. The nice man there didn't even ask to see my ID, although I know he's supposed to. He liked me so much, a good 'ole New Orleans gal, he overlooked that little detail." Corinne smiled what Regan assumed was a big 'ole New Orleans gal smile. "He even threw in the silencer for free when I told him how loud noises made me jump — well almost for free; he had to charge me $200 for the federal stamp for it. He said I could shoot just as well with it on as without it."

"How do you know about Seth Cooper and his mother and about how they're connected to me?"

"Preston may have his faults, but he's a good listener and a better informant. And I can always count on him to come to me first whenever he gets panicked. He overheard you talking about having to go testify against a crazy woman when you were at the Santa Cruz Association office the morning you started in about finding a body in your new house. Everything you said that day was kind of indelibly stamped in his memory after that little mention," Corrine chuckled.

"Charles heard what you said as well, of course, and both of them knew at once who was found in your house and how he got there. Sometimes Charles can be good at keeping it together, so he didn't let on he knew anything. I guess he even managed to keep Preston from turning into a puddle until after they left the building. But that man does have his limitations. When you started asking him questions privately at the open house, he overreacted and threatened you. Bad idea. Stupid idea. I seem to be the only one in our family who can think clearly under pressure," she gave Regan an impish grin and waved the now silencer-free gun around, "or should I say, under the gun?"

"I still don't understand how Seth Cooper …"

"Got involved?" Corinne interrupted. "He was just so handy; I couldn't let the opportunity he presented slip. Meg came back to the office all wide-eyed and told everyone about Seth's little threat to you at his mother's eviction hearing. What do you think of Meg's latest face lift, by the way? I think it's ghastly. She looks like one of those happy face circles; there's no expression left on her face anymore.

"I understand the more time that passes, barring some big shakeup, the less likely it is that the police will solve a crime, the less likely that they'll even think about solving a crime. Sixteen years is a long time for a murder to go unsolved; I felt pretty confident we were home free. But suddenly here you were asking questions the police weren't bothering to ask and flustering Preston and Charles. I've heard about your recent adventures. I figure you like playing detective and would find it absolutely impossible to not poke around, what with a body being found in your own house. I put myself in your shoes: I sure would have been nosing around if I were you.

"We couldn't have that now, could we? We couldn't have you being a shaker. So when Meg talked about Seth threatening you, I got this great idea about how to distract you. I called and pretended to set up a showing with you."

"That was you on the phone, not Linda Cooper?" Regan felt no satisfaction that she had been right about Corinne being her attacker.

"Linda Cooper? Are you kidding? Have you tried to talk to that woman? She can barely function. You can't believe what I had to go through to get her to follow you into town the other night. I had to tell her you had some magical anti-alien powder that required sea water to activate it. I told her the aliens would try to stop you from reaching the ocean and that she had to escort you there to get ocean water. I made her take a pledge that she would sacrifice herself for you if the aliens tried to stop you. Silly woman promised she would.

"When the police grabbed her in the sting you arranged, she completely lost it — that's why Seth hates you so much. So no, it wasn't Linda who called you, it was me. She couldn't have made a coherent call even if I coached her, let alone pushed you off Empire Grade, although she might have tried if I told her you came from another planet," she chuckled.

"You know, I didn't intend to kill you, really. I thought I didn't need to. I thought if I just messed you up enough, you'd stop thinking about Julien. How ironic," she sighed. "I came closer to killing you than I meant to, but I didn't hurt you enough to distract you. C'est la vie."

"You didn't use your little car when you attacked me. Did Preston let you use his Land Rover?"

"Regan, why do you make everything so complicated? I borrowed Charles' Land Rover. I didn't ask his permission. He never knows what's going on."

"But how? The police checked. There wasn't a mark on it," Regan quizzed.

"Well, not on the body, no, but you should have seen the brush guard. Every one of those clunky old 2002 Discoverys come from the factory all set to accept a brush guard. Charles never wanted one, but Preston thought they looked cool so he ordered one for his Rover. He had it on for all of four months before he changed his mind and took it off. He kept it, though.

"Preston knows Charles doesn't like me using his Rover and he knows I won't borrow his — insurance issues. I told him I was going to sneak Charles' Rover because I had to show a Bonny Doon property on an unpaved road and knew my car would never make it, especially not after a good winter rain storm like we had that day. I told him I was worried, though, because I kind of had a premonition about bumping into a big fallen boulder with it." Corinne smiled broadly. "With just the slightest nudge, he came up with this idea *all by himself* that we should put his brush guard on Charles' Rover.

"Preston is such a good boy, dumb as a lump of clay and easier to manipulate, but so accommodating. Two people can trade one of those things out in about fifteen minutes; you don't even need special tools to do it. We put it on, he ran his errands, and I pushed you. When we met up again, I was so upset *and* so relieved that he had suggested the brush guard because, sure enough, I'd had a bit of an accident.

"We took off the guard and my very gracious stepson wouldn't even let me buy him a new one — I offered, of course. He said he never used it and not to worry, that it was going right back into the overhead storage in his garage, right where he stored it before.

"When the police checked Charles' Rover, it was in great shape. And if they bothered to check his purchase records, they'd find out he didn't own a brush guard," Corinne smiled again, "Nicely done, huh?

"Are you good with time, Regan ... with judging the passing of it, I mean? It seems like Preston's been gone a long time. It must almost be time for Seth to make his big entrance. What happened to your purse? You've got a cell in it, don't you? I left my cell in my car and I don't wear a watch. Oh, there it is."

Corinne spotted Regan's purse lying on the floor where she had dropped it when Preston dragged her to the chair. Corinne put the gun on the floor so she could use both hands to rummage through it for Regan's cell phone. "Here we are," she said as she flipped the phone open to read the time.

"Umm, I was wrong. We've probably still got another five to ten minutes to wait. You know how they say time flies when you're having fun? Time's dragging for me, how about for you? This isn't much fun, is it?"

She couldn't see it from where she sat, but Regan thought she felt something change momentarily, something about the air or the light — she thought she heard a barely perceptible scraping noise as Corinne chattered on about her cell and poked through her purse. She thought it was possible the front door had been quietly opened and closed. If she was right, it meant someone had come into the house and was creeping around stealthily. Seth would have blasted through the front door; it couldn't be him. Her policeman must finally have made his entrance.

Regan strained to catch a glimpse of him without attracting Corinne's attention. Did he have a clear view of Corinne and her? She could barely keep from shouting out, "She put the gun down. Get her!"

Her cop was close enough that he was bound to overhear

270

whatever she and Corinne said. He could testify in court about what he heard; he'd make a perfect witness. If she could get Corinne talking about what she had done and what else she intended to do, in court it would no longer just be her word against Corinne's. No matter how good a lawyer she had, Corinne would be convicted of felony murder.

Regan added a note of desperation to her voice to better bait Corinne. "You don't have to go through with this; you don't have to kill Seth and me. You can tell Preston you just couldn't do it, even for Charles' sake. You'll be able to talk him down, I know you will. Please. I'll give you the tapes. No one will know you killed Julien."

"There's no need for you to be so magnanimous, Regan. I've been carefully accumulating money in my private account for years, getting ready to leave Charles and what passes for a life. I'm not greedy; I could pay you off and still have plenty to live on very comfortably. Besides, I'm not really worried about your tapes.

"Oh, Regan, you don't think I'm angry with you for blackmailing me, do you?" Corinne asked with feigned innocence. "I don't have a problem with you doing *that*. You understand what it's like to be with someone you don't respect, someone who doesn't know you at all. I don't fault you for trying to take control of your future like I am mine," Corinne shrugged.

"No, your attempt at blackmail's not the reason I'm going to kill you." Regan saw anger that bordered on hatred flash across Corinne's face. "I'm going to kill you because you placed so little value on Julien's life. He betrayed me and was going to leave me suffocating with Charles ... even so, even

271

after I killed him, I never stopped loving him. $100,000. You think that's all he was worth? You think that's all *we* were worth? That's infuriating."

Regan was certain now. She saw a figure, a man, still in the shadows of the unlit living room, but inching closer to the bedroom door, to the light, and to freeing her. She couldn't restrain her relief. Her shoulders dropped; she took her first deep breath in what seemed like hours.

Corinne didn't notice. "Where is that man?" she asked with annoyance. "What's keeping Seth?" She dropped Regan's phone to the floor and stooped to pick up the gun again. "If he doesn't get here soon, I may shoot you first and him later … that's not how I planned to do it."

The man in the shadows would be able to see Corinne clearly, highlighted by the light in the bedroom. He would know about the gun in her hand. Regan's mind raced to what might come next. She imagined him shouting "Drop it," Corinne spinning and taking aim, and him firing in self-defense. Regan cringed against the sound of gunfire she expected.

Her imagined shootout didn't happen. The figure quietly emerged from the darkness, and for the first time she could see him clearly. Her heart began to pound in her chest. He was no saving cop. He was no friend.

"Seth's not coming, Corinne," Charles Alfrey announced evenly. "Preston didn't call him. He called me, just like last time. I'm here to help you. I'm going to do what's necessary." A long sigh escaped from him. "Give me the gun and go wait in my car."

"Charles, I can explain."

"I'm sure you can." His voice grew demanding, "Do what I say, Corinne. Wait for me in the car."

Corinne seemed amazed by the harshness and authority of his tone; she didn't argue with him. She started to leave as he had ordered but then reached into her pocket and turned back to him. "You may need this." She smiled uncertainly and handed him the silencer.

"Yes," he said. "Now go."

He fitted the silencer to the end of the gun barrel and began twisting it as Corinne watched.

"Leave!" The demand he shouted came from some primal place inside him. Corinne started, as she might have if a great black bear had suddenly spoken and given her an order. Then she turned again, and this time, hurried from the bedroom. She slammed the front door on her way outside.

Charles resumed twisting the silencer onto the gun barrel until it stopped turning. He saw Regan's phone on the floor where Corinne had left it. "That's yours, isn't it?" he quizzed.

Where was her cop? Why wasn't anyone coming to help her? She opened her mouth and tried to find words to dissuade him from what he was about to do, but dread squeezed her throat and she couldn't utter a sound. She responded with a jerky nod.

He moved a step toward her and brought the gun close to her head. His face contorted and his lips quivered as he fought to maintain his composure. "I'm no murderer. And neither is my son." Although he spoke to her, his question was for himself: "How could I have believed he was?"

His hand trembled. Regan's whole body seemed to wince. She raised her shoulder nearest the gun and cowered behind it

273

as if such an ineffectual move might offer her some protection. Then Charles aimed the gun toward the floor and fired. "In case Corinne's listening," he said.

He raised his foot and stomped on the phone. "I can't have you calling anyone; we'll need some time." He still held the gun as he disappeared into the dark living room.

Regan sat on her chair, alone, bound to it by her wrists, hyperventilating to the point of passing out. *Don't you dare!* She commanded herself to hold her breath until she counted to ten before exhaling and taking her next breath. After a few repetitions, her lightheadedness receded and she started figuring out what she needed to do.

Her feet and legs were free; only her wrists held her captive. The chair was part of the staging kit that she and Tom used if a house needed a few pieces of furniture to look homey. They brought it, its mate, and a table to the house so they could sit while they made on-site notes and recorded measurements for house renovations. One of the main criteria for furniture in their staging array was that it be easily transportable — the chair was light; she could stand almost upright and carry it like a turtle carried its shell.

When he left, Charles left the front door slightly ajar — whether by design or accident she didn't know or care. She stuck her foot into the crack and pulled the door fully open, grateful she didn't have to try to grasp the handle and turn it to escape; that would have added minutes and extreme frustration to her exit.

She dragged the chair down the front steps and hobbled toward the street, the chair seat banging the backs of her thighs with each step. At the sidewalk she paused and looked for lights in neighboring houses. The closest one that looked occupied was two doors down and across the street.

She turtle-scuttled her way to the house. It took two failed attempts at a head-on stair climb before she realized she needed to turn sideways to maneuver up the three steps to the porch. As soon as she reached the front door, she turned and banged the chair against it yelling, "Help me!"

An angry resident opened the door within seconds, "Freakin' idiot! What do you think you're doing?" he shouted before he had the door fully open.

Regan dropped the chair to the porch and sat on it, appreciating the relief that gave her wrists and back. "I was kidnapped. Please, undo me. I need to call the police. And can you tell me what time it is?" Her words were calm and unruffled — and not at all the way she felt.

Regan's newly-met neighbor thought her asking the time seemed a little odd given the circumstances of their introduction, but as he undid the tape and freed her from the chair, he humored her.

"Umm, it's about 7:30, I think."

Regan used her new friend's phone to dial their office, the only number she knew from memory. Tom answered on the first ring with an exclamation of her name, "Regan, where are you? What's going on?"

"I'm at our cottage ... was at our cottage. I'm fine. Corinne was going to kill me and make it look like Seth Cooper did it. Then she was going to kill him. Preston was supposed to help, but he called his father instead. Charles smashed my phone but he didn't shoot me ... I thought he was going to, though. I don't remember anyone's number ...

that's what happens when you rely on speed dial. I'm going to the police station. Can you call Dave and Detective Harrison, the real one, and ask them to be there?"

Her statements were disjointed but her directives were clear and calmly delivered. Once she outlined what Tom needed to do, however, her voice became tiny, and like her body, finally coming off its adrenaline surge, unsteady. "Can you meet me there, too? I need to be with you."

32

Dave was leaning against the reception desk at the police station when Regan got there. He jumped to attention as soon as he saw her. She could tell he was rattled even before he said a word. "Regan, I'm sorry ... I tried. I left messages on all your phones ... but after what happened before ... Detective Harrison refused ... I couldn't ..." He clearly wanted to say more, but a police officer poked his head out of a nearby doorway and interrupted him.

"Dave?" The officer motioned for them to come inside, "Detective Harrison needs the witness in here right away."

Dave put his hand against the small of Regan's back and gently steered her toward the briefing room.

Regan didn't know exactly what she expected the real Detective Harrison to look like, but the man in front of her, the one clearly in charge, didn't look right. He was too small for his name somehow, and the military bearing he affected didn't suit him any better than his buzz haircut. If she had been introduced to both of them without knowing who was who, she would have assumed he, rather than Preston Alfrey, was the impostor.

"Ma'am," a young man in a regulation police uniform discreetly got her attention. "Ma'am, would you like some coffee?" he asked softly.

She nodded yes.

Detective Harrison introduced himself and two other officers, but she immediately forgot their names.

The young coffee fetcher returned quickly, stirring a paper cup full of stock station brew. "I hope it's not too sweet. I thought you could use some sugar in your coffee," he smiled at her uncertainly.

Detective Harrison and the two introduced officers began firing questions at her.

"Were all the Alfreys together when they left?"

"Who seemed to be in charge?"

"Were they armed?"

"Did you see more than one weapon?"

"Did they say where they were going?"

"Did they say anything about trying to fly out of the country?"

She felt utterly beleaguered. Regan needed answers of her own, but her questions were overwhelmed by the policemen's relentless staccato. She answered as best she could and asked nothing.

Tom had a difficult time gaining admittance to the briefing room. It took a personal vouch-safe from Dave before he was allowed past the reception desk. Regan wanted to nestle in his arms when she saw him. She could tell he wanted to hold her, too, just to make sure she was real and safe, but they both realized that would have to wait until later, when they were alone. They settled for sitting next to one another and

278

touching hands. That small solace revived her.

She broke into Detective Harrison's command central performance, hesitantly at first, but with mounting determination. "Charles Alfrey knew, Detective Harrison. He knew how Julien Rochette died. I'm sure he did because he said his son was no murderer. How did he know Preston didn't kill Julien?"

It was Dave who answered. "He heard the tapes."

Regan looked at him quizzically. "I thought we agreed to wait ..."

"Decisions about this investigation are not up to you and Officer Everett, Mrs. McHenry," Detective Harrison bristled. "We appreciate that you have produced some useful information for this investigation. However, I am in charge here and will decide how best to use it."

Regan was astounded by Detective Harrison's words. She could feel her face flush. *Produced useful information?* She had solved Julien Rochette's murder and almost been killed in the process. She wanted to return fire but relied instead on a softly intonated statement for her indictment: "Then I assume it was also your decision to withhold police protection for me?"

A female officer burst into the room excitedly and reported, "We have results on the APB for Preston Alfrey. His attorney called to make arrangements for his client's surrender. He'll bring Alfrey in tomorrow morning at ..."

"Unacceptable," Detective Harrison cut her off. "Tell him he's got one hour to produce his client." He added, to no one in particular, "Who knows where that guy will be by tomorrow morning."

"We have an update on the Alfrey plane, too, sir," one of the officers in the briefing room said. "It's a Cessna 172 Skyhawk. The Sheriff got the make, model, and tail numbers from the FAA Aircraft Registry and dispatched a deputy to the Watsonville Airport to look for it, per our request. So far, he's been unable to locate the aircraft. It was a tie down, not kept in a hangar, so Alfrey could have gotten it onto a runway unassisted. He may have taken off without clearance before the deputy reached the airport.

"Alfrey could have gassed up, too, sir. They've got a self-serve pump there, just like at a gas station. There was no staff present when the deputy arrived, but the airport manager is on his way; he'll be able to check the pump to see if Alfrey filled up. On a full tank, the plane's range is 790 miles. Should I notify airports within that radius, sir?"

Detective Harrison gave a quick nod. "Do it."

"Charles said he didn't want me to phone for help right away; he said they needed some time," Regan volunteered. "Maybe he was planning to fly out of the area."

"Thank you for your further insight, Mrs. McHenry. However, we already considered that a strong possibility," Detective Harrison retorted. "Officer Everett, your friends have had a long enough day. If you would be so kind as to show them out — I don't believe we'll need their further assistance, or yours, tonight." Detective Harrison's mastery of sarcasm made Dave seem like a rank amateur.

"What happens now?" Tom asked, once they were back at the police reception desk and he had given his wife a long overdue hug and kiss.

"Now we all go home and leave everything to the pros."

Regan was about to apologize for meddling and for getting Dave into trouble, but he stopped her with a wink, "Who knows, maybe they'll get it right this time."

🏠 🏠 🏠 🏠 🏠 🏠 🏠 🏠 🏠 🏠 🏠

Dave's language in the early morning call to Regan and Tom hinted that he had already gotten over his dressing down and was back in intimate touch with what was happening in the police department.

"Alfrey junior played quite a message from his cell phone when he came in last night. Your buddy Chuck … hey guys, you know what? I don't want to tell you about this over the phone. Invite me up for coffee, will you? Strong coffee. I'm already half way to your house in Bonny Doon. See you in under ten."

Tom, still unshaven, pulled on jeans and a sweatshirt and started coffee brewing by the time Dave walked into their kitchen. Regan put on jeans and a sweater, wrangled her hair into a severe ponytail which she then twisted into a flyaway knot, and managed the most basic face wash and tooth brush. But she didn't have time for makeup or lipstick.

"You look fabulous, Regan," Dave crooned.

"Shut up, Dave."

"I can't do that and tell you what happened, now can I?" He took the cup of coffee Tom handed him, "Thanks." He motioned them to the chairs at their breakfast bar. "You both may want to sit down for this."

Regan and Tom looked at each other but obeyed Dave's suggestion and perched on the high seats. Dave stood on the other side of the island, leaned against the counter behind him and took a sip of his coffee. "We think Corinne and Charles Alfrey are both dead."

"Dead? Not missing or got away? What happened?" Tom asked.

"There's no official confirmation yet, but there's visible scattered debris from a small plane, likely a Cessna, near Point Piños. It's near where John Denver crashed some years back. Water's about thirty feet deep there. They'll send out a crew to pick up what they can, but it's not like they're going to recover much in the way of bodies. If Alfrey did what he told his son he was gonna do, they didn't have an accident, he crashed deliberately. The plane probably went pretty much straight in." Dave looked from Regan to Tom and then back to Regan. "Thing is, when a plane hits like that, it's like an explosion; pieces are all that get found."

"Whew," Tom let his breath out in a soft protracted whistle; Regan stared deeply into her coffee.

"They'll do whatever they can for an autopsy, probably need to run some DNA 'cause heads and hands ... well ... sometimes fingerprints aren't available and teeth get lost, so no dental records. The coroner will declare it death by blunt force trauma for both of them, but he's never gonna know for sure about Corinne Alfrey. For that, all we've got is the cell phone message where Alfrey says he ..."

"He killed her, didn't he?" Regan asked before Dave finished.

"That's what he says he did. He said something about not wanting her to suffer but needing to be sure she didn't hurt anyone else ever again. Alfrey asked Preston to forgive him for lots of things, but mostly for believing he killed Julien Rochette and for letting him believe it, too. Alfrey senior said he strangled his wife. And he said something really bizarre that we don't get: he said he did it lovingly."

Regan nodded, she understood. "Corinne hurt so many people in the past and she was about to deceive and destroy more people; she was going to kill me and then Seth Cooper and make Preston part of her crime. Charles told Corinne he was going to do what was necessary — stopping her was necessary — but I doubt he ever stopped loving her.

"Dave, the police will tell Mrs. Rochette about her son's murder being solved, won't they? Would it be OK if I talked to her, too?"

"You ask permission at the darndest times, Regan. You know her; you have every right to talk to her. I guess you two will feel better after you've talked about how Corinne Alfrey got what she deserved."

"That won't make Mrs. Rochette feel better, Dave. It's complicated for her. I do want to let her know that Corinne made the choices that led to her death. And most importantly, I want her to know that Corinne was still loved when she died, and that in her own way, she never stopped loving Julien. Knowing that might help ease her pain."

Tom put his arm around Regan and pulled her close.

"Well, at least it's all over," Dave said. "You gonna fix up the house now and, what's the term you real estate people use, flip it? You gonna get away from Julien Rochette's murder?"

"The house is too notorious to sell; we'll have to keep it," Regan answered. "But that's OK. Now that the truth about

Julien is out, it's not our murder anymore. We can start filling the cottage with good memories."

"I like that idea," Tom smiled. "Yes, good memories. Regan can fill the house with shells from the beach. Alex can leave a surfboard or two there. We can hang some of Ben's playbills as art. And I'll keep a canoe out back. Maybe I'll even get that boat I always wanted — nothing big, just something I can take out when the bay is calm."

About the author

Nancy Lynn Jarvis has been a Santa Cruz, California, Realtor® for more than twenty years. She owns a real estate company with her husband, Craig.

After earning a BA in behavioral science from San Jose State University, she worked in the advertising department of the *San Jose Mercury News*. A move to Santa Cruz meant a new job as a librarian and later a stint as the business manager for Shakespeare Santa Cruz at UCSC.

Nancy's work history reflects her philosophy: people should try something radically different every few years. Writing is the latest of her adventures.

She invites you to take a peek into the real estate world through the stories that form the backdrop of her Regan McHenry mysteries. Details and ideas come from Nancy's own experiences.

If you're one of her clients or colleagues, read carefully — you may find characters in her books who seem familiar. You may know the people who inspired them — who knows, maybe you inspired a character yourself.

Follow Regan McHenry Real Estate Mysteries on Facebook

or

Visit Nancy Lynn Jarvis' website
www.nancylynnjarvis.com

where you can:

Read the first chapter of the books in the Regan McHenry Mystery Series.

Review reader comments and email your own.

Ask Nancy questions about her books and the next book in the series.

Find out about upcoming events, book club discounts, and arrange for Nancy to talk to your book club or group.

Read or print Regan's recipe for the chocolate chip cookie dough that she and Tom always have ready in their freezer.

Books are available in large print and for your Kindle, iPad, and other e-readers.

For small presses, getting exposure in the market place dominated by big publishers is a challenge; but it is also one where you as a reader can help us enormously by spreading the word.

So, if you have enjoyed this book, please help us to promote it and other Good Read Publishers and Good Read Mysteries titles.

There's a wide range of ways you can do so including:

- Recommending the book to your friends;
- Posting a review on Amazon or other book websites;
- Reviewing it on your blog;
- Tweeting about it and giving a link to our website at http://www.nancylynnjarvis.com
- Suggesting the book to your book club;
- Posting a comment on your Facebook page;
- Liking our Facebook page at http://www.facebook.com/ReganMcHenryRealEstateMysteries?ref=ts.
- Pinning it at Pinterest; or
- Anything else that you think of!

Many thanks for your help – it's much appreciated.

The Good Read Publishers team and Nancy Lynn Jarvis.